The Strawberry Hearts Diner

Center Point
Large Print

Also by Carolyn Brown and available from
Center Point Large Print:

The Wedding Pearls
The Lullaby Sky
The Barefoot Summer
The Lilac Bouquet

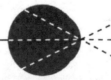

**This Large Print Book carries the
Seal of Approval of N.A.V.H.**

The
Strawberry
Hearts Diner

CAROLYN BROWN

CENTER POINT LARGE PRINT
THORNDIKE, MAINE

The text of this Large Print edition is unabridged.
In other aspects, this book may vary
from the original edition.
Printed in the United States of America
on permanent paper.
Set in 16-point Times New Roman type.
ISBN: 978-1-68324-634-3

Library of Congress Cataloging-in-Publication Data

Names: Brown, Carolyn, 1948- author.
Title: The strawberry hearts diner / Carolyn Brown.
Description: Center Point large print edition. | Thorndike, Maine :
    Center Point Large Print, 2018.
Identifiers: LCCN 2017045931 | ISBN 9781683246343
    (hardcover : alk. paper)
Subjects: LCSH: Large type books. | GSAFD: Love stories.
Classification: LCC PS3552.R685275 S77 2018 | DDC 813/.54—dc23
LC record available at https://lccn.loc.gov/2017045931

To my amazing editor,
Anh Schluep.
In appreciation for continuing to believe in me.

The Strawberry Hearts Diner

Chapter One

L uck, whether good or bad, always came in threes.

Vicky Rawlins was seventeen years old the year that her godmother, Nettie, divorced her worthless, cheating husband in May. Vicky's mother, Thelma, died in June, and Vicky found out she was pregnant in August. Twenty-three years later, she still hated the idea of summer rolling around, dreading the first official day of the season weeks before it actually arrived.

Whoever made the calendar had no idea about seasons in Texas. They thought that spring lasted right up to the twenty-first day of June. If they ever came to visit, they'd learn right quick that there were only two seasons in Pick, Texas—summer and winter.

"Goin' to be a hot one. Starin' at that calendar ain't goin' to make the next week pass by no quicker." Nettie set a cup of steaming-hot coffee in front of her.

"It's still over a month until the first real day of summer, and the bad luck has already started," Vicky muttered.

"I wish you'd get over that crap." Nettie cut and laid out biscuits on a cookie sheet. "Instead of worryin' about luck, think about Emily coming home in a week. We'll have some help then."

Vicky turned away from the feed store calendar hanging on the wall beside the door out into the diner's seating area. "We really need two waitresses."

"Maybe one will drop out of the sky today." Nettie laughed at her own joke.

"That will happen when pigs fly north for the hot summer months." Vicky smiled.

For more than two decades, Nettie had been her surrogate mother, best friend, business partner, and roommate all rolled into one. A tall, raw-boned woman with a round face and short gray hair, Nettie had a backbone of steel and a heart of gold. At seventy she swore that when it was her time to step from earth into heaven, it would be at the end of a fourteen-hour shift right there in the Strawberry Hearts Diner.

Thinking about her daughter, Emily, coming home in a few days lightened Vicky's heart. Maybe this summer would be three months of nothing but working with Emily and enjoying evenings on the porch swing. No bad luck. No good luck. Just a peaceful summer with her daughter and lots of good times.

"Quit your frettin'. It's goin' to be a good-luck

year. I can feel it in my bones." Nettie cut out two dozen biscuits and placed them evenly on a cookie sheet.

"Do your bones ever lie to you?" Vicky asked.

"Haven't yet," Nettie said. "Go open up for business. I'll be glad when Emily gets here on Friday."

"Me, too." Vicky flipped a switch, turning on the lights that flashed **BREAKFAST, LUNCH, DINNER** at the top of three of the windows. The shiny black-and-white-tiled floor evoked the 1950s, right along with the red booths lining one wall. An old silver metal tube of sorts, the diner looked out of place in the modern world, but that was the charm. Folks came from all over the county to eat Nettie's cooking and to taste one of the famous strawberry tarts, which were the diner's real claim to fame.

Heat had melted the adhesive tape holding up the **HELP WANTED** sign, sending it to the floor. Vicky picked it up and carried it back to the cash register, found a roll of duct tape in the gadget basket under the counter, and put it back at eye level on the glass door. It looked like crap, but at least it was visible.

"Is there a line of experienced waitresses waiting at the door for us to interview them? See any pigs flying around up there in the sky?" Nettie yelled from the kitchen.

"No pigs, but you should see this line of folks

wanting a job," Vicky hollered. "It goes from here all the way down the street to the convenience store."

Nettie's hearty laughter filled the diner right along with the aromas of bacon, sausage, and biscuits coming out of the oven. Pretty soon the place would be full and Vicky would be hopping from booths to the counter to the cash register. They needed help so bad that Vicky looked out the window toward the sky, just in case there *was* someone floating down toward them.

"No such luck," she muttered.

Nettie brought two biscuits stuffed with bacon and scrambled eggs from the kitchen to the dining area and set them on the counter. "Better eat up. Got about ten minutes until Woody gets here. I could set my clock by that man."

Vicky bit into a biscuit. "How did you and Mama do all the work by yourselves for all those years?"

"Wasn't easy, but we was determined to never have a year that we weren't making a profit. At the end of the first year, we figured everything up and hired a part-time waitress, Linda," Nettie said. "Whoever said that time takes away the pain of losing someone has cow chips for brains. I miss Thelma every day, especially when I make the crusts for the tarts. She was the one who always did that job."

Vicky twirled around on the bar stool and

braced her back against the counter. "Twenty-three years, Nettie. Can you believe it? Some days it seems like yesterday that I came into the house and told you I was pregnant. Then again, it all feels like at least two lifetimes ago."

Nettie finished off her biscuit and took a sip of coffee. "Wonder how many strawberry tarts we've sold in that time."

"Sixty-four million." Vicky tucked a strand of jet-black hair up under her short ponytail.

"Give or take a few million." Nettie's deep chuckle implied she was a longtime smoker, but truth was she'd never lit up a cigarette in her life.

Jancy Wilson sat down in front of her grandmother's grave in the Pick cemetery and pulled the dandelions away from the tombstone. She would have brought flowers, but she couldn't afford them, and besides, Granny had always said that she wanted her flowers while she was living, not after she was dead.

"Mama is gone," she said softly. "I suppose you know that by now, since it's been four years since she died. Money has been too tight to visit, Granny. I'm sorry. I understand now how she must have missed you when you died. I can't stay long. I'm hoping to get to Louisiana by night so I can sleep in a bed. If y'all have any kind of influence up there"—she glanced up at the cloudless blue sky—"send down some luck that my old car will make it that far. I need a lot of help to get me to where I belong."

She dusted off the seat of her wrinkled jeans and put on a pair of sunglasses that covered half of her delicate face and her green eyes. She settled into the driver's seat and reached across the console for a ball cap. Pink with a rhinestone heart on the brim, it had been her eighteenth birthday present from her mother. Now it was her lucky hat, and she only wore it when she really, really needed good things to happen in her life.

"Okay, let's get this show on the road." She jerked a mousy-brown ponytail through the hole in the back.

While the radio didn't work and the air-conditioning had gone out last summer, the gas tank was full. If those bald tires would just hold up until she got to her cousin's place, that's all she'd ask.

She drove past the place where her granny's trailer used to sit. Now it was nothing but a field of dandelions and weeds. In Jancy's mind a little three-bedroom, single-wide trailer with a flower bed on each side of the wooden porch occupied the lot. She slowed down at the church a block down the street. She and her mother had walked there every Sunday morning. A white-frame building with a steeple and a gravel parking lot, it had been filled to capacity the day they'd had

Granny's funeral, but then, she'd lived in Pick her whole life.

Jancy had always yearned for a life like that, but those things didn't just happen overnight. To be that ingrained into a community, a person had to not only be born there but had to put down roots. She slowed down as she drove through town and passed the familiar places. The old junkyard had entered her rearview mirror when the car first sputtered. She patted the dash and sent up a silent prayer. Evidently God was listening to her mama and granny that day, because it didn't stall out. She glanced over at the tall fence surrounding acres of wrecked or dead vehicles and wondered if Shane Adams still helped his grandpa with the business.

One block down the road was the Strawberry Hearts Diner. If she had had the money, she'd stop there and have breakfast. Her mouth watered just thinking of a plate of biscuits and gravy, but today she'd finish off the cheese crackers and day-old doughnuts in the back seat. She'd refill her water bottles in a gas station restroom. Food and coffee could wait until she reached Minnette's place. She sure hoped that her cousin had been serious the last time they'd talked on the phone when she'd said that Jancy would be welcome to stay with her for a spell.

Jancy caught a whiff of bacon as she drew near to the diner. Her stomach grumbled, but then the strong smell of smoke filled the air. She first thought that someone must be burning old tires back at the junkyard, but then the smoke began to boil from the vents. By the time she braked and swung into the diner parking lot, her eyes were watering and she was coughing so hard that she could hardly breathe. Then she saw flames shooting out from under the hood.

She grabbed her purse and hurriedly made her way to the back of the car. Her hands shook as she unlocked the trunk and started throwing the four duffel bags and a suitcase as far as she could. If the fire hit that full gas tank, the people in Pick would think that a bomb had gone off. Was it parked far enough out in the lot that it wouldn't damage the diner? She broke out in a run for it. Someone had to call the fire department.

God was finally punishing her for the past. Her car burning right there in Pick, Texas—that was too much to be coincidence. It was karma in the purest form coming back around to bite her on the fanny the very week after she was allowed to leave the state of Texas. Two days ago, she'd finally spent her last day in Amarillo and couldn't wait to get on the road to Louisiana to Minnette's place. Now all her plans were going up in smoke in front of her eyes.

When she heard the sirens, she plopped down on her old green duffel bag. With her head in her hands, she wanted to cry, but the tears wouldn't come. Never, not once, in all her wandering had she been so destitute. She had sixteen dollars in her purse, half a pack of gum, and a Texas driver's license that was only good for eight more months. Good luck renewing it without a place to live.

Of all the places in the state of Texas—for that matter, the whole world—Pick, Texas, was the last place she'd want to be stranded with nothing. Hopefully, truckers still stopped at the diner for those blue-plate specials. Maybe she could hitch a ride with one of them.

The red fire truck rolled into the lot, and two volunteer firemen hopped out, unwound the hose, and started spraying water on the vehicle.

"How much gas you got?" one of them yelled.

"Full tank!" She looked up and hollered. That's when she saw Nettie and Vicky start toward her. Vicky knelt beside her and laid a hand on her shoulder. "Can I help you or call someone for you?"

Jancy shook her head slowly. "Nobody to call, and I don't think anyone can help me. Y'all still get truckers coming through every day? I'll hitch a ride with one of them."

"Jancy Wilson?" Nettie frowned.

"That's me, Miz Nettie." She nodded.

"We haven't seen you around here in, what? Five years?" Nettie asked.

"Six," she answered and pointed toward the

diner. "Are y'all really hiring? Where's Emily?"

"Finishing up her last week of the year in college," Nettie answered. "She'll be home on Friday. And yes, we are hiring. You want to apply for the job?"

"Yes, ma'am." Jancy swallowed hard and nodded. It seemed like a lifetime ago that she'd lived in Pick—an eternity since she'd been that young, naive girl who'd wanted so badly to fit in and never did.

That Emily got to go to college didn't surprise her. She'd been the most popular girl in school—a cheerleader, smart enough to win all kinds of awards, pretty and actually kind of sweet even if her group of friends could be downright bitchy. And Jancy would be long gone by Friday. She just needed enough money for a bus ticket to New Iberia. Minnette would drive down and get her from there. With good tips and minimum wage, she should have that much in a few days.

"Got any waitress experience?" Nettie asked.

"Started working in fast food when I was sixteen. Moved up to the better places when I graduated high school. It's all I've ever done."

"Can you start right now?" Vicky asked.

Jancy nodded again. "Got a place I can store my stuff? And would you mind if I throw a pillow in a booth and sleep in the diner a few nights—just until Emily gets here and takes my place?"

"Come on inside where it's cool. We can talk over a cup of coffee," Vicky answered.

"My stuff?" Jancy looked around her as she stood up.

"It's okay right where it is for now." Vicky extended a hand. "Where have you been the past six years?"

"Louisiana and Texas, mainly. A few months in Oklahoma. These last few months, I worked as a waitress at a steak house in Amarillo." She put her hand in Vicky's and let her haul her to a standing position.

"You're Emily's age, aren't you? I remember when y'all moved back here and were in school together for a year or two. How is Elaine these days?" Vicky dropped her hand and led the way to the diner.

"She and my father are both dead. Mama passed right after I graduated from high school, and Daddy died a couple of years later." Jancy opened the door to allow Vicky and Nettie to go inside before her.

Nettie headed straight back to the kitchen. "I'm sorry to hear about her passing. Sounds like you picked up some of that deep southern accent, girl."

"Been a long time since anyone called me a girl." Jancy managed a weak smile.

"Honey, I'm seventy years old. That makes you a kid in my eyes. I was your grandma's friend, and even if you hadn't worked as a waitress, I'd be willin' to train you to get some help in this place," Nettie said.

Jancy took the whole place in with one glance. The last time she'd been inside the place, she and her mother had sat over there in the back booth. That's when she learned they were moving again. Right after her sophomore year in high school.

Her dad had gone down to the other end of town to fill up the gas tank with fuel, and when he pulled up in front of the diner, her mother paid the bill. Ten minutes later Pick wasn't anything but a dot in the rearview. She wouldn't have come back today, but she only had to make a slight detour from the interstate to visit her grandmother's grave. Look where that had gotten her.

"Coffee, tea, breakfast, or maybe a soft drink?" Vicky asked.

Her stomach grumbled again, and hunger overrode pride. "Breakfast, please. I haven't eaten since yesterday morning. I have the cash to pay for it, but if you'd put it on a tab and then take it out of my check, that would really help."

"Come on back to the kitchen and tell me what you want to eat before you put on an apron and get busy," Nettie told her.

"Um, I kind of need an answer about a place to sleep. I'll work hard as many hours as you'll let me, but . . ." Jancy swallowed what was left of her dignity.

"Okay, business first," Nettie said. "Job comes with three squares on the house, but you're limited to one strawberry tart a day. We've got a room up at the house that you can stay in. You can consider that a benefit, since we don't pay insurance or give vacation time."

"Thank you, but you don't have to make my breakfast. I can do that," Jancy said.

Two weeks tops with those benefits. She'd have enough tips to get her cell phone service turned back on and buy a bus ticket to Louisiana. When she grew tired of that place, she might move on to Florida. She'd always wanted to live close to the beach.

"How about we let Nettie fix you up with the breakfast special and you and I go take care of your things? I think it's bothering you that it's all out there, isn't it?" Vicky asked and then went on talking before Jancy could answer. "Until we close up this evening, you can stow it in the little storage shed where we keep extra supplies. It's around back. Another rule is that we don't allow smokin' in here or in our house, so if . . ."

"I don't smoke, but I do like a shot of whiskey or a beer once in a while." Had she really said that out loud? Crimson filled her cheeks. "I'm sorry. I shouldn't have . . ."

Nettie butted in from the kitchen. "No problem with a drink now and then. We'll just expect you to share."

Jancy headed back out to the driveway with Vicky right behind her. "We should be able to get it all in one load. Mostly it's just my clothes and a few little personal things."

The two firemen had taken off their bright-yellow gear to reveal faded jeans, T-shirts, and boots. The taller one tipped his cap at Jancy and motioned toward the still smoldering car. "W-w-would you sell that to m-m-me?"

"Sell it? It's burned-out and worth nothing," she said.

"I'd be w-w-willin' to give you twenty dollars for it and haul it away for free. I got a little scrap yard," he said. "Jancy W-Wilson, is that you?"

"It's me, Shane. How are you?" She'd had a major crush on Shane since she first saw him in the Pick church the summer they got to town. She thought she'd gotten over that years ago, but the extra kick in her heartbeat said there was still a spark there.

"Surprised to see you." He grinned. "Where you been? What happened that summer? You just disappeared after your granny died."

"It's a long story." She forced a smile. "I'll take you up on that deal for the car. When will you haul it away?"

"Soon as we down a couple of glasses of sweet

tea and I can get my tow truck out here. It ought to be cool enough by then," he answered.

"We'll be inside in a minute. Go ahead and help yourself to the tea," Vicky said.

"Wh-where y'all takin' that stuff?" Shane asked.

"Around to the shed," Vicky said.

"Ryder, do you remember Jancy?"

Ryder's gaze started at her feet and traveled all the way to the top of her hair. "No, can't say as I do."

That was no surprise. A couple of years older, Ryder had been the star of the basketball team. There was no way he'd remember a plain Jane. But she remembered him all too well. He'd been the resident bad boy, the one that all mothers warned their daughters about and who had a reputation for talking a girl into the back of his old truck and then leaving her without so much as a phone call. Still, she gave him a sideways glance and sighed. With that brown hair falling down over his forehead, the sweat on his angular cheeks from the heat of the fire, and those come-hither eyes, he'd been her type until she'd sworn off all men a few months ago.

"Hey, w-we'll take that stuff to the shed for you," Shane offered.

Vicky removed a key from a ring in her pocket and handed it to him. "Thanks a bunch. Sweet tea is on the house."

"And a tart?" Shane's shy grin hadn't changed a bit since she'd left. He'd always been a big guy, but good Lord, his arms were so huge now that they stretched the knit of his T-shirt and his broad chest looked to cover about two acres. His round face had developed a few angles, but they hadn't interfered with the dimples.

"You got it," Vicky said. "We'll go on inside and get you set up."

"Thanks, Vicky." Shane picked up three duffel bags, leaving a smaller one and the suitcase for Ryder.

The moment Jancy and Vicky got inside, Nettie stuck her head out the swinging doors and motioned for Jancy to come back there. "You can eat back here and clean up a little bit in the bathroom before you go to work."

"I'd better make a trip through there first and wash my hands," Jancy said.

"Use the sink right there." Nettie pointed at the deep stainless steel sink. "Your food will get cold."

Jancy did a quick washup and pulled up a bar stool. Bacon, eggs, gravy, and biscuits with a plate of pancakes to the side. She set about eating without even looking up, not even when she heard Shane's voice in the dining room. The deep Texas drawl hadn't changed a bit.

A phone rang, and in a moment Shane raised his voice. "Hey, Vicky. W-we'll be back real soon for that tea and tart, but right now there's a grass fire down south of town w-we got to take care of quick. See you in a few m-minutes."

Vicky stuck her head out the serving window. "See you later, then."

Jancy polished off her breakfast, downed the coffee, and went straight to the ladies' room out at the far end of the diner. A moan escaped her at her reflection in the mirror. Her shoulder-length hair was stringy, and she could see bags under her eyes. She'd washed up the night before in a rest stop bathroom, and although clean, her jeans and shirt left no doubt that she'd slept in them. It was a wonder Nettie hadn't told her to get out there on the road with her thumb out rather than hiring her.

She adjusted the temperature of the water and bent under the faucet, filled her hand with soap from the dispenser, and quickly shampooed her hair. After she'd rinsed it and dried it on paper towels, she pulled a brush from her purse to get the tangles out and then flipped it up into a ponytail. She brought out a makeup kit and smeared concealer under her eyes, working fast to make herself presentable.

"Best I can do. I'll never be an Emily, but at least I don't look like the homeless orphan that I am." She opened the door, got an approving nod from Vicky, and went back to the kitchen. Tying an apron around her waist, she pushed through the swinging doors just as Shane and Ryder reentered the diner. *Why couldn't Shane have gained sixty pounds and started dipping snuff?* With a sigh, she picked up an order pad from a stack on a shelf under the cash register and slipped it into one pocket and a pen in the other.

"Iced tea and tarts, right?" Jancy set a dome to the side and eased a heart-shaped tart onto each of two small plates, filled two of the largest glasses with ice and sweet tea, and put it all on a tray.

Shane nodded. "Here comes W-Woody. Do you remember him, Jancy?"

"Of course. He and Irma were friends with my grandmother," she said.

"Irma's been dead two years now." Shane slid a long look from Jancy's toes to her ponytail.

It had been six years since that infatuation, but not to her suddenly sweaty palms. She had to concentrate on walking or she would have dropped the tray.

"You are late," Nettie called from the kitchen when Woody pushed through the doors, bringing in a rush of hot air behind him.

"Had to go up to the church to help them with some plumbing," Woody said. "I'm starving. Give me your biggest breakfast, the one with pancakes on the side, and a cup of coffee. Who owns that car out there? Looks like it ain't good for nothing but the junkyard now."

Woody, a tall, rail-thin guy who looked like he needed rocks in his pockets to keep from blowing away when the north wind cut through the rolling hills of Anderson County, eyed her up and down twice before he took a booth behind Ryder and Shane. "You the new waitress here?"

"I am," Jancy said. "Cream or sugar?"

Woody removed his Texas A&M cap and raked his fingers through his thick gray hair. "You look familiar."

"This is Jancy W-Wilson. Her grandma was Lucy, and her mama was Elaine," Shane piped up from the booth next to where Woody took a seat.

"I remember them both. Always thought it was strange when Elaine married a man with the same last name, but Lucy said there wasn't no way they were related. Guess it is a pretty common name, ain't it? What are you doin' back in Pick?" Woody asked.

"That's her burned-out car in the parkin' lot," Shane said.

"Do you answer anything for yourself?" Woody asked.

"I'm workin' here. Coffee, black. Breakfast special, right?" She pasted on the brightest smile she could muster. She'd forgotten what small-town chatter was like.

"That's right." Woody nodded. "Hey, Vicky, when is Emily comin' home?"

"Friday. One more year and she'll have college done with, but she'll be here for the summer," Vicky said. "You want those eggs scrambled or fried this mornin'?"

Jancy blushed. She should have thought to ask that.

"Scrambled is fine, and don't forget the picante sauce. Where are you going to live, girl?" Woody cocked his head like a gangly bird. "Your granny's trailer has been gone since two weeks after she died. Some fishermen bought the thing and moved it up by the lake for a weekend place."

"Jancy will be stayin' with us," Vicky said.

"I heard Emily turned down one of them internship things down at NASA this summer. Has the girl gone goofy? That's a big deal." Woody's stream of conversation flowed right on, no matter the response.

Vicky shrugged. "She says she'd get homesick. Besides, she hates big cities."

"So do I," Ryder said.

Jancy picked up Woody's order from the shelf, added a cup of coffee to the tray, and carried it to his booth. She'd only lived in one small town her entire life, and that was Pick. Before and after that, her father had favored the big cities where he could find a job easily, most of the time on an oil rig.

Woody picked up his knife and fork. "So how's the offshore business going, Ryder?"

"Real good, but I'm not going back out anymore. The oil company is putting in an office in Frankston, and I'm going to manage it for them," Ryder answered.

"Then you'll be home for the festival?" Woody asked.

"Oh, yeah! Wouldn't miss that even if I had to quit my job," Ryder chuckled.

Jancy had attended the annual Strawberry Festival only once. Money was always tight in their house, but her mother had given her enough to buy either cotton candy or maybe a fried pickle and lemonade. She'd wandered around all evening alone wishing she had a group of friends like Emily had surrounding her. Finally, she'd bought cotton candy with her money, taken it home, and shared it with her mother.

"So where's your mama and daddy these days?" Woody asked Jancy when she set the food and coffee in front of him.

"Both gone. Mama went right after I graduated from high school. Daddy died two years ago," Jancy said.

"Sorry," Woody mumbled.

A lump the size of a grapefruit formed in Jancy's throat, like it always did when she thought of her mother, who had still been in her thirties when the blood clot went through her heart. Jancy had been flipping burgers when her father called and said, "Your mother is dead. You'd better come on home."

She'd wanted to bring her mama home to Pick to bury her, but her dad wouldn't have it. He'd insisted on cremation, and there wasn't even a memorial service. No dinner. No friends. Nothing but a widower and a daughter standing at the edge of the sandbar in Galveston, Texas, dumping her mother's ashes into the salty water.

They'd lived in a motel for a week and then he moved them into an apartment. Two months later he was ready to move again, but she didn't go with him that time. She didn't hear from him again until she got a call that he'd died with liver cancer in Pampa, Texas. She had him cremated and shook his ashes out near the same spot where they'd left her mother.

She and Vicky crossed paths as she headed back to the counter. "The parking lot is starting to fill up. You take the booths to the left of the cash register. I'll take the right side. And I'm sorry to hear about your folks. I always liked Elaine. She was shy but had a good heart."

"Thanks." Jancy swallowed hard, but the baseball-size lump in her throat wouldn't budge. She managed to keep the tears at bay as she went through a crazy roller coaster of emotions.

Chapter Two

The minute the breakfast rush was done, Jancy grabbed a broom and started sweeping. When she finished that, she went to the mudroom at the back of the kitchen, got out a bucket and mop, and set about cleaning the floor. And she did it without being told, which spoke volumes to Vicky.

Jancy wiped down all the tables again, cleaned a few smudges off the windows, and had just cleaned the door when it swung open. A guy wearing a light-gray three-piece suit and a big smile took in the place and then slid into a booth on Vicky's end of the diner.

"Sit anywhere. I'll be right with you," Jancy said.

Vicky picked up a menu, carrying it to the booth. "What can I get you to drink?"

"Are you Victoria Rawlins?" His smile got bigger.

"I'm Vicky. We have coffee, sweet and unsweet tea, and Coke products. We stopped serving breakfast thirty minutes ago and our lunch special won't be ready for another hour, but we do have hamburgers and cheeseburgers until then," she said.

"I'll have a cup of coffee." His fake smile did not match the cool assessment of his steely-blue eyes.

She poured a mug full of coffee and carried it to his booth. "Sugar, artificial sweeteners, and half-and-half are on the table. Anything else?"

"Please join me." He motioned toward the other side of the booth.

"Thank you, but I've got work to do. Enjoy the coffee and let me know if I can get you anything else."

Emily would call it Vicky's spidey senses, but something wasn't quite right. This fellow wasn't there for a cup of coffee and an attempt to flirt with that big toothy grin—that much Vicky could feel in her spidey bones. Maybe the guy was from the IRS and was there to tell her that he was going to audit her books. Or maybe he was a health inspector or one of those people who go into a business and then rate the service.

She backed up and propped a hip on a bar stool.

"He could be flirting," Jancy whispered as she cleaned fingerprints from the domed cake stands right behind Vicky.

"It's not workin'," Vicky said in a loud voice.

He leaned toward her and winked. "This is a pretty nice little setup you got here, and I understand that you also own the land to the north of the café."

Be danged if the sunlight flowing in through the windows didn't make his fingernails shine. That mesmerized Vicky. There wasn't a man in Pick, Texas, who would be caught dead with polished nails—not even if they were high-gloss clear.

"No, sir, I do not," she answered. "But I would appreciate it if you'd state your business, because we're about to get knee-deep in a lunch rush around here. You sure you don't want to see a menu? Nettie makes a mean cheeseburger with bacon."

He looked to be about fifty with that sprinkling of gray hair at his temples and the thinning spot on the top of his head. Maybe that naked patch was what made his eyes look too close together. "I'm Carlton Wolfe. Haven't you seen my picture in the newspaper ads?"

His tone said that he was somebody real important. Heck, he might have even descended right from a personal visit with Jesus with all the importance that he was throwing around.

"Well, Mr. Carlton Wolfe, what can I do for you? And no, I haven't seen your picture in the newspaper."

"You own this place, right?"

"I am a co-owner."

He wasn't IRS or he'd already know that, so

she wasn't about to be audited. If he was a health inspector, he could put on his white gloves and run his fancy little fingers around the place. He wouldn't get a bit of dust on them.

"And who is your partner?"

He looked like a wolf with those beady little eyes and that nose with the indentation at the end. If Vicky believed in shape-shifters, she'd think that he'd been a mangy old gray wolf just before he walked into her business and the transition wasn't quite finished. He had on clothing, but that nose—there was something about it.

"I'm not sure I want to answer your questions, Mr. Carlton Wolfe. What business is it of yours who owns the diner? Just exactly what are you selling?" she asked.

He tipped back his head and flashed an even brighter grin at her. The nose had a slight indentation at the tip that gave it the appearance of a penis. Rather than feeling intimidated, she wanted to giggle. If she squinted, she could imagine his wide, full lips turning into what usually sat below a penis. Maybe if he grew a scraggly beard it would complete the whole picture.

"I'd like to take you to dinner and discuss a business proposition. Maybe I can pick you up at seven tonight?" He lowered his voice. "And candlelight and a bottle of good vintage wine."

"No, thank you. Just exactly what are you selling?"

"Not selling, honey—buying. But I'd far rather have this conversation this evening, or if you are busy, tomorrow would be great, too," he said.

"Buying what?" Vicky asked.

"Aha." He snapped his fingers. "I've got your interest. Pick you up at seven. You live in the little white frame house down the lane from this diner, right? Wear something pretty and plan on being out past midnight."

"Mr. Wolfe, I'm not going anywhere with you. I don't know you." Vicky pushed away from the bar stool. "Enjoy your coffee, and if you change your mind, just holler."

"Okay, but I would have enjoyed taking a beautiful woman like you to dinner and chatting in a quieter atmosphere," he said with wistfulness. "I'm a real estate entrepreneur, and I'd like to buy this section of land from you, the undeveloped property to the north, this café, and your house in a package deal. I'm prepared to offer you one hundred and fifty thousand dollars for the whole parcel, and I will write a check for ten percent of that today if you will be off the land in thirty days," he said. "You could think about that and go with me to dinner tonight to seal the deal. I'll have my team draw up the contract and bring it with me."

"And what makes you think I want to sell my house and café?"

"You probably didn't until I mentioned that

amount of money. I know property, Miz Rawlins, and what I just offered you is twenty percent above the fair market value of that land. You just give it some thought. Call me when you want to talk or go to dinner—either one." He pulled out a business card and laid it on the table as he stood up without taking even one sip of his coffee.

"The answer won't change in a week or in a year. We're not interested in selling our land or our business," Vicky said.

"We'll see." Carlton strutted across the floor with a wave over his shoulder. He passed Shane on the porch but didn't even glance his way.

"Hey, did y'all know that m-man? I spoke to him and he didn't even say a w-word. I bet the sweat from that fancy suit has m-messed up his hearin'." Shane laughed at his own joke.

"He came to buy the diner, my house, and Nettie's land," Vicky said.

"Wh-what for?" Shane asked.

"Over a hundred thousand dollars," Vicky answered.

"No, wh-what for as in wh-what's he goin' to do w-with it wh-when he gets it? Is he goin' to start plantin' strawberries?"

Vicky slapped the booth where Carlton had been sitting. "I didn't even think to ask him that. It don't matter, though. I'm not sellin'."

"Phew!" Shane wiped his forehead with a

laugh. "I'd sure miss this place if y'all sold it. W-wouldn't never be the same without you and Nettie and Emily and—" He nodded toward Jancy. "And now Jancy."

"And we'd miss seein' all the folks around here." Vicky clamped a hand on Shane's shoulder as she passed him and went to wait on a couple who'd entered the café and were looking around to see where they should sit. "Jancy will take your order."

"Just iced tea and a big order of fries, Jancy." He raised his voice.

"Sweet?" Jancy asked.

"Yes, you are." Shane grinned.

Jancy blushed, and Vicky smiled as she motioned for the couple to sit on her end of the diner and took their order.

"So you wantin' to sell our little piece of heaven?" Vicky asked Nettie when she took the order to the kitchen rather than pinning it on the carousel.

"Last time someone came in here wantin' to buy our place was the week before your mama passed away. Wasn't interested then and time ain't changed my mind," Nettie said. "We're goin' to get hit hard here in a few minutes. Folks will be wantin' to see the burned-up car and check out our new waitress. Your mama would tell us that fate brought her to us and that's good luck."

"I still hate summer," Vicky said. "And it won't even officially start for another month."

"But we always get through it, don't we?" Nettie winked.

Jancy turned around slowly in the middle of the bedroom. A four-poster bed took up a lot of space, though there was still room for a chest of drawers and a dresser with a big mirror above it, plus a dark-green velvet recliner in the corner. It even had a little table beside it and a lamp. She turned down the bed to find soft sheets and a fluffy blanket, all of which called out to her. But first she was going to have a real bath or a warm shower, whichever one was offered, because she had only had washups in gas station restrooms for a week.

She'd made forty dollars in tips that day. If the whole week was that good, she'd have enough to get her cell phone service back, and a week after that she could be on her way to see Minnette. Life was beginning to look up—at least a little bit.

She sighed as she set a small framed picture of her and her mother on the bedside table. It was the last one they'd had taken together. They'd been all dressed up for church on Sunday. Her father had griped about his job again all that hot morning. Her mother had held him off about moving that time until Jancy graduated, but it hadn't been easy. He'd been drinking a lot more in those weeks up to the middle of May.

She'd felt so empty when they'd dumped her mother's ashes from the crematorium's wooden box. Her father had simply said, "She always wanted us to travel down this way so she could wade in the salt water. Well, now she's happy."

That was it. No poem. No hymn. No Bible verses. Elaine would have liked something scriptural said over her ashes, so Jancy had silently recited the twenty-third Psalm and added a few drops of salty tears to the water.

"Now let's go look for jobs. We'll have to sleep in the truck if we can't get a motel that'll let you do some cleaning to cover a room until we can get a paycheck," her father had said that day.

She took her broken heart and the empty box with her to a cheap motel on the outskirts of Galveston and cried herself to sleep every night for the next week. When her father got his first paycheck, they moved into a trailer and she went to work at a fast-food place as a waitress. It was life, and there was no changing it back then.

Next she took out the stack of letters and cards tied with a faded pink ribbon. Those went into the drawer beside her bed except for the one marked with a small heart on the corner. She slumped down in the chair beside the window and opened it. Every first night in a new place she read that letter to remind her that her mother was with her no matter where the winds took her.

She carefully removed the lined paper from the envelope and held it to her heart before she unfolded it. Her lips moved as she read the all-too-familiar words.

My darling daughter,

If you are reading this, then I'm gone. When your father and I got married, I thought we'd settle down like most folks. He seemed to favor bigger cities and I didn't care where we lived as long as we were happy. As you well know, he never could put down roots anywhere, but I'd vowed to stay with him through the bad as well as the good, and we did have some good times in our marriage. I loved him even if I didn't love the nomadic way of life. But no matter where we lived, my mama wrote me a letter every week. When she died, the letters that she'd written to me over the years were such a comfort. Just seeing her handwriting and reading over her advice and feeling the love in her words have helped me so much. I want you to have that. There will be a letter for each major milestone in your life and a birthday card for a few years.

The happiest years of my life were those two that we lived in Pick, Texas. It was where I was raised and I got to spend that time with my mother. Even though your father is a wandering soul, I appreciate him staying there with me. Don't fault him for what he does, Jancy. Some folks think the grass is greener on the other side of the fence. I hope that you don't get too much of that in your grown-up life and, if you do, that you never get married. You and your loved ones will be miserable.

Please know that you are the biggest blessing God could ever give me. I chose this life. Maybe I was too young to make that decision at eighteen, but I made my bed and I'll sleep in it—no matter how many times that bed has to change. But I want you to remember that choices have consequences and I'm sorry that you had to pay for mine.

Jancy read through the last paragraph, slipped the letter back into the envelope, and put it with the rest of the letters. Swiping away a lonesome tear that escaped from behind her lashes, she touched her mother's picture with her forefinger. "Mama, would things have been different if you hadn't gotten pregnant with me? Was I really a blessing or a curse? Maybe you wouldn't have married Daddy that summer otherwise."

She finished unpacking, stuffed the duffel bags

inside the suitcase, and set it in the closet. Taking a deep breath, she headed down the long hallway to the kitchen. Vicky and Nettie were sitting at the table, a pot of coffee and three cups sitting in the middle with a chocolate cake underneath one of those plastic cake carriers.

Vicky pointed. "We started without you. I'm only having half a cup or I'll be awake half the night."

"I'm immune to caffeine. This is my second cup," Nettie said.

"Me, too." Jancy pulled out a chair, sat down, and poured a full cup of coffee. "I know you've got questions, so fire away."

"You done a good job today. Folks liked you," Nettie said. "I reckon that's all that's important right now."

"Except that we do need you to fill out some tax forms. We'll do that tomorrow during down-time." Vicky cut a thick slice of the layer cake and put it on a saucer. "We didn't have leftover tarts today, but this is very good. You'll like it."

"Leftover tarts?" Jancy expected them to ask her personal questions, some that she'd probably not even want to answer.

"We usually bring home two to four in the evenings. We never serve leftovers. I make about fifty, and the rule is that a person can only take out two. We don't cater them or sell them for parties, and when those fifty are gone, then there's no dessert on the menu. Folks can eat as many as they want to buy in the diner or take two home with them, but no more. That's rule number one," Nettie answered.

"How many rules are there?" Jancy asked.

"Only a few, but they're important. Go on and cut your own slice. I don't know how much you want, but I'll tell you right now, this is my second piece, and it's really good." Vicky took a bite. "Did you do something different with the recipe for this, Nettie?"

"Added a little bit of almond extract to the icing. You like it?"

"This is fantastic," Jancy said. "It's delicious, but I can't wait to try a tart."

"Didn't you eat one back when you lived here?" Vicky froze in surprise with her fork halfway back to her plate.

Jancy shook her head. "Never had enough money to buy one, but I'm lookin' forward to getting to taste them sometime in the next couple of weeks."

"Well, honey, I'll save one back for you tomorrow so you can see what you missed. Think about it long and hard first before you partake of a tart from the Strawberry Hearts Diner." Nettie sounded like a preacher converting a house full of sinners.

"Why's that?" Jancy asked.

"Because word has it that they are magic. If

you ever eat the first one, then you'll always crave them and want to come back to Pick to get another one," Vicky said. "Want another piece of cake?"

"No, thanks. I've eaten more today than I have in a week combined," Jancy answered. "Who taught you to make the tarts, Nettie?"

"Vicky's mama and I perfected the recipe, and now I'm the only one who knows exactly how to make them. We always wanted to have a diner, not a café—a real silver diner—and name it the Strawberry Hearts. When Thelma's husband died and left her a chunk of insurance money, we put one in and did just that."

"I get the recipe when she kicks the bucket. Until then it's locked in a safe-deposit box up in Tyler," Vicky said.

"When did you start working in the diner, Vicky?" Jancy asked.

"I worked after school and summers from the time Mama and Nettie started the business. The summer before my eighteenth birthday my mother died and I went to work full-time. Nettie had been named my guardian until I could take over my half of the diner. I was pregnant before that even happened."

"That means . . ." Jancy frowned.

"I was orphaned. Pregnant. Married. Widowed all in a three-month period. Then Emily was born when I was eighteen, and I was a mother. Thank

44

God for Nettie and the diner or I'd never have lived through everything. I've hated summer ever since then."

Jancy swallowed the lump in her throat. She should open up and share some of her life with these strong women, but she couldn't—not yet. Maybe not ever. It was too painful and too embarrassing to talk about. Jancy changed the subject. "Do you realize that you could sell this chocolate cake in the diner?"

"Yep, but Thelma and I made a deal that we'd only sell our tarts as desserts in the diner. That's the way it's always been, ever since we had that diner built and set up on the corner of my land."

"And there ain't an entrepreneur in the whole great state of Texas who's going to buy it for any amount of money." Vicky sipped her coffee.

Jancy giggled. "I wouldn't mess with either of you—or with Shane. Lord, did you see the size of his arms? They'd make a weight lifter look like a sissy. He's really packed on the muscle since I lived here."

"He's a hardworkin' boy, always has been," Nettie said. "Awful self-conscious of that stutter, but when him and Ryder was in grade school, folks learned right quick that they'd better not tease him about it. Ryder didn't take to anybody makin' fun of his best friend."

"What happened to Shane's grandpa?" Jancy asked.

"He's in a nursing home in Palestine. He's got severe arthritis. Made his work just too hard. When he first realized what was happening to him, he signed over the whole business to Shane. That boy has expanded it from a junkyard into a body shop. He's real good at what he does," Vicky told her.

Jancy finished off her coffee and gathered up all the dirty dishes to take to the dishwasher. "Sign out at the edge of town still says there's three hundred and six people. They didn't change it when the three of us left, did they?"

"No, didn't add to it when y'all came to take care of Granny Wilson, either." Vicky put the cover back on the cake. "Nothing new in six years. Still got the feed store, post office, two churches, and the diner on this end of the highway through town. Shane's business is up north of us, along with the volunteer fire station. South is Leonard's convenience store and gas station combined. We keep hoping a business or two will go in the empty buildings between us and the convenience store, but nothing has happened yet."

"You forgot the bank," Nettie said.

"Yes, I did." Vicky nodded. "It's a branch bank from the one in Frankston. Set up in one of them portable buildings, but it's got an ATM and everything that a big bank has. Where were you last night, Jancy?"

That was an abrupt change of subject, but then they deserved a few answers.

"Roadside rest stop up on the interstate." She leaned on the counter separating the kitchen from the kitchen nook. The house was a whole lot bigger than the trailers where she and her parents had lived in most of the towns her dad thought looked interesting. She'd usually had a tiny little room on one end that wasn't much bigger than a closet. The twin-size bed occupied most of the space, but she hadn't spent much time in any of the rooms, so it didn't matter. If she wasn't in school, she was at whatever job she could find, and her paycheck went to keep groceries in the place.

"You slept in your car?" Nettie gasped.

"A few nights. I lost my job a couple of weeks ago. The rent was due, so I had to move out of the apartment. I thought I could pick up another one, but when my money was almost gone, I figured I'd better head out toward Louisiana. I have a cousin there who told me I was welcome at her place."

"But in your car? That's dangerous," Vicky said.

"It wasn't so bad. We did it pretty often when we'd move into a town where my dad had to save up paychecks until he could rent a place. Few times he made a deal with a run-down motel. If Mama and I cleaned for them, they'd give us a couple of rooms. It was the way it was. Other than Pick for those two years, I usually went to three or four schools a year. Mama was determined I'd get my diploma. Daddy was just as determined that I'd earn my keep."

A vision of her mother flashed through her mind. Elaine hadn't even been forty when she died, and she'd looked sixty. Jancy glanced over at Vicky. How could she be forty years old? They'd probably ID her at a club before they'd serve her a beer. Had Emily held on to her beauty the past six years? She'd sure never looked like her mother. Folks said that she took after her maternal grandmother with all that height, those big blue eyes and blonde hair. Vicky wasn't a bit taller than Jancy, had jet-black hair and brown eyes.

"Well, tonight you'll have your choice of a nice long bath or shower and a decent bed to sleep in," Nettie said. "Towels are in the linen closet right outside the bathroom door."

"Thank you"—Jancy smiled—"for everything. I've got a question for you before I go sink into a tub of water. What on earth kept y'all in Pick all these years?"

"It's home," Nettie said simply. "Now I'm going to bed. See y'all at six tomorrow mornin' when we open up for breakfast. Vicky and I usually walk to the diner together. If you want to go with us, we leave at five thirty. It's fine

48

if you want to sleep until the last minute, too."

"I'll be ready at five thirty," Jancy said.

Vicky yawned and pushed back her chair. "I've got some book work to do, so I'm going to my room. Help yourself to more coffee or there's milk in the fridge. We don't keep much soda pop in the house."

Jancy wiped down the table and then went to her new bedroom, gathered up her things, and carried them to the bathroom. She filled the old claw-foot tub half-full of water and then sank down into the warm water and sighed. Dunking completely under the water to get her hair wet and then resurfacing, she felt as if she'd been baptized. She was leaving the old behind, and of all the crazy places in the world to land, it felt good to be back in Pick.

Chapter Three

"Mama, are you crazy?" Emily yelled. "Don't y'all ever watch the news? Jancy mighta been a quiet-type girl in high school, but she might be a criminal now or maybe even working for that horrible man who tried to buy the diner. Give her enough money to get her out of town or at least to a cheap Frankston motel."

Vicky held the phone out from her ear. "And how is she supposed to get to work tomorrow morning? Her car burned up in the diner parking lot. If you were stranded in a town with no motel, I'd sure hope someone would help you out. Besides, her granny was Nettie's friend and Jancy lived right here in Pick for two years."

"Will you at least promise me that you will lock your bedroom door and call me first thing in the morning?" Emily moaned.

"Before dawn?"

Another groan. "Yes, or earlier if something insane happens, like she kicks in your door or points a gun at your face. Call Shane or Ryder if something goes wrong. They can be there in five minutes and hold the place down until the Frankston police arrive."

"You've been watching too many cop shows," Vicky laughed.

"Don't make me come down there." Emily laughed with her. "But, seriously, Mama, I am worried."

"Don't be. I'm pretty good at reading people, and I don't think Jancy is going to kill us in our sleep for the chocolate cake out there in the kitchen," Vicky said.

"You are mean to mention Nettie's chocolate cake. I like it even better than tarts," Emily whined. "It's not fair that Jancy gets tarts and cake and I'm a million miles away."

"Nettie will make another chocolate cake on Friday, and you are not a million miles away. You are only in Tyler. The semester is over in four days. You'll be home and we'll have the whole summer together."

"I'm holding you to that promise. And, Mama, I sure hope Nettie hasn't lost her touch when it comes to reading people. Good night."

Vicky kissed her finger and touched Emily's forehead in the picture beside her bed. "Good night. Sweet dreams."

Nettie stuck her head in the door just as Vicky laid the phone on the nightstand. Dressed in her favorite nightgown that barely had any of the original lilac color in it at all, she shut the door

51

behind her and twisted a red bandanna in her hands. Her short gray hair stuck up all over her head in wet spikes from her shower. All it needed was pink or purple streaks to make her look like a punk rocker.

"Nettie, what is wrong? Are you sick?"

"Did I make a mistake?" She crossed the room and sat on the edge of the bed. "I'm second-guessing myself."

"About selling the diner for a development that won't do our town a bit of good? I don't think so. The people who buy the fancy houses will stay to themselves. They'll get up early to go to work and come home late. They'll buy whatever they need in Tyler or Frankston and they'll take their kids up there to private schools." Vicky stopped for a breath. "And what would we do? We'd be lost without the diner."

"Not that! About inviting Jancy to stay here. She's lived a hard life. What if she's addicted to drugs or what if she's got crazy people out lookin' for her? Maybe we've brought them right here to our home." The handkerchief was knotted up into a ball. "I've never done something so impulsive in my life—other than getting married when I was past forty, and you know what happened there."

"Emily is having a fit about it, too, but I don't have any bad vibes. If it was my child on the road like Jancy, I'd sure be glad if a couple of old women gave her a job and a bedroom," Vicky answered.

"Who are you callin' old?" Nettie shot a dirty look her way. "And you're right. I knew when I was standing beside that sumbitch at the courthouse that I was making a mistake, but I didn't want to admit it to my mama. She always hated him. I should've listened to her."

Vicky sat down beside her and took the bandanna from her. "Until we got home this evening, you didn't worry, did you?"

"Not a bit. She's a hard worker, an excellent waitress, and everyone that came in felt right at home with her. Her grandma was the salt of the earth, even if she did wind up with a worthless son-in-law."

Vicky put an arm around Nettie's shoulders. "So your intuition has never really been wrong. Don't doubt yourself now. She's not going to kill us in our sleep and steal our van."

"Thank you. Now give me back that old hankie. I was dustin' my dresser with it when I started doubtin' myself." She took the bandanna from Vicky and smoothed it out before she stood up. "I'm going to bed now. Tomorrow will be as busy as it was today. Some folks were doin' Bible school at the church and they didn't get to see Jancy."

Vicky smiled and then chuckled. "And next week the other church has Bible school. Crazy, isn't it? They coordinate so all the kids in the community can go to both, but they have to have separate buildings for Sunday morning worship."

"Tarts and chocolate cake." Nettie started for the door.

Vicky frowned. "What?"

"Some folks like tarts. Others like chocolate cake. They'll argue which one is best until the cows come home. Same with religion. Some folks like it served up one way, others like it another, but when it's all said and done, it's just dessert."

"Amen!" Vicky said.

She waited until she heard Nettie's bedroom door shut and then turned the latch to lock her door. "It's for Emily's peace of mind," she told herself as she picked up the book she'd been reading.

The diner did not have a break room for the staff like the steak house in Amarillo. When the morning rush was over, Nettie came from the kitchen, put a platter of pancakes on the counter, and sat down on one of the stools. Vicky brought out three plates of bacon and eggs along with a small side of sausage gravy and biscuits for each of them. Jancy poured three cups of coffee.

"I'm goin' to gain fifty pounds eatin' like this." Jancy slung a leg over the stool and got comfortable.

"Skinny as you are, it wouldn't hurt." Nettie poured warmed maple syrup over the stack of pancakes. "You've mentioned Louisiana a couple of times. Did y'all go there when you left here?"

"Yes, ma'am. Daddy had a brother down there, but we only got to stay three months. I do have one blood relative left in those parts, though. A girl cousin that I really liked. We stayed in touch over the years. That's where I'll be going when I leave here." She took a bite of food. "These are some really good biscuits."

"Homemade, not frozen," Nettie said.

"Will you teach me how to make them or is the recipe as secret as the tarts?"

"Nope, it's my mama's biscuit recipe and I don't mind sharing it," Nettie said.

Woody arrived and went to the coffee machine to pour a cup. He sat down, back to the counter, and crossed one leg over the other. "Sorry I'm late again. I swear to God, I'm busier now that I retired than I ever was as a workin' man. I brought news. That fancy man who was in here yesterday, Carlton something or other, went down to Leonard's convenience store and offered him a fortune for his store and the thirty acres he's got down south of town. He said that he'd already made a deal with Vicky and they'd be signin' a contract here in a couple of days. I can't believe that you are sellin' out, Vicky. This here is your home place. Why, you was raised in that house back there—" He paused to take a breath.

Vicky laid a hand on Woody's thin arm. "Honey, I'm not sellin' to anyone."

"What did Leonard tell him?" Nettie asked.

"That he could take his offer and shove it where the sun don't shine. I'm spreadin' the news that we're havin' a town meetin' at the fire hall tonight at eight o'clock. We got to stand together or before long there won't be a Pick, Texas. They'll change the name to something like Pecan Grove or whatever the hell they name their estates."

"Estates?" Vicky asked.

"Leonard did some askin' around after he left and found out he's one of them fellers who buys up land and puts in them fancy houses so the folks in places like Tyler can get out of the bigger cities to raise their kids," Woody said.

"He's wantin' to turn Pick into a bedroom community?" Nettie frowned.

Vicky removed her hand and went back to eating. "Sounds to me like he's tryin' to cause trouble and get rumors started."

Nettie nodded. "Divide and conquer. You are right, Woody. We need a town meeting so we all know where we're standing."

Woody slapped the top of the counter. "Crazy fool is up to no good, and I wouldn't be surprised if he didn't change Pick to Carlton."

Nettie's head bobbed up and down again. "Or

56

maybe just Estates, Texas, if that's the name of the game he's playin'. They'll try to smother us right out of existence. We'll close up a little early to be there. We'll sure tell everyone that comes in today about it, too."

"They might not even rename the place or get a post office for it. They could just get their mail out of Frankston on a rural route delivery," Jancy said.

Woody shivered. "I was born right here in Pick and raised three kids here. The idea of us losing our town, my Irma's town, is downright scary."

"Terrifies me, too," Nettie said. "But we'll stand together as a community."

He downed the rest of his coffee and put some coins on the counter. "I got to get down to the church and let all the Bible school folks know about the meetin'."

"See you tonight." Vicky waved.

He held the door for a stranger who stepped inside the diner, removed his straw cowboy hat, and nodded at the ladies. His dark hair was a little too long and his angular face a lot too sexy. He wore his jeans stacked up just right over polished cowboy boots and his white pearl-snap shirt had creases down the sleeves.

Vicky's pulse jacked up a notch, and her heart kicked in an extra beat. She couldn't help it. She'd always been attracted to cowboys with dark hair, and those green eyes didn't slow the flash of heat inside her, either. But with her luck, he was probably one of the developer's minions.

She stood up slowly and circled around to the back of the counter where he'd sat down. "What can I get you this mornin'?"

"Hot one, ain't it?" he said with a smile.

Don't even think a grin will persuade me to listen to your offer. I don't give a rat's rear if you offer six million dollars.

"Looks like it's shapin' up to be," she said. "Iced tea?"

"Yes, please with a twist of lime."

"Lime, not lemon?"

"Never did learn to like the flavor of lemon," he said. "And I'll have one of those strawberry tarts."

"Be right out," she said.

"I pass this place at least once a month and have sworn for years that I'd stop by. Today I decided to just do it. I own a little pastry shop in Palestine, so I bet this could be considered research," he said. "I'm Andy Butler, by the way. Are you the owner here?"

"Part owner." She sliced a lime and put it into a small bowl, filled a glass with crushed ice and tea, and carefully put a tart on a saucer. She added a paper napkin wrapped around a set of cutlery.

Nettie and Jancy had gone to the kitchen. She could hear them talking about biscuits and the recipes for pancakes and omelets. But Vicky's eye was on the cowboy and his reaction to the tart.

He rolled his eyes in appreciation at the first bite of the tart. "My God, this is fantastic."

"Thank you," she said.

"If you aren't married, I'm proposing to you."

"I'll have to warn you that I've turned down more romantic proposals than that," she said.

"How did your husband propose?" He put another bite in his mouth.

"I think his words were, 'I guess we'd best go tell Nettie that you're pregnant and then we'd better find us a preacher.' But then that was twenty-three years ago."

"You aren't old enough to have been married that long."

"Forty in September," she said.

He raised a wait-a-second finger while he chewed and swallowed. "Forty-two in October. So does your husband make these delicious tarts, or do you?"

"Nettie, co-owner of the diner, makes them. My husband died six weeks after we married."

"I'm so sorry." His gaze seemed sincere. "The people who told me about these did not exaggerate. They really are fabulous."

"Thank you." She refilled his tea glass.

"Want to sell me the recipe?"

"I do not!" Vicky growled. "And I'm not

selling the diner. You can tell Carlton Wolfe that he's got some nerve sending his peon in here to do his dirty work. It don't matter if he comes in here in his three-piece suit or if he sends in a sexy cowboy or even a Dallas Cowboy in full football gear, my business or my recipe either one are not for sale," she said coldly.

"Whoa, lady." Both hands shot up like a cowboy in an old western as he dropped the pie. "I don't want to buy your business. I was jokin' with you, but I would definitely buy this recipe if you did want to sell it."

"Sorry about my temper," she said. "The tart recipe is not for sale at any price you could offer. We don't even cater them and we limit the number that folks can carry out of here."

"And that is?"

She glared at him. How dare he stroll in her place of business and try to buy their recipe. Lord, what next? Was someone going to come in and offer to set her up as the madam of a brothel? She'd had an offer for her property, now her recipe. All that was left was her body.

"Two. Most of the time only one goes out the door and it's for when a guy proposes to a lady or when a couple have a big anniversary," she said with a coldness her flushed cheeks definitely didn't share.

"Well, then could I please have two of these to take with me?"

"Proposing or celebrating an anniversary?" she asked as she popped two small boxes into shape and put a tart in each one.

"Neither. I just know that when I get back to the shop, they're going to ask me about them and I'll want to let them see for themselves." He smiled brightly. "They are something else. I'd love to sell them in my shop. Maybe even ship them out to specialty places around the state." He laid a fancy business card on the counter. "If you ever change your mind."

"I won't." She tucked the card into her back pocket.

"Then I guess I'll have to make a trip up here every week or two to satisfy my sweet tooth." He settled his hat on his head, tipped the brim toward her, and said, "Y'all have a good day, now."

Vicky couldn't take her eyes off his swagger as he walked out the door, got into a big white crew-cab truck, and drove away. She wasn't even aware that Jancy had joined her at the counter until the girl giggled.

"If he was twenty years younger, I'd have the same look on my face."

"He's the devil. He wants to buy the tart recipe. Even took two with him, but he won't figure out the secret that makes them so good," Vicky declared.

"The devil in blue jeans like in that old song 'Somebody's Knockin'.' Downright temptin', ain't he? But don't pay no attention to me. I'm the worst person in the whole state, maybe the whole world, when it comes to figurin' out a man," Jancy said.

Vicky grabbed a white bar rag and went to work cleaning up the booth. "You're not old enough to know that song. I wouldn't know it if Nettie hadn't played it when I was a kid."

"My mama liked jazz. I heard y'all arguing about the recipe for the tarts."

"Not even pillow talk would get me to give him the recipe," Vicky said.

Nettie poked her face up to the order window. "Which she can't do anyway because she doesn't know what all I put in the filling or the crust. Is that a bad-luck thing or a good-luck thing for the summer?"

"Luck thing?" Jancy asked.

"Vicky hates summer. It's the time of year when luck, either bad or good, comes to her in threes. Been that way since she was seventeen. How about your good-luck/bad-luck stories, Jancy? You got any? Maybe we'll uncork a bottle of cheap strawberry wine some evening and have a girls' night in when Emily gets home," Nettie said.

"As in Boone's Farm?" Jancy asked.

"As in one of the few bottles left in the cellar that my mama and Nettie made back in the day," Vicky answered.

"You go wipin' the dust off one of them bottles, you better be sure Emily is home for one of them girls' nights," Nettie said. "Here comes the first of the lunch run. I bet we don't take a single tart home tonight. And I mean it about that wine, girl. I won't have y'all sneakin' a bottle out without tellin' me."

"I wouldn't dream of poppin' the cork without you there to tell us the story of how you and Mama nearly put in a winery instead of a diner." Vicky picked up four menus and headed toward the booth where two couples were settling in for an early lunch.

Woody took his place behind the podium that evening at exactly eight o'clock. He looked out over the packed firehouse room and frowned. "I don't want our town to be turned into a bedroom community for Tyler folks who don't want to live in the city. And I sure do not want us to become a divided town because of rumors. Out of fairness, we will let Mr. Carlton Wolfe say his piece to all of us at one time instead of meetin' with us individually. It'll make it so that we aren't hearin' rumors and we all know what everyone is thinkin' on this matter. So we'll let him talk first, and then he can answer all our questions."

Vicky had chosen a seat near the back, and Jancy sat beside her. Nettie, God love her heart, plowed right up to the front row so she could look that developer in the eye. Vicky just hoped that was all she'd put in his eye. With her temper, he might get a good sharp fingernail or even a poke with the little pink pearl-handled knife Nettie carried in her purse.

The hall was attached to the side of the metal building that housed the two fire trucks and a small office that made up the volunteer fire department. Ten years ago Woody had written a grant along with the help of Gary Drummond, a lawyer who'd come home to Pick when he retired twenty years before. They'd gotten enough money to build both the fire building and a town hall at the same time. It wasn't fancy, but there'd been lots of anniversaries, birthday parties, and meetings held in the building, and the residents of Pick were grateful to have it.

That night folding chairs had been set up in rows with a center aisle. When Woody introduced Carlton, he appeared from the back corner, out of the shadows, and strutted up the aisle like a banty rooster. He carried his arrogance to the podium, where he adjusted the sleeves of his dark-gray suit, a different one than what he'd worn to the diner the day before. His shirt was bloodred, and his gray-and-white paisley tie had a splash of red.

Feathers, Vicky thought. *Any minute now he is going to throw back his head, point that penis nose at the ceiling, and start crowing.*

Quite the polished politician, he smiled

64

dramatically out over the crowd. Silence filled the room with only an occasional cough or sigh as everyone waited to hear what he'd say.

There is no way those pearly whites are real. Someone probably knocked the original ones out when he tried to sweet-talk them into buying their property. Vicky hoped they'd scattered all over the street when it happened.

The whole place fell eerily quiet while they waited for him to speak. Then he clapped his hands in front of the microphone three times so fast that it sounded like gunfire. Several folks covered their ears, and two older ladies yelped like they'd been shot.

Nettie gave him an evil look. "You do that again and I'll make sure you are shovelin' coal in hell before nightfall. Scarin' us old people ain't goin' to persuade us into lettin' you have our land and our heritage."

"Amen, Miz Nettie," Woody said.

He leaned forward and said into the microphone, "Just like that—you can all be rich. You can retire early, buy a travel trailer, go on that vacation you always dreamed about. I'm gathering investors not only to buy Vicky Rawlins's property but also the convenience store. I'm interested in the rest of this place, too. It will be a community of beautiful homes and every one of you that sells to me will have the option of buying a new house at a ten percent discount. My company will even take applications to carry the mortgage for you. You don't get a better deal than that, folks. It's a win-win situation."

Vicky felt someone's presence before she turned her head and saw that handsome cowboy baker, Andy Butler, had sat down beside her. Cowboy baker? What had gotten into her? He'd changed into khaki slacks and a knit shirt with three buttons at the neck. She tried to listen to Carlton going on about the benefits the citizens of Pick would have if they'd only sign away their hearts and souls, but it was useless.

She'd been right. Andy was in cahoots with Carlton. Why else would he be at a Pick town meeting? He wouldn't have a bit of interest in what went on in their little town.

"He's a smooth talker. I bet he could sell oceanfront property right here in east Texas," Andy whispered.

"What are you doin' here?" she asked.

"Do you know my dad, Wesley Butler?"

"Heard of him. He owns the Butler Ranch north of Palestine, right? Can't say as I've ever met him. What does your father have to do with this community meeting?"

"Carlton Wolfe approached my dad about being an investor, so I came to see what's going on. I think this is all a show. He'll run off with the investors' money as well as the down payments

66

the folks in town give him for new homes. But what do I know? I make cakes and doughnuts for a livin'." Andy smiled.

"Then if we were to sell our places to him, he would . . ." She paused.

"He'd give you a twenty-page contract full of legal jargon that not even the best lawyers could decipher and you'd never see a dime. But your property would be tied up in court for years while someone tried to sort the whole thing out. I can't find a thing on him, not where he's done other deals or anything. Makes you suspicious. I doubt that Carlton Wolfe is even his name."

"Hey, I got a question for you, Mr. Wolfe." Vicky interrupted him in the middle of a sentence as she stood. "If we did sell to you—and for the record, I'm not at all interested in selling my property and neither is Nettie—but I was wondering how long is it going to take to see the houses ready to live in?"

"We will have time for questions and answers later, Victoria Rawlins, so take your seat and wait until I have finished talking," he said.

"My name is Vicky and you want my land, so I want answers. What kind of guarantees do we have that we'd have first chance at the houses you will build? And what's the price range?"

She enjoyed the fact that she was riling him. Maybe he'd get mad enough to storm out and never come back again.

"Very good questions indeed, and I'm prepared to answer each of them." His smile didn't fade, but his jaw worked in anger.

Vicky folded her hands over her chest. "Then have at it. I'm waiting. How about the rest of y'all? You want some answers tonight?"

"Yeah, we do," Ryder yelled.

"All y'all who w-want him to get down to the details, raise your hand," Shane said.

Every hand in the place went up.

Vicky expected Carlton to clap again, but he just smiled and nodded. "I have a wonderful surprise for all you folks here in Pick." His lips peeled back even farther over his perfect teeth, resembling a possum snarling. "I will host a big barbecue feast for the whole town at the city park on Sunday afternoon at one o'clock. I will bring my team to answer any questions, and I'll have copies of a sample contract that you can all read over. I assure you, my plan will put your little town on the map."

Nettie started talking as she stood up and marched to the front of the room. "We're already on the map. We have the Strawberry Festival every year and folks come from miles away to get a strawberry tart or any number of other things made with strawberries at the vendors. We have a carnival and the whole nine yards." She stopped and stood in front of the lectern. "We'll come to your barbecue and we'll eat your food.

68

But we don't take charity here in Pick, so let's call it a community potluck. What do you say, folks? We haven't had a good old Sunday get-together in a long time."

Applause came close to raising the roof. Nettie was a genius. Vicky had never wanted to hug her as much as she did right then. Vicky clapped with everyone else and even threw in one of her shrill catcalls. When the noise died down, she winked at Woody. "We might bust out some of our strawberry wine, right, Woody?"

"You got it. I'll bring six bottles, the last of what Irma made before she died. Myrtle, you can bring a couple of them blackberry cobblers," he said.

"I'll bring four if Darlene and Leonard will freeze up some homemade ice cream to go with it," Myrtle piped up from the middle of the room.

"Wait a minute." Carlton looked like steam might start flowing out of his ears at any minute. "This is my party to show you all that I'm serious about this venture."

That man had some really hard lessons to learn—tonight was number one. He couldn't waltz into their town and take over.

"Naw, it's our party now. You bring the barbecue, and we'll bring the rest and we'll all have a good time," Woody said. "It's the way we do things in Pick, Texas. Hey, Ryder, if you're in town, you can bring along your guitar."

"Sounds good to me. Shane can tune up his fiddle and if Dusty will get out his banjo, we'll use the pavilion for a little dancin'." Ryder nodded.

"One o'clock right after church on Sunday, it is. We can have us a good old time and anyone that wants to talk to Mr. Wolfe can do so," Nettie said. "Oh, and I'm sure you won't mind if we call on our own local lawyer to read through that contract for us, will you, Mr. Wolfe? I think you are wastin' your time because we're kind of proud of our town and the way we do things, but we'll be glad to party with you."

Jancy leaned over and whispered. "What just happened?"

"We put him in his place the Pick, Texas, way," Vicky told her. "I doubt he even shows up with the barbecue since Nettie mentioned a lawyer."

"Who'll bring the meat for the party then?"

"Nobody ever goes home hungry from our get-togethers," Vicky said. "We'll shut the diner at one o'clock and bring along a couple of big pans of meat loaf in case he doesn't show."

"I've never seen anything like this," Jancy said.

"Stick around Pick, honey. We do right by what is ours," Vicky told her.

"I will look forward to Sunday then. I want all of you"—Carlton raised his arms dramatically as if gathering in his lost brothers—"to think about how much my deal can improve your lives. I will

70

turn this over to Woody again. I appreciate you letting me talk to you."

Woody picked up the gavel and hit the oak lectern with it. "Meeting is adjourned. Let's all go home and polish up our dancin' boots. We might even talk the kids into doing some clog dancin' for us."

"And that's the way to steal a man's thunder," Andy chuckled as he stood to his feet, towering over Vicky's short stature. "Why don't you invite me to the party on Sunday? Since it's only for citizens of Pick, I would need an invitation."

"What are you goin' to advise your father to do about the investment?" Jancy stood up and was tall enough that it was no trouble to look him right in the eye.

"To superglue all his bank accounts shut," Andy told her.

"Then I'll invite you to the hoopla. Bring your daddy with you if you want to and he can see for himself that Carlton is just a bag of wind," Jancy said.

"I'll bring two sheet cakes and a dozen or two frosted doughnuts," he said. "Good night, ladies. See y'all on Sunday." That he wasn't wearing jeans did not hinder that swagger one bit as he left the fire hall.

"You are welcome," Jancy said with a big grin.

"For what?" Nettie asked as she joined them.

"She was too shy to invite that man to the party

71

on Sunday, so I did it for her." Jancy giggled. "And he's bringing cakes and doughnuts."

"Long as he don't come empty-handed, he's welcome," Nettie said.

Vicky frowned. "She's been here two days. She doesn't get to make this kind of decision."

"Long as she holds a job in Pick and lives in Pick, she gets a vote in what we do. You goin' to side with Carlton, Jancy?" Nettie asked.

"Hell, no! I've seen smooth talkers like him before. He's a snake, a poisonous one, and I hope that none of these good folks get taken in by his promises," Jancy said.

"Well said for a kid your age," Nettie said. "Now let's go home and have a shot of Jack Daniel's. I need to get the taste of this evening out of my mouth. Fancy houses, indeed. We don't need all that crap in Pick. We just need good neighbors and good friends, and we done got both. Don't that man have a lick of sense?"

"Some men are just born jackasses and age doesn't do anything but make them bray louder." Jancy followed Vicky and Nettie out of the building.

"Amen!" they said in unison.

Chapter Four

The diner sat completely empty in the middle of the afternoon on Friday. Rain poured down in sheets, big drops sounding like bullets as they hit the tin roof. The door flew open, and a big red-and-white umbrella preceded a lady into the place. Jancy jumped up from the booth where she'd stretched out her long legs and headed for the counter to get a menu.

"Emily! You're early!" Vicky squealed from the kitchen.

With Nettie right behind her, they were soon all tangled up in a hug. Water droplets flew from the umbrella when Emily dropped it and threw back the hood of her yellow slicker, showing off thick blonde hair that floated to her shoulders in big, bouncy waves.

The rain hadn't smeared a bit of her makeup. But then, the angels in heaven had always smiled on Emily Rawlins. It was a wonder they hadn't stopped the rain and parted the clouds so she could walk to the diner from her cute little red car in sunshine.

"My last final was over at ten, but I was already

packed and ready to leave. I drove the whole way in this hellacious rain." She backed up a step and removed the raincoat.

She had big blue eyes and a face that would make a photographer drool, no change from the last time Jancy had seen her. It had been on a Saturday. She'd driven the same little car that was out there in the parking lot up to the diner, gotten out, and rushed inside to tell her mother that she and her friends were going to a mall in Tyler. She hadn't even looked at Jancy or acknowledged that she was in the diner.

Jancy's mama had reached across the table and squeezed her hand. "Time will ease the pain, honey. Life changes, and it's okay to hurt."

Jancy didn't have the heart to tell her it wasn't that they were moving that brought the pain to her expression that afternoon. It was the ache to belong to a place like Emily Rawlins did.

"Your dad is a difficult man, but someday he might change," Elaine had said.

"How do you do this? How do you live with him, Mama?" Jancy asked.

Jancy would never forget what her mother said to her that day. "I loved him enough to say vows, and I won't break them. What doesn't kill us makes us stronger."

"You drove way too fast," Nettie scolded, bringing her back to the moment. "Have you had lunch?"

The way Vicky smiled at Emily reminded Jancy of her mother. She'd had that same look on her face the night Jancy got her high school diploma.

Emily shook her head. "I hope you saved me a piece of meat loaf. I've been starving for your cookin' for the past four weeks. God, I missed this place. I wish I never had to go back to school."

Vicky kept an arm around her shoulders and led her toward the kitchen. "It's only one more year and then you'll have a fancy business degree. You'll be able to get a job anywhere in the whole world."

Emily stopped at the swinging doors and locked eyes with Jancy. "Hello. You haven't changed a bit since you were sixteen."

"Just six years older and fifty years wiser. You haven't changed, either." Jancy blew off the comment with a wave of the hand. "Y'all go visit. I'll sweep up and man the front while we've got a little bit of downtime."

"Thank you," Emily said. "I smell meat loaf and real mashed potatoes and green beans with bacon. I'm never leaving the city limits again." Emily led the parade through the doors. She grabbed up a platter instead of a plate and went straight for the pots on the stove.

Jancy picked up the broom and started at the north end of the diner. There was little on the floor, but she needed to keep busy. Tuesday when she'd gone to the town meeting, she'd felt like she fit in. Wednesday and Thursday she and Vicky had worked out an unspoken arrangement in the diner, and she'd even entertained notions of staying longer than two weeks. But when Emily arrived, all the old insecurities surfaced. She became again that nerdy, shy girl who wasn't accepted in any of the high school cliques.

And I was crazy to think I'd ever be more than that. Why can't I learn not to trust people? It was my mama's failing. She was constantly getting hurt by people she put her faith in. I should have learned from her mistakes.

Emily brought the loaded platter out into the diner and sat down at a booth. Nettie and Vicky followed along after her like a couple of hungry little puppy dogs and slid in on the opposite side.

"Did you do well on all your finals?" Vicky asked.

"I'm still holding on to a three-point average." She grabbed the saltshaker and shook it over her food.

"You could have a four-point if you'd work harder. You have the brains," Nettie fussed.

Jancy kept at it until she reached the middle of the room, and then she swept her small pile of trash into the kitchen. After she'd cleaned it up, she set about tidying up the workstation and washing the pans that had been piled into the sink. She didn't want to hear their conversation, but with no one else in the diner, Emily's voice floated right on back to her.

"Now, Nettie, start talkin'. Tell me all the gossip that I've missed."

"You've heard about Carlton Wolfe?" Nettie asked.

"Mama told me about him. Has he been back? Do we need to make some oleander tea special for him, or maybe fix him a strawberry tart with oleander in the crust? Now that would be poetic justice, wouldn't it? He would probably tear down our diner, and instead our diner takes him down."

Jancy peeked out the serving window to see Emily shovel a forkful of mashed potatoes covered with gravy into her mouth, shut her eyes, and groan. "I mean it, Mama. I'm going to pitch a tent on the forty acres and get fat and sassy on diner food."

"Hush! You are going to be a big shot executive somewhere like New York City. Or maybe London," Vicky said.

Emily looked up in time to lock gazes with Jancy. "I wish I'd majored in culinary arts so you'd let me come home and work right here the rest of my life."

Jancy quickly bent out of sight and duckwalked over to the workstation, where she pulled out a stool and sat down. It wasn't that Emily had ever been mean to her, but indifference could be even more painful. Emily had always looked through Jancy, not at her. If she did speak to her, it was with a curt hello and nothing more when they passed in the hallways.

Deep in her own thoughts, she didn't hear Emily come back through the swinging doors until she was already in the kitchen. When she realized all three women were joining her in the tiny space, she hopped off the stool and grabbed the broom.

"I'll get that other half now that y'all are finished. We should be getting the afternoon coffee drinkers here soon," Jancy said.

"You don't have to leave," Nettie said.

"No problem. I'll get everything ready for the supper run." Jancy managed at least half a smile.

"Don't put on that apron," Vicky said.

At first Jancy thought she was talking to her, but then she glanced over her shoulder to see that Vicky was shaking a finger at Emily.

"You go on to the house and get settled in. Tomorrow is soon enough for you to start working here," Vicky said.

Well, rats! Now I know I'm leaving at the end of next week. I'd hoped that she'd have her own things to do—like keeping her toenails and fingernails all pretty and maybe washing that gorgeous thick hair twice a day. But working here already? That I do not need or want.

"I'll unload my things after work. I'm not leavin', Mama. This diner is like vitamin pills to me. I love waitressing. I get to see everyone and talk to the people." Emily came through the doors wearing a bright-red apron, picked up an order pad and stuck it in her pocket along with a pen, and then swept her hair up into a ponytail that she secured with a tie from the pocket of her jeans.

"What needs to be done now, Jancy?" she asked.

Was the queen talking to her? Had she held out the golden scepter and given her permission to speak?

"I just work here. Vicky is the boss," Jancy said.

"Okay, then, Mama, do you want me in the front or in the kitchen?" Emily asked as she picked up a bar rag and dusted off the cake domes, a job that Jancy had just finished.

"You and Jancy can work the front. I'll help Nettie in the kitchen," Vicky answered.

Jancy bit back a groan at that idea. But she'd only have to work with Emily one more day, because payday was Saturday night in most restaurants. That meant she could hitch a ride to Palestine and catch a bus to Louisiana on Sunday morning. Now that Queen Emily was in Pick, they didn't need her anyway.

That would be jealousy rearing its ugly head.

Her mother's voice rang loud and clear in her head. *Anyone can run from a problem, but you might make friends if you stick around awhile.*

But Emily doesn't like me, she argued.

The voice in her head didn't say another word.

Nettie had never seen Emily tossing about such craziness. Lord love a duck! There was no way she'd ever live in a tent or that Vicky would let her work in the diner after having put her through all that schooling.

Emily dusted everything in sight but kept an eye on the windows as if she expected someone. And whoever it was that she was looking for sure made her nervous. "I can't wait until Sunday to see everyone at church. I haven't been home in two weekends."

Nettie went up front and took a seat on a bar stool. Something had that girl just plumb jumpy. She was a bear when she was hungry—always had been. But this new blast of energy was something else, and Nettie intended to get to the bottom of it.

"You can't begin to know how much I've missed home, Mama." Emily started cleaning the cash register.

Whatever it was with that girl had nothing to do with Carlton Wolfe, because the whole town had spoken their minds about that. The way she was acting, Nettie would bet it wasn't a little thing like Emily wanting to trade her car in, either. She'd approached that before and Vicky had told her she could have a new vehicle when she could pay for it herself. The little economy car that she'd gotten for her sixteenth birthday had come with the notice that it wouldn't be replaced until Emily finished college. Whatever was going on with her was riding on the tail of a class-five tornado.

"So you don't like big-city life?" Jancy asked.

"Hate it. Can't imagine living in a place like New York City. I don't even like Tyler," she said.

Nettie gripped the edge of the counter and remembered the day Vicky had told her she was expecting a baby. It was exactly the way that Emily was behaving.

"You'll get used to it," Vicky said.

"No, I won't," Emily argued. "I wish you would have just let me help with the diner right out of high school."

"In today's world you need a job that does not involve carrying tea and coffee to people for more than twelve hours a day, seven days a week," Vicky argued.

Emily shrugged. "Look, there's Shane and Ryder driving up in the lot."

She met them as they came in and hugged them both. "It's so good to see y'all. Ryder, I heard you are thinkin' about a desk job up in Frankston."

"Thinkin' about it." Ryder smiled.

"My dream car is gettin' close to finished." Shane made a beeline to the counter. "We got busy doin' some stuff in the shop since it was rainin' and haven't had lunch. Got any meat loaf left?"

"Sure do. Want the special?" Jancy asked.

"Sounds w-wonderful. Make it two and I'll pay today, so put it on one ticket," Shane said.

Nettie's feeling deepened. Surely to God it wasn't Ryder and Emily. It couldn't be that—not in a million years would she ever lose her mind and go out with Ryder Jensen. No decent girl would be caught with him. He was one of those wild boys only interested in sex. But maybe she'd confided in him and Shane about whoever she was dating. Only a man could make a girl act like that. Vicky was going to have a hissy if Emily had gotten serious about some guy in Pick this close to getting her pushed through college.

Nettie eased out of the booth and headed for the kitchen, where she quickly put two plates together, giving the boys extra-large portions. Emily followed behind her, lining a red plastic basket with papers and loading it up with hot dinner rolls from the warmer.

"Now you are really home," Nettie said.

Emily threw an arm around her shoulders and sighed. "Yes, I am, and Mama's not going to like what I've got to say while I'm here. I'm

82

depending on you to keep her from going into a really big funk, Nettie."

"And what are you going to tell her that's all that bad?" Nettie whispered.

"That I didn't enroll for next semester," she whispered.

"Hell's bells!" Nettie gasped.

"And that's not all, but right now that's all I'm sayin'. Baby steps, Nettie. Just little bitty baby steps. Here she comes."

"Woody is on his way in. Are we going to have enough food for another blue-plate special?" Vicky's head popped up in the window.

"Plenty. I overcooked and then it rained," Nettie answered.

"Emily!" Woody hurried across the floor and wrapped his arms around her. "It's good to have you home for the summer. We miss you around here during the school year. How'd you do on the finals?"

Jancy checked her arms and hands to see if she was turning pea green. With the amount of jealousy shooting through her veins, it wouldn't have surprised her one bit to look like a Martian that afternoon. Not even the brief moment when her mother's voice came back to scold her had helped erase the feelings in her heart.

The last song she'd heard before her car radio went dead had been "This Ain't Nothin'" by

Craig Morgan. The lyrics talked about an old man who'd lost everything to a tornado and said, "This ain't nothin'." Working with Emily wasn't even a tiny little dark cloud in the big picture of Jancy's life. She could endure another week or two, and when she started thinking about things, she'd let that song play through her mind.

"So what are you doin' on your first night home, Em?" Ryder asked.

"Unpackin' and sittin' on the porch swing," she answered. "Y'all should come on over and have a glass of tea with us."

"W-we'd love to," Shane said. "Eight?"

"Maybe seven thirty-ish, and we can watch the sun set together. Lord, I miss a decent sunset and sweet tea that don't come out of a gallon jug from the store," Emily said. "If you get there early, you can help me unload the car. Don't look at me like that, Mama. I can always put things away tomorrow evening."

Jancy wanted to slap Emily. If she had a mama like Vicky, she'd spend the time with her, not a couple of local guys like Shane and Ryder. Did she have a crush on one of them?

Either one would cause Vicky to stroke out for sure. Shane would never be good enough for the amazing Emily. And Ryder was the resident bad boy of the whole damn county. But what Emily did or didn't do wasn't her problem. Jancy was there for one more week, and then she'd have enough money in her sock drawer to catch a bus to Louisiana.

The afternoon got busy, and Emily took over one end of the diner while Jancy handled the other. Vicky had gone to the kitchen with Nettie. Then suddenly it was closing time and they were on the way home. She hung back and let the three of them walk ahead of her. When they reached the porch, she went straight on inside to her bedroom and closed the door.

Gathering up her stuff for the bathroom, she was fussing at herself for ever coming down through Pick to begin with. She opened the door just as Nettie raised her hand to knock, and it startled both of them. "I was coming to see what we'd done wrong. You've acted strange all afternoon."

"Nothing." Jancy backed up and sat down on the edge of the bed. "It's not you. It's me. Come on in, Nettie."

The older woman ran a hand through her short gray hair and frowned. "I thought we were getting along good."

"We were."

"Emily? She's not herself, either. Is there something going on between y'all two?"

"Maybe we're both jealous," Jancy said.

"Jealous! What in the devil for?"

"I'm jealous because she has y'all, and she might be jealous because I'm in her house and she's afraid I'll mess with the dynamics y'all have," Jancy said.

"That's a crock of bull crap," Nettie said. "That's like sayin' we only got space in our hearts for one person. You both need to get over it."

"I'll try," Jancy said. "But she's got first dibs on the whole enchilada. I'm just the hired help."

"Your grandmother was my friend. You are my friend." Nettie's finger was a blur as it shook in front of her face. "Now get your butt out there on the porch and stop pouting. And keep your eyes and ears open. I want to know why Emily is acting so weird."

"Nettie! I told you why she's acting strange."

"No, you told me why *you* are. I think her problem goes a lot deeper than a little snit of jealousy," she said. "Go!"

"I don't want to. I haven't been invited."

"I'm tellin' you, not invitin' you. And if you see anything or find out what's goin' on with her, I want to know."

"What makes you think I'd rat her out if I did find out something?" Jancy asked.

"You don't want to see Vicky drop dead with a heart attack that we could have prevented if we'd known the facts."

"Okay, but only because I respect you and Vicky so much," Jancy said on a sigh.

"And get that long face straightened up before you get out there."

"Yes, ma'am," she said, but it wasn't with a smile.

Vicky was in the kitchen talking to someone on the phone about a delivery. The bathroom door slammed loudly, so evidently Nettie had claimed that room. Jancy pushed the front door open to find Ryder and Shane sitting on the porch steps and Emily on the swing.

"Come on out here with us," Shane said. "You can sit here beside me."

Emily patted the place beside her. "There's room on the swing."

The golden scepter had been extended once again. Did she bow her head and accept the favor, or did she ignore the queen and sit beside Shane? One didn't sound any better than the other, but Nettie had given her orders, so she sat down on the swing.

"So what do you w-want to be wh-when you grow up?" Shane asked.

"Why'd you ask that?" Jancy kept the swing going with a foot.

"We were talkin' about how things change after we get out of high school. I couldn't wait to get out of Pick, but after six weeks of college, I just wanted to come home and work in the diner," Emily said.

"And you, Ryder?" Jancy asked.

"Same. I went to school to be a marine biologist and wound up taking an offshore rig job. I like it fine, but I hate being away from home. That's why I'm going to take a desk job in Frankston the first of August," he answered Jancy, but his eyes were on Emily the whole time.

"Shane?" Jancy asked.

"I always w-wanted to do body w-work on cars, so I'm the success story." He grinned. "Now you, Jancy."

"I'm a waitress. I'll probably always be a waitress. I like what I do just fine. My mama wanted me to be a hairdresser, but . . ." She shrugged. "Tips aren't nearly as good and I don't even like doin' *my* hair. I can't imagine doin' something I don't like all day."

"Anything else you'd like to do in the future?" Emily asked.

"I want to be a wife and a mother, but I'm not in a hurry for either."

"Me, too, but I am in a hurry."

Jancy could have sworn that she saw her look right at Ryder—or was it Shane?

Chapter Five

"Mornin', Vicky." Jancy yawned as she stepped out of the bathroom. "Looks like the weatherman might be right. It's not raining. We need a hot and sunny day for the big picnic."

"It should be interesting to see if old P-Nose even shows up," Vicky said.

"P-Nose?" Jancy cocked her head to one side.

"Think about it," Vicky said.

"Oh!" Jancy clapped a hand over her mouth. "It does look like one, doesn't it?"

"A short one." Vicky nodded and closed the bathroom door behind her.

Giggling, Jancy turned to find Emily coming from the kitchen. She had bags under her eyes, and she was wearing the same clothes she'd had on the night before.

The giggling stopped. "Are you sneakin' in or did you fall asleep on the porch?"

"Shh . . ." Emily put a finger over her lips. "I'm pleading the Fifth."

"Good mornin'." Nettie threw open her bedroom door.

Emily slipped inside her room.

Nettie rubbed sleep from her eyes. "I thought I heard voices."

"Vicky and I were laughing at Carlton's nose."

"Why his nose?" Nettie asked.

"Vicky calls him P-Nose. Think about it," Jancy said.

Nettie nodded. "It ought to look like that. Way he pokes his nose into everyone's business and tries to screw them."

"Nettie!" Jancy gasped.

"It's the truth." She knocked on Emily's door. "Rise and shine, mornin' glory. If you are goin' to walk to work with the rest of us, you'd best get up and around."

Jancy waited on the porch swing for the other three. Trees had begun to take on individual forms instead of blending together into big black shapeless blobs. In an hour the sun would pop up as an orange sliver at first, and then it would rise with heat and power to knock out the darkness. As Jancy sat on the porch that morning, the pungent scents of wet grass and dirt all around her, she admitted that getting stranded in Pick was a good thing.

Her life had been a black blob for a long time, but in the past five days she'd begun to feel like the trees were taking shape. The sun wasn't up yet, but it was rising, and it might reveal that she wasn't supposed to spend the rest of her life at the diner. Yet she wasn't sure what she'd do if that's what was laid on her heart.

"Hey." Emily sat down on the other end of the swing. "I guess I owe you an explanation. You know I did not spend the night on the swing."

"Emily, this is your home. You don't owe me anything," Jancy said.

"Well, then I've got a confession. I wasn't sure about you living here. I remembered you from when you lived here before, and you were kind of standoffish. Anyway, after working with you and listening to Shane talk about you, I'll admit I was wrong."

"Shane talked about me?" Jancy asked.

"Honey, Shane had a big, big crush on you when we were sophomores and he and Ryder were seniors."

"Really?" Jancy gasped. "Are you serious?"

"Oh, yeah." Emily smiled.

"Why didn't he say something?"

"Because he stutters and it would have broken his heart if you'd laughed at him or rejected him. I've talked to him every night since you took the job. He says that you are a hard worker and that Mama and Nettie are lucky to have you."

"You must like him a lot," Jancy said.

"I really do," Emily told her.

"Y'all ready?" Nettie and Vicky came out at the same time.

"Ready." Jancy quickly stood up.

Vicky and Emily walked on ahead with Nettie and Jancy a few feet behind. They were about halfway to the diner when Nettie raised an eyebrow. Jancy shrugged and shook her head. Jancy wasn't ready to get in the middle of family problems. She'd been in that place before, and all it got her was a lot of misery.

She sucked in one more lungful of fresh morning air as Nettie unlocked the back door to the diner. "Want me to get out the pans of meat loaf and put them in the oven?"

Nettie looped a clean apron over her neck. "Not until we get the biscuits done for breakfast. You can make the dough up while I start a pot of gravy."

Emily removed a stick of sausage from the refrigerator, pulled out a stockpot, and crumbled the meat into it. "I'll make the gravy. I got hungry for sausage gravy and biscuits last spring and decided I'd make some."

"And you made a pot this size, right?" Jancy carefully mixed the ingredients for the biscuits.

"Oh, yeah. Didn't even think to size the recipe down. The whole dorm had biscuits and gravy that morning." Emily laughed. "You must've made the same mistake, right?"

Jancy nodded. "Only it was with salsa. We served it at the Mexican restaurant where I worked and they shared the recipe. I was the only one who liked it at home, and there I was with a whole gallon."

She remembered how her father had fussed for weeks about having to move it to the side every time he wanted a beer from the tiny refrigerator in the smallest trailer they'd ever lived in. With his ideas about a woman's place being in the home and the man making a living, it was a miracle that he even allowed Jancy to get a job when she was sixteen. But they needed that paycheck. *Old enough to work; old enough to make her own way*—that became his philosophy.

As soon as the dough was ready, Jancy slid it over toward her area of the worktable, rolled it out, and cut it into perfect little circles.

"The other places I worked used frozen biscuits," Jancy said.

"I mentioned that years ago and got shot down in a hurry." Emily didn't even look up from stirring the sausage. "In this diner everything is made from scratch."

"Cash register is counted and loaded. I'll get the tart shells put into the convection oven." Vicky looped the strings of a bibbed apron over her head. "Y'all did a good job yesterday of taking care of the customers, so I'll leave the front to y'all and help Nettie get things done back here."

Jancy smiled at the compliment. Not that she was vain enough to ever think she'd be anything but an employee—well, maybe a friend—for the next couple of weeks, but it was nice to be appreciated.

Couple of weeks? In one more week, you'll have the money to go. Don't let moss grow on you, girl, or you'll never leave. You were lookin' for a job when you found this one, and there's plenty more to be had. Her father's voice came through loud and clear in her head.

But a few weeks won't matter, she argued.

"Are we taking tarts to the picnic?" she blurted to get her father out of her head.

Vicky shook her head. "Rule says that only two can go out the door with anyone, and Nettie says that includes us. But she has a lemon sheet cake ready to go."

"What about for the Strawberry Festival?" Jancy asked.

"We close up an hour or so early."

"And I make extra for that day," Nettie said.

Vicky flipped on all the lights and unlocked the door. "Shane and Ryder are already here."

"And Woody is parking right beside them," Emily said.

"Woody is early. Must be makin' up for the fact that he was late a couple of days last week," Nettie said.

Jancy caught a glimpse of Shane patting Woody on the shoulder as they made their way toward the diner. But she kept a close watch on Emily, whose eyes were glued on the trio. Something was definitely going on. Although she kept reminding herself that it was none of her business, despite Nellie's instructions, curiosity was rising at a fast speed.

"Hey, Jancy, coffee for all three of us," Woody said as they headed for a booth.

"Black, right?" she asked.

"Sunday morning pancakes or the big breakfast?" Nettie yelled from the back.

"You know us too well," Woody hollered. "I'm goin' to gain ten pounds today with a big breakfast and then another fifteen with the get-together at the park. Y'all goin' to open back up for supper? I might just clog up my arteries real good if you are."

Nettie poked her head out the door. "You could gain fifty pounds and still be too skinny. Biscuits are in the oven. Give 'em five minutes and they'll come out to you pipin' hot. And we aren't opening back up after the picnic."

"M-m-mornin'." Shane flashed a bright smile past Nettie and toward the cash register area where Jancy and Emily were standing side by side. Jancy couldn't tell if he was flirting with her or Emily or merely happy to be in the diner with breakfast on the way.

Ryder waved at Nettie. "Pancakes with sausage for me."

"Pancakes w-with bacon, M-Miz Nettie. I'll help you take the coffee to the table, Jancy."

Shane covered the distance from the booth to the counter in three long strides.

"You goin' to the picnic?" Shane asked Jancy, derailing her train of thought. "I'll be playin' the fiddle for the dancin'."

"Yes, I am and lookin' forward to it," she answered. "I had no idea you played the fiddle."

"Grandpa taught m-me. I don't read music. I just play by ear." Shane smiled. "Reckon you could save m-m-me a dance?"

"Be glad to," Jancy said. "But if you are dancin', who will play?"

"I'll step in and do my best," Woody said. "I ain't the musician this boy is, but I can do well enough for a set or two."

"Do you still know how to clog?" Shane asked.

"How do you . . ." She paused. She'd never danced anywhere but in the backyard until she'd left Pick. She'd seen the kids clogging on the stage at the park at the festival the one year that she'd attended, and it looked like so much fun that she'd taught herself the steps.

"It's a long story. I'll tell you sometime if you'll save a dance for m-me," Shane said.

"Haven't danced a clog in years," she said.

"It's like ridin' a bicycle. It all comes back to you," Emily said as she picked up Woody's breakfast and took it to the booth. "I can't wait to dance. You going to be my partner, Ryder?"

"Sure, I will, darlin'." He grinned.

There was a moment when their eyes locked, but it was gone so quickly that Jancy couldn't be sure that it had even happened. The diner started filling up so fast then that she only caught a glimpse of the guys when they left. It turned into a constant hustle to keep coffee cups and orders filled. Then, boom, things began to slow down and Emily slipped a five-dollar bill into her pocket.

"I believe this belongs to you, since you took their order. Woody handed it to me when he left. Because we both kind of waited on the table, he didn't know who to give it to, but that side belongs to you."

"Thanks. I didn't think we'd be this busy on a Sunday with a big thing later this afternoon." Jancy filled three glasses with sweet tea.

"Neither did Nettie. It's a good thing that we're here to work the front. Now it's over—except for any truckers that we'll get—because everyone is off to Sunday school and then church."

Jancy picked up a wet bar rag and a small tub to clean off the last table. "I don't think I ever worked so hard or got so many tips in three hours in my life."

"I'll help get the tables cleared and then we can take a break and eat," Emily said. "We got off track this morning about me comin' in so late," she whispered as she put cups and plates into the tub.

Jancy had made a promise to Nettie that she'd find out what was going on with Emily, but she wasn't sure she wanted to hear about it. Knowing meant she had an obligation to tell, and she liked where things were with all three of them. Tattling somehow didn't seem right, and yet, she'd agreed to help Nettie. Talk about being between the old rock and a hard place.

That's what she'd told the police when they came to question her about her boyfriend's job. They'd offered her a deal and she'd made her choice, but it had come with a dump truck load of guilt attached to it. A rock on one side and a hard place on the other, and she'd have to make a choice because it was evident that Emily wanted to talk about things.

"Hey, y'all, the biscuits are done," Nettie called.

"Later," Emily whispered.

Jancy nodded and followed Emily to the kitchen. She hiked a hip on a bar stool and grabbed a biscuit from the pan.

Nettie sat down beside her. "Butter?"

"No, these are like eating cake. They don't need anything else," Jancy answered.

Vicky pulled up the third stool. "My feet hurt and I'm starving."

Emily hoisted the pitcher filled with batter. "Pancakes, anyone?"

"Yes," Jancy said. "I'll fry eggs when we finish eating."

"Good. There's plenty of leftover bacon and sausage gravy for the four of us, too," Nettie said.

"Shane was flirting with Jancy." Emily poured batter onto the griddle.

"He was not." Jancy blushed. "And if he was, it was useless. I have sworn off all men forever, amen."

"Bad relationship?" Nettie asked.

Jancy nodded. "More than one."

"Want to talk about it?" Emily asked.

"Not today. Maybe later. Today is all about the picnic and trying to remember the clogging steps that I haven't practiced in six years," Jancy said.

"Want to practice out in the diner? I haven't clogged in years, either," Emily said.

Jancy wasn't quite sure how she felt about this new offer of friendship and camaraderie. Six years ago she would have stumbled over her own two feet for an offer to be Emily Rawlins's friend, but there'd been a lot of water under the bridge since then. And Emily might not be so quick to offer her friendship if she knew everything about Jancy. Still, it wouldn't hurt to at least be nice.

"I'd love it, but let's eat first," Jancy said.

Vicky and Nettie sat on bar stools and watched Emily and Jancy dancing to a clogging song that Emily had pulled up on her phone. The whining fiddles took Vicky off the stool on the second dance, and by the beginning of the third, Nettie had joined them.

Nettie was breathless when the song ended and collapsed with her feet up in a booth. "Man, that takes the energy right out of a person. Wasn't sure that I'd remember the steps, but it's a lot like riding a bicycle. And just as hard on the legs and knees."

Vicky slid into another booth. "Amen to that. You girls did a fine job. I don't think either of you will be embarrassed this afternoon. Just take your cowboy boots so you can make lots of noise on the wood floor."

"Who needs a gym class?" Jancy panted as she popped up on a bar stool.

"Now that we're limbered up and we've got a few minutes, you want to tell us about those bad relationships, Jancy?" Nettie asked.

"Why ruin the perfect moment?" Jancy smiled.

"Amen. That was fun," Vicky agreed.

"Besides," Emily panted, "why worry with past relationships when there's a new one off the horizon for Jancy? Shane really was flirting with her this morning."

"Shane has roots. I've grown a pretty good set of wings," she said.

"Wings can be clipped," Nettie said.

"Not unless you stand still and let someone do it," Jancy answered. "How about you, Emily? You got wings or roots?"

"My roots are so deep in Pick that they run down halfway to China. No one could ever get me out of here permanently." Emily went to the drink machine and filled four glasses with lemonade.

"Oh, honey, don't give up your wings," Vicky said. "You are still young. There is plenty of time to settle down. Let those wings take you to places where you'll build beautiful memories."

Emily set a glass in front of Vicky and kissed her on the top of the head. "Memories can grow like a big old oak tree with roots here just as easily as they can on the wings of someone who can't ever find a place to settle."

She was right, but not all memories were good ones. Jancy was the poster child for bad ones. Maybe that's why she kept moving around— outrunning what she didn't want to remember.

Chapter Six

Vicky's heart had gone out to Jancy as they were drinking lemonade. There was a lot of pain in her face—the kind that no one her age should have to deal with. She should have been in college with Emily, having fun and worrying about whether she passed a test, not sleeping in her car and worrying about where her next meal would come from. Vicky felt a desperate tugging on her heartstrings to help Jancy find her roots, almost as much as the pull for Emily to find her wings.

"It hasn't changed," Jancy said when Vicky pulled the van into a parking place at the park.

"Not much does in Pick." Emily slid open the side door. "And I hope it stays like this forever."

Vicky was fighting with Carlton over the same thing, so she couldn't say a word. If she didn't win the fight, there wouldn't be a park in a few years. With two swing sets, a slide, and a merry-go-round, it wasn't a big park, but it did have a pavilion with three picnic tables and a basketball court. The city paid to keep the lights on until ten o'clock every night. The parents of the kids who gathered there on the weekends to sneak a beer or make out would have gladly paid their share to the power company. Darkness bred all kinds of mischief that the lights kept at a minimum.

"Hey." Shane waved and hurried over to the van to help unload the food. "Is that Nettie's meat loaf? Man, who wants barbecue when we got this?"

"Our host isn't here yet?" Vicky asked.

"No, he'll wait until the park is full and then make a grand entrance," Ryder said as he took the sheet cake from Nettie's hands.

"What makes you say that?" Emily asked.

"Because if I was a con man trying to fleece a bunch of country bumpkins, that's what I'd do," Ryder answered. "This goes to Darlene, right? She's been cuttin' cakes and pies since I got here."

"That's right, and I see at least two hams and a turkey over there on the tables, so he don't need to show with his store-bought barbecue," Nettie said.

"I'm pretending that this is my welcome-home party," Emily laughed.

"It is, darlin'," Ryder teased. "I'll be right back and take that meat loaf over for you, Nettie. Don't let Shane carry it. As clumsy as he is, he might drop one. Folks'll look down on me for eating it off the ground with my fingers."

"I'm lighter on my feet than you are," Shane

argued. "And if I drop it, then it's all mine."

"Boys!" Vicky smiled. "I'm glad I had a daughter."

"I was thinkin' that I'd fight both of them for it. A little dirt and grass would just add fiber," Emily said.

Vicky shuddered. "You guys carry that gently. If I see my prissy daughter eating off the ground, I'll shoot whoever dropped it."

"What can I do?" Woody rounded the side of the van.

"We got it taken care of," Ryder said. "Did you bring the strawberry wine?"

"It's over there in a cooler gettin' a good chill on it," Woody said. "Y'all got to watch the kids. If they ain't twenty-one, they don't even get a sip. It's some pretty strong stuff."

"I'll m-m-make sure they don't get any," Shane said. "Just set it by the band and w-w-we'll guard it."

Woody chuckled down deep in his chest. "I imagine you will."

"M-m-might keep me from stutterin'," Shane teased. "Don't forget that you promised m-me a dance, Jancy."

"I've even been practicin'." She smiled.

"How long do we have to wait on this wolf man to get here?" Emily asked.

"We'll give him half an hour," Nettie answered. "If he's not here by then, we'll declare that we've won the war against him and get the party started."

Ten minutes later a big white limo pulled up in the parking lot. A van with the logo **JUNIOR'S RIBS** emblazoned on the side parked right beside it. Four people hopped out of the van and threw open the back, and two of them removed a long folding table. They carried it to a spot under a big oak shade tree, set it up, and tossed a snow-white tablecloth over it with a flourish. The other two carried two pans of barbecue to the table, and then all four went back to bring out potato salad, baked beans, and coleslaw.

"Pretty good spread, but that wouldn't be enough to go around one time for this crowd," Vicky said. "And that white cloth is doomed. Barbecue stains will ruin it."

"I'll give you two hundred dollars to accidentally fall against the back side of the table and send every bit of it into the dirt," Nettie whispered to Jancy.

"I can't waste good food, but I'll work other angles," Jancy laughed. "Where is the host for this extravaganza?"

As if on cue, the driver stepped out of the limo, swung open the back door, and held his hand out. A red-haired woman wearing a cute little black suit and high heels made a few of the young guys' eyes pop out. The skintight skirt barely reached her knees, and the top two buttons of the jacket were undone, with a little black lace camisole peeking out from underneath. The next person who crawled out didn't need a hand to help him. The man stood over six feet tall and wore shiny black cowboy boots, starched jeans, and a tailored plaid shirt with pearl snaps.

"A little eye candy for the ladies and something to entice the men," Vicky said. "Smart man, but none of us just fell off the turnip wagon."

Jancy smiled. "You know what they say about knowing the enemy. I bet we could get some good information out of those two."

"Oh, yes, we can." Emily nodded. "And there's Sarah, Teresa, and Waynette to help us tear the rest of this business apart at the foundation."

Three girls that Emily had been friends with her entire life hurried from the edge of the park to hug her, putting their heads together in whispers.

"Hey, Jancy, come on over here." Emily motioned.

"I'm fine. Y'all have things to talk about," Jancy said.

"And there's the man of the hour." Nettie nodded at the car.

Carlton held both hands up in a wave to everyone as he got out of the limo. He wore khaki pants, a blue knit shirt, and loafers.

Nettie folded her arms across her chest. "Evidently he thinks if he fits in with the local yokels, maybe they'll sell their souls to him."

"Yep, the devil does take on different forms," Jancy said.

Emily left her friends and came over to the tables. She looped her arm in Jancy's and pulled her toward the group waiting beside the merry-go-round. "We need your help. None of us can flirt with that henchman of Carlton's, but you can," Emily said on the way back to the group. "We want you to infiltrate their camp and see what's going on."

"Why can't you do it? He's never even seen you?"

"Because she's involved with another man who's goin' to want to monopolize all her time," Sarah whispered.

Emily blushed. "Do y'all remember Jancy? She was here for our freshman and sophomore years in high school before she moved away."

"I remember wishing you would tutor me in chemistry. My mama told me if I ever brought home a C on my report card we'd have a funeral at our house," Sarah said. "I got a D and she was so glad that I didn't flunk that we almost had a party, but I wouldn't have sweated all the way home that day if I'd had your brains. Lord, you were a whiz kid in that class. Did you major in it at college?"

"Didn't go to college. Barely got through high school," Jancy said.

All of them looked like they'd been cut from the same bolt of cloth. About the same height. Shades of blonde hair ranging from honey to strawberry. Perfect makeup and cute little outfits that matched from their earrings to their shoes.

"Sarah and Teresa each got married this past year," Emily said. "And Waynette has a two-year-old and another one on the way."

All those awkward and uncomfortable high school feelings crashed into her like a wave. "Congratulations."

"I just found out. No baby bump yet," Waynette said. "You still single like Emily?"

Jancy nodded. "So what do you want me to do . . ."

"Good afternoon to all of you." Carlton spoke into a microphone that he'd taken from the driver's hand. "Welcome to my party. This is my lawyer, Rebecca, and my associate, Hilton. We will be mingling among all of you to answer questions, but before that, let's all eat up and enjoy this lovely summer day."

The caterers brought out a small card table and set it up close to the limo. Rebecca put her pretty pink briefcase in the middle and headed toward the barbecue. Evidently she wasn't accustomed to walking in those high heels, because when one of them sank into the earth, it threw her off balance. She pitched forward, and if Ryder hadn't been standing close, she'd have landed facedown in the dirt. He caught her, set her aright with a big grin, and took a step back.

"You'd do better to kick off them shoes and go barefoot, ma'am," he said loudly as he tipped his hat and then walked away.

Jancy noticed the daggers that shot from Emily's eyes. So it just might be Ryder, after all. If that was the case, Vicky was going to have a first-rate Texas hissy when she found out.

Nettie stepped out from under the pavilion, and the whole place went silent. She did not need a microphone for her voice to reach out across the whole park. "We'll have grace before we dig in. After we eat, the local boys will provide us with some music and we can socialize all afternoon. I'll ask Woody to bless this food today."

Men removed their hats, and heads bowed. Woody said a short prayer, and the whole crowd said a hearty "Amen!" Then folks lined up on both sides of the tables under the pavilion. After they'd loaded their plates with home cooking, some of them wandered over to the barbecue table. They carried their food to quilts that had been thrown out under the big shade trees or to lawn chairs they'd brought from home. Jancy wasn't sure where she belonged in the scheme of things until Shane laid a hand on her shoulder.

"Fall in right here in front of me. W-we'll get us a plate and go over to the quilt that Ryder brought for us to share with the ladies. It'll be crowded, but we'll all fit," he said.

"Thank you," Jancy muttered.

"Nope, thank you for bein' with m-me today. Sometimes it gets old bein' the third wh-wheel at everything," he said.

"Don't I know it." Jancy smiled up at him.

"There's plenty of room," Sarah said. "Just crowd right in here beside me and Jimmy. Good thing that we brought two quilts. Jancy, meet my husband. That one right there belongs to Teresa. His name is Quaid. And that one"—she pointed—"has been married to Waynette for three years, and he's Will."

"Hello." Jancy took them all in with one smile. "Thanks for making room for us."

"Hey, we've got to stick together. I hear that you are going to be our spy of the day," Ryder said.

"I'll do my best. Do I need a badge or a gun?" she teased.

"Naw, just your smile. That old cowboy w-won't even know wh-what hit him." Shane nudged her on the shoulder.

Jancy still wasn't sure if Shane was just flirting with her or if he was sincere, but the sparks sure danced around the park when his shoulder touched hers. Still, if he really had a crush on her like Emily said, wouldn't he be at least a little jealous of her flirting with another man?

110

"So what do y'all want me to find out? We already know that the wolf is sniffing around wanting to buy land. What else can we discover?" she asked as she shoved a fork loaded with potato salad into her mouth. The good home cooking reminded her of suppers when her mother was alive.

"Find out if Carlton is legit," Shane said.

"Or if this is his first attempt to build a bedroom community," Jimmy said.

"And if he's really got investors or if he's just a con man." Quaid threw in his two cents.

"But, most of all, find out why he chose Pick. Does he think we're all just a bunch of rednecks who'll fall at his feet?" Ryder asked.

"I'll do my best." Despite the tall order, Jancy felt like she really was part of the group.

"But don't fall for him," Shane whispered for her ears only.

Two dots of crimson filled her cheeks. "Never. I don't like fake cowboys." Mercy, could Shane really be jealous? He shouldn't be. A man like Hilton would lose in any contest with Shane—looks, eyes, muscles, and even his voice.

"I'm bringing Misty back to you, Waynette." A teenage girl set a cute blonde toddler on the quilt. "She's been fussin' for her mama."

"Thanks for watching her while I ate." Waynette picked up the child and began to rock back and forth with her. "It's nap time, isn't it, pretty girl?"

Jancy forgot all about everything but the picture in front of her. She wanted a stable life, a good honest husband who loved her and wasn't a damn crook, and a houseful of babies like that little child.

Vicky was looking around for a place to sit when someone touched her on the arm. She looked around to find Andy Butler smiling and nodding toward the tailgate of his pickup truck.

"Want to join me?" he asked.

"I thought you were Jancy's date for the day. I wouldn't want to get between y'all," Vicky answered.

"She's done thrown me over for a younger man." He nodded toward the quilt where several young couples were sitting. "My heart is broken, but if you'll sit with me, maybe it won't be quite as painful," Andy teased.

"Well, I can't have you poutin'. It wouldn't be good for our little town's reputation for hospitality. Lead the way, Mr. Butler," she said.

"That's Andy to you, ma'am," he said.

"Then I'm Vicky, not ma'am," she shot back.

When they'd set their food down on the tail-gate, he took a couple of lawn chairs from the back seat, popped them open, and motioned for her to sit in one. "Thanks for joinin' me. You are the only person near my age I know very well."

"Why are you here?" Vicky sat down and pulled her plate a little closer.

"Brought my dad, Wesley. He's the gray-haired feller over there . . ." Andy pointed.

"Beside Woody? Do they know each other?"

"They've sat on a couple of committees together in this area, so he's over there visiting with him about this estate thing."

"Didn't you tell him that Carlton is probably runnin' a scam?"

Andy chuckled. "He and I . . . it's complicated. I gave him my opinion after the town hall meeting, but he needs to see for himself."

"Well, Woody will definitely give him a double earful." Vicky started with a bite of brisket. "You didn't make it over to Carlton's table?"

"I don't get meat loaf very often, so I bypassed the other table," he said.

"Nettie makes it every Saturday," Vicky said.

"Well, that gives me a good reason to stop by when I'm traveling from the new shop in Frankston to Palestine." He put a bite into his mouth. "Oh. My. God! This is great. What is her secret?"

"That is as classified as the tart recipe," Vicky told him.

"Oh, really?" Andy raised an eyebrow.

"Good grief!" she sputtered.

"What?" He followed her eyes to the table on the other side of the park.

"Now Jancy is over at that table flirting with Carlton's cowboy."

"I'd say that she's infiltrating their camp," Andy laughed. "She'd make a good actress. She comes off kind of shy and backward. That will bring that man's guard down real fast."

"If I could have your attention, please." Carlton was leaning against the back fender of the limo with the microphone in his hand again. "I see that you're enjoying the barbecue, and we'd love to tell you all about how our plans can benefit both your community and you personally. We'll be mixing in the crowd if you'd like to catch us for a moment."

"Why is he so hell-bent on having Pick, Texas?" Vicky wondered aloud.

"It's a prime location and he thinks he'll get the land cheap. He's most likely already conned a few investors or he wouldn't be spending so much on limos and a caterer to try to buy you with barbecue and big words."

"We've spoken our piece. He should go on down the road for his McMansion business," Vicky said.

"Amen to that. I told my father that he was all hat and no cattle. He said he wanted to see for himself." Andy swiped a paper towel across his mouth. "But to answer your question, from a business standpoint, it's like this. The lake is to the north and land up there will be more expensive, plus folks looking for a bedroom community aren't interested in the sounds of motorboats and the smell of fish. To the south is Frankston, which is fine for buying supplies on the way home but already a little congested for what Carlton is looking for. This is the perfect spot. Not too far to Tyler, and if Palestine grows much more, it could accommodate their overflow as well."

"So he's all hat and no cattle?" She'd heard that expression before, but it put a smile on her face. "And you really think that Jancy is over there playing spy?"

"I'd bet my business on it." Andy smiled.

"Oh!" Vicky gasped.

"What?" Andy glanced around.

"I just made the connection. You are that guy," she said.

"What guy?"

"The one who owns the wedding cake and bakery business," she said.

"Yep, I'm that guy. The one who everyone thinks should be wranglin' cows and stretchin' barbed-wire fences, not making fancy cakes."

Vicky smiled. "Everyone should mind their own business."

"Well, thank you very much for that. Mama said that if you love what you do, then you are a success, no matter if it's diggin' ditches or sittin' in the Oval Office. With that in mind, I am a success and I'd be an even bigger one if I had the recipe for your tarts. But I understand you hanging on to it. I have recipes that a million bucks couldn't buy, too."

Shane drew the bow across the strings and it really did give an evil hiss, silencing Andy and the rest of the crowd in the park. He did his rendition of "The Devil Went Down to Georgia" while Ryder tuned his guitar and Jimmy set up a keyboard. By the time Shane had finished, they all went straight into a country two-stepping song that brought the dancers out to the cleared area in front of the band.

"They're pretty good," Andy said. "Do they do gigs or what?"

"No, they just play for fun and occasionally in church," Vicky said. "Shane can play a gospel tune that will bring the most avid sinner to his knees."

"Can he heal a shattered heart? My date is dancing with Mr. Muscle Man," Andy joked. "You have to dance with me so I can show Jancy up." He hopped down off the tailgate and held out his hand. "One dance? So I can save face."

"Just one. I wouldn't want you to go home with a bad taste in your mouth about Pick. And then we'll have desserts with a glass of strawberry wine. You really should try the blackberry cobbler." She put her hand in his and led him to the dance area.

"I'd rather have a piece of chocolate cake with my strawberry wine. I'm not one for cobblers. Too much dough."

Vicky scolded herself for dancing with anyone, especially someone who was most likely trying to sweet-talk her out of a recipe. Maybe the gossip would center on Jancy and not her.

Don't bet on it, the voice in her head said. *They'll see you with Andy, and tomorrow morning's gossip will have it that you are selling your diner and moving to Palestine to work for him. Jancy's flirting is juicy gossip, but yours will set the phone lines on fire.*

He was so smooth on his feet that she felt as if she were gliding two inches above the grass. The song ended too soon, but he didn't ask for another dance like the cowboy who had Jancy pulled up too close.

"That wine is disappearing pretty fast. We should get in line if we're goin' to. And would you look at that? Rachel isn't busy. We could go over there and visit with her." Andy's green eyes glittered with mischief.

"Her name is Rebecca, not Rachel, and you have to taste Woody's strawberry wine. His late wife, Irma, made the best in the whole state."

One second she was looking up into Andy's eyes—the next someone had grabbed her arm and swung her out to the music. She blinked twice, but Carlton's big smile didn't fade. She didn't fight him when he brought her back to his chest with a thud.

"You look beautiful this afternoon, Victoria," he said with one of those big smiles.

"I've told you repeatedly, it's Vicky, not Victoria, and I'm not selling you my property so you can build a gated community of McMansions."

"I detest that word." He swung her out again.

"The answer is no. Not today or tomorrow or next year," she told him.

"Have dinner with me, darlin', and I'll up the price to two hundred thousand. I might even consider making you a partner. You are both gorgeous and smart. I can see us working well together."

"There are some things in life that money cannot buy."

"Money," he whispered into her hair, "can buy anything. I'm really attracted to you, Vicky."

"You are crazy for thinking you could ever change my mind." She deftly hooked one leg behind his knees and ground down into the arch of his other foot with her heel as he stumbled. If Hilton hadn't caught his arm, he would have pitched right into Shane and sent the band members scrambling.

Well, crap! Vicky thought as she turned back to Andy. *If I had it to do over again, I would have waited until we were closer to Shane. I could buy him a new fiddle and it might have kept Carlton out of Pick.*

"You bitch," Carlton mumbled.

She turned around and in two steps was nose to nose with him. "You *ask* a lady if she wants to dance. You don't grab her like that. Go crawl back to whatever rock you came out from under, Mr. Wolfe, and stay away from our town."

"Oh, honey." He reached out to pat her cheek, but she grabbed his hand in a vise grip, twisting it until he leaned in.

"Don't touch me. Don't speak to me. And damn sure do not call me honey," she whispered just for his ears.

"You are breaking my fingers," he growled.

"I will if you try to lay a hand on me again for any reason."

Shane caught her eye and raised an eyebrow.

"Keep playin'," she mouthed.

"Looks like you've been samplin' too much strawberry wine, Mr. Wolfe," she said loudly. "Better sit a spell and let the effects wear off before you try to dance with someone again."

A few folks laughed, though Vicky didn't think it shook their interest in her dinner partner. The Butlers were big-name folks in Anderson County, so everyone would be filled with questions. Carlton stomped back to the table where Rebecca sat with one leg crossed over the other, fanning herself with a bunch of papers. He reminded

Emily of that Cheshire cat in a movie she saw as a child—all teeth with that fake smile. He looked mad enough to chew up railroad spikes and spit out thumbtacks.

Poor Rebecca looked so bored and so dang hot that Nettie felt sorry for her. She picked up three plastic cups of wine and carried them to the table.

She pulled out a chair and sat down across from Rebecca. "Y'all look like you're about to burn up."

"I am," Rebecca said.

"But we can endure the heat. The limo doesn't leave until four o'clock." Carlton's whole body language changed. "I don't believe that we have met." He extended a hand. "I'm Carlton Wolfe, and you are . . ."

"Nettie," she said.

He frowned as they shook. "So, are you interested in letting me explain a little about our proposition here in Pick?"

"Not really. I just thought y'all might like a little strawberry wine. It's good and cold and will sure help cool you down," Nettie answered.

Carlton threw back the wine like it was a shot of whiskey. "Not bad. I saw the two musicians up there on the stage talking to you. I understand one of them owns an automobile junkyard and the other one works for him. Would you introduce me to them?"

"That's Ryder and Shane. Don't think they're interested in talking to you. Shane's business is Pick Auto Parts and Repair. Give him a call and make an appointment if you want to talk to him."

"Tell me about them," Carlton said.

"Well, Shane's grandpa owned the junkyard until he had to go to an assisted living place down in Palestine."

Carlton almost rubbed his hands together. "So is Shane now the owner, or is the grandpa?"

Nettie played along. "Oh, he signed it all over to Shane a while back. And Ryder is his best friend and helps out for room and board at Shane's house."

"So that young man owns the property?"

"Looks that way."

"And the other one, does he own property?" Carlton asked.

Nettie took a sip of the wine. "Not anymore. His dad sold his place to Shane's grandpa when he remarried and left town. It's only ten acres next to the junkyard and all grown up in weeds, but I reckon Shane will use it someday for his wrecked cars."

Carlton wiggled in his chair. "I think I'll go mingle in the crowd and, when these boys stop playing, get to know them a little better."

Rebecca downed her wine in three gulps. "Not bad for homemade wine. It wouldn't ever hold a place in Dallas, but it's cold."

"How long have you been workin' for Carlton?"

A sheepish expression crossed her face. "One month."

Nettie slid the second cup of wine over to her. "Sip it and you'll like it better."

Like a rebellious teenager, she finished it off without even coming up for air. "It still tastes like crap."

"I guess some folks don't have the palate for it," Nettie said. "So what's in this contract?"

"Basically it says the same thing that Carlton has already told you." She fanned faster as the weather and the wine began to combine. "Tell me about that Ryder guy. I would have fallen on my face if he hadn't caught me."

"His mama was from Dallas. His daddy was raised here. They married, moved here to do a little farmin', had Ryder, and she was miserable. When Ryder was about five, she couldn't take any more. She got a divorce and moved back to Dallas. His dad remarried later on down the road, when Ryder was about seventeen. He sold everything and moved to Montana. The new wife had a spread up there. Ryder stayed behind and lived with Shane and his grandpa his senior year. He's got a few cousins scattered around Dallas, but not much other family. Both of his parents are dead now."

"Why didn't he go with his dad?" she asked.

"He was just starting his senior year when they left and he already had a scholarship to Texas A&M and"—Nettie lowered her voice—"he didn't like the new stepmama very much."

"Poor baby," Rebecca sighed.

Nettie quickly changed the subject. "Where did you get your law degree?"

"I'm plannin' on goin' to law school someday. Right now I just do whatever Carlton needs." Her shoulders slumped. "I wasn't supposed to say that."

"Is your name really Rebecca?"

She nodded. "Of course it is. Would you like to go over this contract or not?"

Nettie shook her head. "Be a waste of time, since I don't have any property to sell. You see that tall, dark, and handsome guy over there sitting with the short lady?"

"The one she was dancin' with?" Rebecca fanned faster and faster.

"Well, honey, he couldn't even talk me and my partner in business out of a recipe for strawberry tarts. We are pretty set in our ways here in Pick, and we don't want to sell what we've got."

"I'd give that guy whatever he wanted just to get to dance with him." Rebecca giggled and leaned forward. "And honey"—she dragged out the last word—"I'd bet you that Hilton could sweet-talk a woman's underpants down around her ankles, so don't be so sure your neighbors

123

won't sell that property. That girl who's been dancin' with him all afternoon is about to spend a little time with him in our motel in Tyler. She might be the first one to put her name on the dotted line. What does she own?"

Nettie chose to ignore the last question. "The party is just getting into full swing, so you'll be here for a while. You might as well get rid of those shoes, feel the grass under your feet, and dance a little, because no one is interested in those papers you are usin' to cool down."

"They will be." Rebecca giggled again. Evidently, she couldn't hold her strawberry wine too well. "Carlton has big plans, and he's willin' to do whatever it takes. Don't push him."

"And that means?"

"He'll have his big score even if bodies start piling up. He doesn't do so well with folks tellin' him no."

"Well, honey"—Nettie stood up and smiled—"I didn't touch that cup of wine right there, so you enjoy it. And don't hold your breath until Carlton has bought all the property in Pick. With your coloring, you'd look horrible in that shade of blue."

Rebecca sipped the wine. "Tell that good-lookin' Ryder that he can bring me another cup when he takes a break. The guitar player in a band always takes my eye."

Nettie waved over her shoulder as she walked

away. She hoped that Carlton did talk to Shane about the junkyard property. Shane might stutter, but he'd singe the hair right out of Carlton's ears with the heated words he'd use.

Vicky caught Carlton glaring at her from near the limo and waved at him. If he thought he could intimidate her, he'd better bring his best game and a sack lunch.

Jancy put a cup of wine in her hands as she passed and whispered, "Carlton told Hilton that if he can make you and Leonard cave, then the rest of the town will go down like a row of dominoes."

"Hilton thinks he's got you eating out of his hand," Vicky observed.

"Exactly what I want him to think. I'm going to dance some more with him. What did the woman tell Nettie?" Jancy asked.

"What?" Vicky frowned.

"My job is to flirt with Hilton. She took Rebecca and Carlton a cup of wine. I'm sure it was her way of finding out even more," Jancy said. "Think I should go out on a date with him if he asks?"

"No." Emily walked up and caught the last line of the conversation. "Not under any circumstance. Nettie just now told me that Rebecca said that Carlton would have what he wanted even if it meant dead bodies. I don't want you to be the first one. And from what I hear, Hilton is trying to get you into a motel room and seduce you."

"I can take care of myself." Jancy smiled. "I've met his kind before. If we could buy all three of these folks for what they're worth and sell them for what they think they're worth, we'd be rich as Midas."

Vicky laid a hand on her arm. "Please don't go out with him. Today is enough."

"Then I will make today count for all it's worth. And he's all talk and no walk, Vicky. Even if he did have some powerful juju, he ain't never dealt with the four women of the diner before." Jancy touched her cup of wine to Vicky's.

A wide smile covered Vicky's face. Jancy was putting down roots and clipping her own wings. Funny how living in Pick did that to a person.

"Now back to work," Jancy said.

"And I'm going back over there with Waynette and Misty. I want a dozen babies," Emily said.

"But not until you get through college," Vicky said. "Until then you can enjoy Waynette's kids."

Vicky intended to help the ladies over at the tables, but when she reached the picnic benches, Andy touched her arm and motioned toward the seat beside him. "Come sit a spell. I've been getting acquainted with Leonard. He was telling me that his grandparents were some of the original folks here and they raised strawberries."

She sat down, and Leonard put a cup of wine in her hands. "So did Vicky's. Her grandpa had that acreage out to the north of the diner," Leonard said. "Pick was called Strawberry Flats in the beginning. Lots of folks around here had acres and acres of strawberry fields, and folks came from miles away to pick them. They'd bring their own containers and pay by the quart. When they went to get a post office, the folks wouldn't let them call it Strawberry Flats on account of another town, so Grandpa chose the name Pick. Granny said it didn't have a thing to do with anything other than Pick was short and easy to spell."

"Makes sense to me. Did Pick still have a high school back when you went to school?" Andy asked Leonard.

"Oh, yes, but by the time Vicky got to that point, we only had the elementary school. She went to Frankston for junior high and high school," Leonard said.

Andy turned to face Vicky. "We used to play Frankston in summer baseball. Our paths might have crossed way back then."

"Maybe so," Vicky said as she kept a watch on Hilton, who was leading Jancy over to a tree stump, where the two of them sat down—too close to suit Vicky, for sure.

A tall, lanky man with thinning hair and an angular face, Leonard liked to talk. "Looks like

Jancy has took up with that fool. Don't she know better? I swear, the young people today don't see past a pretty face. You'll have to have a talk with her, Vicky. She ain't got a mama or a granny, so it's up to you to set her straight about men like that."

"Already did. She knows what she's doin'," Vicky said.

"I wouldn't bank on it, the way she's lookin' at him like she could eat him plumb up."

"Maybe she's playin' him like he thinks he is doing to her," Andy said.

Leonard stood up and looked around. "Well, now, if that's the case, she's a smart woman. I wondered why Shane wasn't puttin' down that fiddle and moppin' up this park with that man."

"Oh?" Andy raised an eyebrow.

"Boy has had a crush on that girl since back when they was kids. His grandpa used to jaw about it. Well, now if I'm goin' to get a dance in before this party ends, I'd best find Darlene."

Vicky looked over the crowd, but didn't see Leonard's wife or Andy's dad. "Where's your dad? I wanted to meet him."

"He ate and went on back home for his Sunday nap. We don't mess with his schedule," Andy answered. "But he found out enough to know that he's not putting his money into this scheme. A lot of Carlton's potential investors will dry up— if Dad doesn't invest in it, then they won't."

"They must trust his judgment a lot," Vicky said.

"He's good at what he does," Andy answered.

"Like father, like son." She grinned.

"Tell that to him if you ever get to know him."

Vicky nodded toward the band. "Look! Woody is going to take over for Shane. We'll have to move."

"Why?" Andy asked.

"Because clogging on grass does not have the same effect that it does on a wood floor. All those guys coming this way are about to move the tables out from under the pavilion so the dancers can do their thing on this wood floor."

"Do you clog?" Andy asked.

"A little, but not today. Emily and the kids around here are really good at it. You are in for a show."

Before Woody could get the fiddle up to his neck, Carlton had his microphone out again. "I see that the band is about to make some changes before the party. We've all gotten to know one another a little better this afternoon, and I'll visit with each of you in town next week. This investment is a big decision, but I know you will each recognize that it's a once-in-a-lifetime opportunity that you can't turn down."

Nettie walked up beside Vicky and Andy. "Is he going to put a horse's head in our beds if we turn him down?"

Andy chuckled. "He said a lot about nothin'."

"Why are they changin' fiddlers?" Andy asked.

"Shane is very good at clogging. He'll want to dance, not play," Vicky explained.

Carlton looked out over the crowd as if he expected applause to rattle up out of the buzz of whispers. Nettie slowly stood, and even the children quieted.

"It's been a good afternoon. We should do this again in the fall. Be sure to put your fans in this basket." She pointed. "And pick up all your trash. Thanks to everyone who brought food and wine. We'll see all y'all in church tonight. Now Woody is going to play and let our kids strut their stuff as a closing number."

Applause and whistle calls drowned out whatever it was that Carlton tried to say next, and then Woody wound up a whining fiddle to a nice slow country song. Shane crossed the lawn and held out his hand to Jancy, who turned her back on Hilton and looped her arms around his neck.

"I thought they were going to clog," Andy said.

"They will. The kids all need a couple of slow dances to get them ready. It won't be long," Vicky told him.

Woody broke into a good two-stepping country song, "Country Roads." Tapping his foot to keep time, he shut his old eyes and really got into the music.

"May I?" Andy got to his feet.

Vicky tucked her hand in his and kicked off her sandals. "Don't seem fittin' to dance to that song with shoes on."

He settled his face into her dark hair, and the warmth of his breath made her scalp tingle. With the grass soft on her bare feet, she wished the song would go on forever, but all too soon it ended. Andy took a step back, picked up her hand, and kissed the palm.

"Thank you for a lovely afternoon, Miz Vicky Rawlins," he whispered.

Hilton tapped Shane on the shoulder when the next slow song started, but Jancy shook her head. "I promised the last couple of dances to this man, but it's been real nice gettin' to know you, Hilton," Jancy said.

"Find out m-much?" Shane asked when Hilton sauntered away, casting a look around for his next target.

"Just that Carlton is determined to own Pick and that he doesn't give up easy," she said and smiled. "I love this song."

"I asked the guys who are standing in to play a couple of extra songs so I could dance with you." Shane grinned.

"After wallowing in the mud with that man all afternoon, this is wonderful." Jancy snuggled in close to Shane's chest. Sparks danced around them, and she felt as if she was floating six inches off the ground. She was really dancing with Shane, the guy that she'd never been able to get out of her mind.

The song ended, but Woody and the older guys went right into one more, and Shane kept Jancy in his arms. Leonard picked up the microphone and did a fine job with an old George Jones tune, "Tennessee Whiskey."

Shane sang along with the lyrics that said she was sweet as Tennessee whiskey and strawberry wine. Princess dreams filled Jancy for those three or four minutes with Shane as her knight in shining armor.

"Okay, folks," Leonard said when the song was finished. "Woody is warmed up, and I'll turn this microphone over to a man who can call a clog better than I can. Choose your partners and let's close this party out in real Pick style."

Shane grabbed Jancy's hand and led her to the pavilion. Ryder quickly laced his fingers in Emily's and fell in behind Shane and Jancy. The other three couples joined them, with two more bringing up the rear.

"I practiced a little this mornin', but it's been a long time," Jancy said.

"You'll rem-m-member real quick."

Woody pulled the bow across the fiddle. Pretty soon the sound of fast music and feet clogging on the wooden stage joined the clapping of the folks keeping time and filled the whole park. If Carlton

Wolfe didn't get the message, he was just plain stupid. Pick, Texas, had a heartbeat of its own, and the folks there didn't need a pacemaker.

Shane and Jancy stole the show. She grabbed the skirt of her sundress and sashayed around like she'd been born to bluegrass clog dancing. If the folks in Pick hadn't already accepted her into the flock and fold, they would now for sure.

When the music stopped, Woody held up his fiddle and pointed his bow to Shane and Jancy. "And that, folks, is the way to end a party here in our part of the world."

Shane kept her hand in his as he led her across the lawn. "That was the best part of the whole afternoon. You are a great dance partner."

Vicky walked up beside them. "You were both pretty amazing. So were y'all, Ryder and Emily."

"So are we going to church?" Jancy asked, amazed after that fast dancing that she had breath left.

Vicky nodded. "We always close at six on Sunday so we can go to the night service."

"Reckon I could pick you up at six thirty and take you?" Shane asked.

Jancy turned to Vicky. "Does he go to the same one y'all do?"

"Yes, I do," Shane answered.

"Then I'll be ready," she told Shane.

A bright smile covered his face as he headed toward Woody to claim his fiddle.

"Who'd have ever guessed that you could clog," Vicky said.

"Louisiana, remember?" She smiled. "I'm surprised that your new boyfriend didn't jump up here on the stage with you."

"Number one, he's not my boyfriend. He's courtin' my recipe for tarts, not me. Number two, he's a city guy. I doubt he knows how to dance like that."

"With number two you might be right. But with number one, you couldn't be more wrong. Look at him over there helping the old gals carry stuff to their cars. Men who are out for a recipe don't do things like that. They act more like Mr. P-Nose." Jancy looped her arm in Vicky's. "I can't believe I'm going to church with Shane."

"Why?"

"Because he could have his pick of all the single girls in this part of Texas."

"I don't think he's got eyes for anyone else," said Vicky.

Chapter Seven

The last time Jancy had attended church was the week before her mother had died. Yet it wasn't so different from the one where she and Shane sat on a back pew that hot Sunday evening. A center aisle separated the sturdy oak pews. The choir sat behind the pulpit in a small section reserved for about a dozen people. An old upright piano stood off to the right, and Darlene, Leonard's wife, leafed through pages of the hymnal. Jancy figured there were about seventy-five people in the congregation, which was pretty close to the number of folks who'd attended the church back when she and her mother sat on the back pew every Sunday morning.

The preacher finally came forward and took his place behind the lectern. "Evenin', folks. We had a right nice time at the park this afternoon. All those folks there standing together—well, it caused me to think of what Jesus said about loving your neighbor. But before I get into that, let's all open our songbooks to hymn number two eighty and sing loud enough that the angels in heaven can hear us."

"Wasn't he the one who was callin' the dance steps?" Jancy whispered.

Shane picked a hymnal from the back of the pew in front of them and found the page. "Yes, but that's only because his wife wasn't up to dancin'. They're both really good at it."

Strange, but Shane didn't stutter one time when he was singing. Maybe he was kin to that old country music artist Mel Tillis. She kept stealing glances over at him, sitting there as if he was proud to have her beside him. The creases in his jeans stood out sharp, and his boots shined. The sky blue in his plaid shirt matched his eyes, and the rolled-up sleeves clung tight to his biceps.

Jancy scarcely heard a word of the sermon. She'd never been to church with a guy before. Men that she was drawn to were far more interested in a cheap motel. She chanced another sideways glance at him. The grown-up Shane was far more handsome than the boy had been. He'd always been tall, but this guy had grown into his own. On a smaller man, his curly brown hair might look a little girly, but Shane wore it with sexiness.

He caught her gaze and held it for several seconds before he took her hand in his and rested it on his knee. The heat was enough to set the whole church ablaze, but she couldn't force herself to move it. Lord, what a mess. When he found out what all she'd done in the past six years, there would be no more flirting or dates for church. Finally, the preacher asked Woody to say a final prayer, and then folks were on their feet.

Shane pulled her up, let go of her hand, and draped an arm around her shoulders. "I couldn't keep my m-mind on wh-what the preacher w-was sayin' w-with you right beside m-me."

If anyone else had said that to her, she'd have chalked it up to a pickup line, but everything that Shane said and did left no doubt he was sincere. Her heart lifted a little despite her thoughts.

The preacher shook her hand as they left and said, "I remember you and your mama from years ago. She was such a good woman—helped clean the church on Friday mornings and was always helping with food for funeral dinners. And you and Shane made a good couple out there on the dance floor this afternoon."

"Thank you," Jancy said. "Mama loved Pick better than anywhere we ever lived."

"I understand that she's passed on," the preacher said. "I'm so sorry for your loss."

"Thank you." She moved on a few steps.

Shane didn't tarry long with the preacher, saying only a sentence or two, and then his hand went to the small of her back, guiding her out to his old truck at the far edge of the parking lot.

"W-want to drive up to Frankston for an ice cream? It's still early and it ain't even dark yet,"

Shane asked as he opened the truck door for her.

"Five o'clock in the morning comes pretty quick. A rain check?" She wanted to spend more time with him—lots more time—and he gave her self-confidence such a boost, but the wariness and shame in her heart didn't want to let go.

"You got it," he said. "Can I have your phone number, Jancy?"

"I'll give it to you when I get the service turned back on. In the meantime, call on the house phone. I don't know that number, but it's in the phone book, I'm sure," she said.

He started the engine and put it in reverse.

"Shane, are you in love with Emily?" she blurted out before they even left the parking lot.

"Hell, no!" He braked so fast that she was glad the old truck had seat belts. "Sorry about that, but wh-why'd you ask that question?"

"I needed to know. Something isn't right with that girl. I don't know her, so to me, she's—too many words." She flipped her hands in the air. "Short story, Nettie asked me to figure out what's making Emily so jumpy. I thought maybe you were flirting with me to—well, you know."

"I w-would never use you like that." He started backing up again. "I kinda had a crush on you a long time ago. I w-was afraid to ask you out because"—he smiled—"I stutter and you were so far out of my league."

"I kinda had a crush on you, too," she admitted.

"But that was a long time ago. And honey, if anyone was out of a league, it was me out of yours."

"Look, we were just kids. The time w-wasn't right then. Maybe it is now. We can at least see if it is." He drove so slowly that she could have gotten home faster on the back of a snail.

Home. She hadn't thought that word in years.

"Right?" he prompted as he parked in the driveway.

"Yes, but I probably won't stay in Pick more than a few weeks."

"I'll take what I can get." He grinned as he opened the truck door and rounded the back to help her out. "Maybe, if it's all right, I'll come around tomorrow night and we can walk up to Leonard's for an ice cream?"

That might be the perfect time to tell him that she wasn't right for him. "I'd like that," she said instead. "Thanks, Shane."

"See you then." He whistled all the way back to the truck.

"You should have given him a good night kiss," Nettie said from the shadows of the porch. "He's a good person."

Jancy jumped. "Nettie, you scared me."

"Come sit beside me and talk to me. It's not Shane, is it?"

"He says it isn't." She hiked a hip on the porch rail.

"I was kind of hoping it was. That means it's probably Ryder."

"Why does it have to be anyone? She's nervous about disappointing Vicky about not going to school. She really doesn't want to go back. That much is right out there in the air even if Vicky doesn't want to see it." Jancy kicked off one sandal. "Where are they?"

"In the kitchen. We might as well join them." Nettie sighed. "You might be right, but I know that girl and there's something more than hating college up her sleeve."

"All I can tell you is that I asked Shane straight out. He was very convincing when he denied they were interested in each other." Jancy picked up her shoes and held the door for Nettie.

When she reached the kitchen, she went straight to the refrigerator and poured a tall glass of milk. As she turned around to sit at the table, they were all staring at her as if she had dirt on her face.

"What?"

"So how did the date go?" Emily asked.

"He didn't kiss her good night," Nettie told them.

"It was a first date. Kisses aren't until at least the second and maybe the third," Vicky said.

Jancy gulped down a third of the milk. In her world, kisses were reserved for the second thirty minutes. "It's not fair to start something that has a fast finish line. I probably won't stay in Pick past the summer. Daddy had a wandering soul. Still, my mama loved him even if he couldn't sit still very long. I have to admit, I didn't listen to much of what the preacher said tonight," Jancy said.

"Come on over here and sit down." Emily nodded toward the last chair at the table. "And explain why you think those wings are still there; we're all seeing some roots growing."

"I've always been attracted to bad boys. After Mama died, we took her ashes to Galveston and poured them out in the gulf. Daddy said that anything that was salt water was ocean and that she'd always wanted to see water that went on to the edge of the sky. We had a big fight when he got tired of that place, and he went on without me. I moved in with a guy and worked in a fast-food joint, and we moved from there to Amarillo."

"What kind of job did he have?" Nettie asked.

Jancy pinched the bridge of her nose. "Bad boys do bad-boy things. He was stealing cars and got busted. He's still doing jail time."

"Did you stay in that area?" Emily asked.

"I had to because . . ." Her hands went clammy, and her chest tightened. The timing was perfect to spit it out, but the words caught in her chest.

"Because what?" Emily asked.

"I wasn't stealing cars, but I knew what he was doing and the people he was working for and . . ." She ran out of air and took a deep breath. "So I gave the cops what they wanted to stop the theft ring and got off on probation. I had to stay in the area for a year. I had my final visit with my probation officer last week."

"Oh, my." Vicky gasped.

"You did what was right," Emily said. "You shut down the bad guys' operation."

"That's not all." Jancy inhaled and started again. "I figured I knew all about men after that experience. But I was dead wrong. A couple of months after he went to jail, I got a job in a small, family-owned restaurant and started dating a friend of the owner. He put me up in a little apartment in a complex that he owned. The first time he sent a friend to my door to . . ." She swallowed hard and tears flooded her eyes, but she refused to let them spill down her cheeks.

Nettie laid a hand on her arm. "You don't have to tell us this."

"But I want to. Y'all need to understand why Shane is too good for me," she said. "If he asks me out again, I should say no. I did not let my new boyfriend turn me into a prostitute, but that's when I found myself right back out on the street. I had enough money to rent a trailer in a fairly decent part of town, got a job at the steak house where I told you I worked last, and I ate at work to save buying groceries. Shane needs a woman who is all sweet and innocent. I'm not that person."

"Everyone has a past." Nettie yawned.

"And it sounds like you learned from the mistakes you made," Emily said.

"Maybe so, but Shane is the sweetest man I've ever been around. Who's next?" she asked.

"Next?" Emily fidgeted with the saltshaker.

"Any of y'all got anything to share in this group therapy?" Jancy looked right at her.

"Nothing from me except that if I was going to confessional, I'd have to ask forgiveness for wanting to kill Carlton Wolfe," Vicky answered.

"I've got a doctor's appointment in the afternoon on Tuesday, so I'll need all y'all to cover. Does that count?" Nettie asked.

Emily pushed the saltshaker back to the middle of the table. "Are you okay, Nettie? Why are you goin' to the doctor?"

"Checkup time. He won't refill my blood pressure meds if I don't come in and get checked every six months," Nettie said. "Now your turn. You been home a couple of very hectic days. You ready for a plain old calm week?"

"I'll take hectic or boring, either one, as long as it's in Pick. Jancy, so what if you have a past that's not too shiny? That's no reason to walk away from Shane. I think he really likes you."

Jancy held up a finger. "What if I hurt him?"

Another finger. "What if things don't work out and I'm unhappy?"

Third finger. "What if I'm more like my dad than I want to be and I feel miserable sitting still in one place?"

Fourth. "What if he changes his mind and my heart is broken?"

Her thumb went up. "What if I disappoint all y'all?"

When she held up the other hand, Nettie reached over and closed both into fists.

"We can't let the past run our lives. We have choices. You can decide not to be like your dad. You can decide to sit still right here in Pick and see if you like it. You can decide to leave after you give me a six-month notice. All of those are your choices, but remember with each one comes a different set of consequences."

Jancy pulled her hands free and hugged Nettie. "Thank you, but my decisions haven't netted me much other than heartache. I learned to be tough and take care of myself, but I wasn't always the sharpest knife in the drawer when it came to reading people." She stepped back and gave Nettie a sharp look. "Six months?"

Nettie patted her on the back. "That's the least notice I'll take. Anything less and I won't give you a decent recommendation for another job. So suck it up, kiddo! That's rule number two. And honey, I'm the least smart of anyone in this room. I was smart enough to stay single until I was forty and then spent some miserable years before Vicky's mama, Thelma, helped me get rid of the sorry sucker. So I can't give advice on relationships. I can tell you that I don't think Shane gives a damn about your past."

"Is that why there are two shovels out there in the shed? Did you and Thelma get rid of him permanently?" Jancy teased.

"No, just used a real good divorce lawyer. Of course Thelma was ready to use the shovels when she saw the bruises he left on me. He liked whiskey more than me," Nettie answered. "But this is probably enough of a group therapy session for one night. That afternoon in the heat wore me out worse than working in the kitchen all day. I'm going to take a fast shower and go to bed." She pushed back her chair and straightened up. "Jancy, I'm glad you are here and that you trust us enough to talk to us. Don't shut the door of opportunity until you see what's on the other side."

"Crazy, ain't it," Jancy said. "I feel like y'all are family and I ain't even been here a week. Is it all right if Shane calls me on the house phone? He asked for my cell number, but I couldn't pay the last bill, so they cut it off. I'll have enough money saved next week to take care of that."

"We could give you an advance . . . ," Vicky started.

Jancy quickly shook her head. "No, ma'am. You've done enough."

· · ·

Vicky flipped on the light switch in her bedroom and took a look at the pictures scattered around the room of Emily—when she was a baby, her first day of school, her first date, her high school proms, high school graduation, and the last one, a picture of her the previous summer taken in front of the diner.

She settled down in the rocking chair at the end of her bed and propped her feet on the bedpost. A gentle knock on the door was followed by her blonde-haired daughter, who crossed the room and crawled into the middle of the bed.

Emily inhaled deeply and let it out slowly. Something was on her mind, but Vicky had learned long ago not to apply pressure. The past had proven that if Emily was ever going to open up about whatever was bothering her, it had to be her idea.

"She's had it rough. I'm glad that I never had to live like she has. Isn't it good that Shane knows her from back when?" Emily asked.

"It is, but what will happen if she tells him what she told us?"

Emily shook her head slowly from side to side. "I don't think it will matter one bit. If I was Shane and got a second chance with someone I'd always had a big crush on, it wouldn't matter to me."

"But you are not Shane or Jancy," Vicky said.

"Still, I'm glad you hired her and I'm sorry I told you to lock your door at night. She's a good person."

Vicky got up from her chair and joined Emily on the bed, giving her a hug. "My child, I've always been a good judge of people."

"Except with my dad," Emily shot back.

"Oh, I was a good judge there, too. I knew exactly what Creed Rawlins was when I fell in love with him. It wasn't that I was blindsided. And he might've been the wildest boy in the whole state of Texas and the biggest daredevil in the world, but he had a soft spot when it came to loving me. He didn't hesitate when I told him I was pregnant. He did what was right, so give him that much. And remember he was young, only eighteen when he died."

"Racing motorcycles on a dirt road without a helmet," Emily said. "I grew up without a dad because he was wild."

"But you had a mama and an aunt Nettie who adored you, so you don't have much to bitch about," Vicky scolded. "Are you trying to start a fight with me, Emily Rawlins?"

"Okay, you win. I'll change the subject," Emily said. "I researched Carlton Wolfe. I can't find anything on the man. That's probably not even his name. You should hire a private investigator and expose the sorry sucker for what he is."

Vicky nodded. "I'm not wasting my money. That's the same thing Andy Butler told me. Carlton will figure out that he's not going to con any of us in Pick."

Emily slid off the bed and headed toward the door. "So to sum up the weekend, Shane might be fallin' for Jancy, who may or may not stay in Pick, Carlton's a con man, and I'm not going back to school in the fall."

"You got that right . . . what did you say?" Vicky stammered.

"I said that I'm not going back to college."

"Good God, Emily Diane Rawlins. You've got one year left. Only twenty-four college hours! You cannot quit now."

"I'll get my degree in a couple of years. I'm going to work in the diner and do evening classes on the computer to finish that way," she said. "And I'm not changing my mind, Mama. I hate being away from Pick."

Vicky felt her world crumbling. "You could make it one more year. You come home every holiday, even just those single days off, so you are never away for more than three months at the most."

Emily's mouth set in a firm line. "I love you and I hate to disappoint you, but it ain't happenin'. I'll take two classes a semester until I get finished, and that will take two years. I'll have the degree and I can be right here."

"Why now?" Vicky groaned. "With just one year left?"

Emily started for the door. "Because it's what my heart tells me to do. It shouldn't come as a surprise. You know how I've felt since day one."

"Can we talk about it later in the summer?"

"We can talk about it every day until I'm old and gray, but I'm not changing my mind." She turned and planted a kiss on her mother's forehead. "Good night and I love you, Mama."

"We definitely will discuss this more." Vicky wasn't giving in to this crazy idea easily. She'd regroup and come up with a plan to keep her daughter in school one more year.

"I'm sure we will. See you in the morning," Emily said as she closed the door behind her.

Chapter Eight

The diner was packed fifteen minutes after Vicky opened the doors the next morning. Emily ran the booths, and Vicky took care of the customers who were sitting at the bar. It might be Memorial Day, but except for Christmas, the diner was always open.

It wasn't the first time the diner had served as a conference hall in the twenty-five years it had been in business. But Vicky had never answered the same question or reassured the residents of Pick more times in her life. No, she was not one bit interested in Carlton Wolfe's offer, and she was not going to cave in no matter what he threatened.

"He's a wolf in sheep's clothing," Ryder chuckled.

"Absolutely," Vicky said. "If that's his real name, he should change it. If it's not, then he chose the wrong one."

"He ain't goin' to fleece us, is he?" Shane asked. "Wh-where's Jancy?"

"We'll hang his sorry carcass on one of the barbed-wire fences in town before we let him get a toe in our town," Vicky said. "And Jancy took a few minutes off to run up to the bank to do some business."

"Mark the spot and me and Shane will take care of that mangy old wolf." Ryder's big brown eyes sparkled. "And we won't even charge you for it. I hate it when someone like that sucker comes into our little place."

"It makes us appreciate what we got and reminds us that we might have to do battle for anything that is worthwhile," Vicky said.

"You got that right," Ryder said.

Shane nodded. "Just sometimes the fight is kind of scary."

"But if we stick together, we can win." Vicky smiled, and Ryder unexpectedly weighed in with a yawn.

"Long night?" Vicky asked.

"Yes, ma'am." Ryder blushed.

"Regular old roustabout." A wide grin split Shane's face. "He even m-m-missed church last night."

One booth of folks left and another pushed into the diner at the same time. Vicky hurried over to clean the table and get it ready for the newcomers. She glanced at the clock. Ten thirty. By this time most days, she was sitting at a booth or the counter with Nettie and Jancy having breakfast. It was beginning to look like there would be no letup until the noon rush. How on earth Nettie kept up with the orders and still had time to get her blue-plate special going was a miracle. The scent of ham, sweet potato casserole, and baked beans blended with all the breakfast food and made Vicky's stomach grumble.

Jancy breezed back into the diner and through the swinging doors. She tied an apron around her waist and was about to start helping Nettie when Vicky stuck her face in the window. "You come on out here and take care of the counter. I'll do kitchen duty."

"I don't mind," Jancy said.

"My daughter and I need some space," she said.

"Oh, yeah?" Jancy's brows shot up.

Vicky joined Jancy and Nettie in the kitchen. "She says she's not going back to school in the fall."

"It's a long time until then. She might change her mind," Jancy said.

"She's a lot like you, Vicky. When she makes up her mind, wild horses couldn't get her to change it." Nettie stirred the pot of beans.

"Got any advice, Jancy?" Vicky asked.

"Fightin' her could make her set her heels even harder. Might be smarter to let it alone for a while and let her figure out for herself that it's not such a good decision," Jancy said.

Nettie chuckled. "The way they both like to argue a point until it's died a dozen times, that won't be easy."

"I just like things settled and planned out," Vicky said.

"Don't know what to tell you about that," Jancy said. "In my world, things were never settled or planned."

"Will you talk to her?" Vicky asked.

"Every day." Jancy smiled.

"I mean about this crazy notion." Vicky sighed.

"I'm the last person you should ask to do that. You know about . . ." Jancy stumbled over the words.

"You are probably the best person for the job," Nettie said.

Emily poked her face into the window. "Hey, I could use some help out here."

"Sure thing." Jancy passed her on the way back out into the dining room, where she picked up an order pad, wrote on it, and then handed it to Shane.

Shane shook his head. "It's Ryder's turn to pay for breakfast. Give it to him."

"This is not a bill. It's my new cell phone number," Jancy said.

Ryder reached for it, but Shane snatched it away.

His fingertips grazed hers, and the little bit of chemistry did not surprise her one bit. "Thank you, Jancy. I'll get it programmed into my phone soon as we leave."

She refilled their coffee cups and carried the

pot down the counter, making sure everyone had a warm-up. When she reached the end, Ryder was standing there with his billfold in his hand. "Shane was right. It's my morning to pay. And Jancy"— he lowered his voice—"don't break his heart. He's my friend and . . ."

She rang up the amount and took the bills he offered. "I won't. I promise."

"W-we ready to go?" Shane walked up behind Ryder as Jancy made change. "I'll call you this evenin'."

"Be lookin' for it." Jancy smiled.

Half an hour later, the diner was suddenly empty. Vicky cleaned off the last table in the deafening silence and grabbed the broom to give the floors a quick sweeping before the next onslaught of customers, but Nettie took it from her hands.

"It don't look too bad. Let's eat right here in the kitchen. Jancy, would you pour four cups of coffee? Emily, you help her bring them back here."

"Yes, ma'am," Emily groaned. "I didn't know there were even that many people in Pick."

"There's not. Some of them were from Frankston and up in Berryville," Vicky said. "Some of them are most likely sent from Carlton to see what's going on today and to pick up any gossip. I hope they heard Ryder offer to hang his carcass on a barbed-wire fence."

"Like they do coyotes?" Emily brought in two cups of coffee.

"Exactly," Nettie said. "I'd pay Ryder in free lunches if he'd put him on the fence for me."

"Nettie!" Jancy exclaimed.

"It's the truth." Nettie shrugged.

"Why don't I give y'all another truth to shriek about," Vicky said with a sidelong look at her daughter. "Emily says that she's finishing up the last of her degree with online classes."

"At least she isn't quittin' altogether," Nettie said. "Y'all had better get busy eatin'. The next rush will hit in half an hour."

"You can do that? Take classes online?" Jancy put two sausage patties on her plate along with a scoop of scrambled eggs and a couple of biscuits.

"Sure. You want to take some with me?" Emily crammed a biscuit full of eggs and bacon and ate it while three pancakes cooked on the griddle.

"Probably not right now, but I might sometime in the future." Jancy carried her plate to the table, pulled up a bar stool, and concentrated on eating.

"Do you have a boyfriend here in Pick? Is that why you don't want to go back to school? Who is it?" Vicky demanded, barely nibbling on a piece of toast.

"I wondered if that's what was making her so antsy," Nettie said. "Shane is interested in Jancy. All the other guys that amount to anything at all are married, and she's got better sense than to get tangled up with Ryder."

"Emily is twenty-one, isn't she?" Jancy asked.

"Twenty-two on May 1," Emily said over her shoulder. "And I'm right here. I can hear you talkin' about me."

"I was twenty-two on Valentine's Day," Jancy said. "No disrespect, Vicky, but I think we are both old enough to date. We could even get into a bar, order a drink, and vote."

Emily set a plate in front of Nettie. "Thank you, Jancy. Bacon or sausage, Nettie?"

"Both. I expect the doctor is going to fuss at me tomorrow about my cholesterol, so today I'll eat what I want," Nettie answered. "And if Emily had a boyfriend, she couldn't keep it a secret from us. Lord, she even told us when she went to get birth control pills."

"For real? My mama had no idea that I went to the health department and got pills," Jancy said.

"I should've gotten . . . no, I'm wrong," Vicky said. "If I hadn't gotten pregnant and had Emily, I never would have survived that year after my mother and my husband both died. Knowing that I had a little bit of him . . . Well, anyway, that's what kept me going. Along with Nettie's constant naggin' at me."

Nettie pointed a fork at Vicky. "I did not nag."

"Yes, you did." Vicky's fork shot up to do battle with Nettie's. "And thank God for it, because

156

it was what brought me out of the dark places. What time is your appointment tomorrow? Do you want me to go with you?"

"Hell, no!" Nettie said. "You'll have to run the kitchen from right after the breakfast run until the middle of the afternoon when I get back. That means you'll be doing the lunch without me."

"It'll be tough, but we'll manage. Long as it's only one day and you don't go shopping instead of coming home," Emily teased.

"I hate shopping," Nettie growled.

Later that evening, Jancy carried a cold beer out to the porch and settled in on the old wooden swing on the south end. She pulled her long legs up and propped one elbow on her knees. Chin in her hand, she watched a star fall from the sky, leaving a long streak behind it.

"Did you m-m-make a w-w-wish?" Shane stammered as he rounded the end of the house.

"Where did you come from?" she asked.

"Been out for a w-w-walk. Clearin' the cobwebs outta m-my head," he said. "Can I join you?"

She scooted to the end of the swing. "Want a beer?"

"No, thanks, but a little company would be nice. Evenin's get lonely. I w-was goin' to call. Hope it's all right that I just stopped by." He eased down, his body only a few inches from hers.

Delicious little shivers chased down her spine as the air between them came alive with electricity. She tried to think about something other than the way the earth shifted, but it didn't work. She liked all those hot tingles when he'd drawn her into his arms at the picnic or when he'd slung an arm around her shoulders as he walked her to the door after the church date.

"Shane," she said, intending to tell him that she was the wrong person for him.

"Jancy." He moved a few inches toward her, cupped her face in his big hands, and lowered his lips to hers.

Fire surged between them when the kiss deepened and his tongue touched her lower lip, asking politely for permission to enter. She shifted positions so that she was facing him, and her arms snaked up around his neck. She tasted a mixture of cinnamon with a hint of brown sugar and sweet tea as she pressed closer to him.

When the kiss ended, he drew her to his chest. "I've w-w-wanted to do that since I saw you in the parking lot wh-wh-when your car was on fire."

"Really?" Her heart was going like a steam engine, beating twice as fast as it should, and emotions she'd never felt with anyone were rattling around in her chest.

"Never saw a w-woman beautiful as you," he said.

"Shane Adams, is that a pickup line?"

"Nope. Never have been too good with girls. My stutter puts them off."

"Not me," she said.

He pulled her even closer. "Just holdin' you is a dream come true. I'd sure enough like it if you stuck around Pick for a wh-while."

"I'm not goin' anywhere until the end of summer at the least," she whispered.

"Good." He kissed the top of her head, and even that sent vibes dancing around the porch like a million shooting stars.

They sat like that, swinging, watching the stars twinkle for a long time before he finally leaned back, tipped her chin up with his fist, and kissed her again. This time it was a sweet kiss, but it still created a flutter down deep in her stomach.

Lord! Her insides turned to hot mush, and her hands were shaking.

"Good night, Jancy. I'm glad your name starts with a *J* so I don't mess it up. Reckon we could do this again tomorrow night?" he asked.

"I'll be right here," she said.

"We could go for a little stroll down to Leonard's and get us a beer, take it to the park, and talk a spell," he said.

"Sounds like a date to me." She stood up with him and walked him to the edge of the porch.

He waved over his shoulder as he disappeared into the twilight of the summer evening. She picked up the half-empty bottle of beer and carried it into the house, plopped down on the sofa, and leaned her head back. Vicky looked up from the recliner where she'd curled up with a book.

"I thought I heard voices out there on the porch. Were you talkin' to yourself?"

"Strangest thing just happened. I wanted to tell Shane that there wasn't any chemistry between us and I couldn't lead him on. So I was about to spit it out that we could be friends and nothing more." She sat up and pulled her feet up under her to sit cross-legged.

"And?"

"He kissed me."

"I figured that would have happened when he brought you home from church last night. Shocked me a little when Nettie said he didn't even try," Vicky said.

"There were sparks like I've never experienced before."

Vicky laid her book to the side. "Shane is not a bad-boy type. Don't hurt him."

"That I might cause him any kind of pain scares me. What do I do?"

"Follow your heart."

"I can't trust it. It's led me astray too many times."

Vicky moved from the chair to the other end of the sofa. "Have you ever listened to it? Really paid attention? When you were letting that boy-friend talk you into living in his apartment, didn't you know somewhere down deep that it wasn't right? Or when that other boyfriend was stealin' cars, didn't your conscience tell you to do something about it?"

"Probably." Jancy nodded.

"Nettie told me that the heart never steers us wrong. Sometimes it doesn't answer us as fast as we want it to, but we have to give it time and be patient. It doesn't see, hear, or smell, but it has an acute sense of feelin' and it will never lie to us."

Jancy hugged Vicky. "You and Nettie are the best things that have happened to me in years. I'm so glad that fate put me in that parking lot last week."

"So are we." Vicky headed for the kitchen. "Let's have a glass of strawberry wine for each of us to celebrate the kiss."

Jancy finished off the beer and set the empty bottle on the coffee table. "Oh, no!" She clamped a hand over her mouth.

"What?" Vicky stopped in the middle of the floor.

"What if the stars are lined up all wrong? What if I'm fallin' for a good guy at last and the timing is wrong? What if folks find out that I was on probation and they look down on him because of me? I can't do that to him."

"Do what to whom?" Emily appeared in the doorway coming from the hall. "Shane kissed you, didn't he?"

Jancy nodded.

"We're going to have a glass of wine to celebrate." Vicky brought out a quart jar from under the counter and poured a little into four glasses.

"Do we get wine when I kiss my boyfriend?" Emily joked.

"Depends on who it is," Vicky shot back. "What number are we at?"

"Only two down," Emily said.

"Then you've got a few to go."

"What are you talking about?" Jancy asked.

"She's hung up on that old movie *Lucky Seven*."

"I am not," Vicky said.

"Yes, she is," Emily said. "She thinks I need to see the world and have lots of boyfriends before I settle down. In the movie, the mama is dying and she tells the daughter that at certain times in her life she will meet a man—like number three will be her first sexual experience in college. But it will be the seventh man who will be her soul mate and the one she will marry."

"I know. I checked that movie out at the library and watched it about six times before I had to take it back," Jancy said. "Why do you want Emily to wait until number seven? Is it because

162

you only had that first real love in your life and then you had a baby to take care of?"

"Pretty much," Vicky said. "I want her to experience lots of life before she settles down."

"Sometimes life isn't a substitute for love," Jancy whispered as she sipped the wine.

Vicky's head bobbed a couple of times. "And sometimes love ain't a substitute for life."

Those words stuck in Jancy's mind as she made her way to her bedroom, opened the drawer, and took out the second letter from the bottom. She turned on the bedside lamp and propped a pillow against the tall headboard.

"I need to hear your voice, Mama. Even if it's through words on paper that don't say a thing about relationships. Shane kissed me and I felt something new and strange. Is that what you felt with Daddy even though you knew he was probably the wrong boy for you?"

She unfolded the letter and read slowly.

Happy birthday, Jancy! I hope that you are having cake and ice cream. Take this ten dollars and buy a fancy cupcake and a pint of rocky road ice cream. Today I'm sitting here in the trailer with the smell of a chocolate cake filling the whole place. It's your eighteenth-birthday cake. We'll move again as soon as you graduate. Your father is getting antsy, but he's promised me that we'll stay right here so you can finish your education. I've got a feeling if we move this close to the end of the year, you'll never finish, and I so want to see you walk across that stage and get your diploma.

Tonight we'll have cake and ice cream and I've made a little throw for you from scraps that I bought from a remnant bin. It reminds me of the tiny baby clothing that I stitched for you before you were born. You came home in a pretty smocked outfit and you were wrapped in a pink quilt. Each square had a special bit of embroidery. You completely wore that quilt out. I hope you do the same with this throw and that you think of me every time that you use it.

Enough sadness. I'm gone and it's your birthday. Wherever you are, be happy. Eat cake and ice cream and remember all the good times we've had.

Her mother was right. Just remembering that chocolate cake and ice cream on her eighteenth birthday made her happy. She tucked the letter back into the envelope and into the drawer beside the throw that was one of her prized possessions. She ran her fingers over the stitches. She used the throw when she was so homesick for her mother that sadness filled her whole being, and it never failed to bring her comfort and happiness. "But Mama, what do I do? You gave me love and memories, but I need your advice."

Be happy, her mother's voice whispered in her head.

Jancy picked up the picture and looked into her mother's eyes. "I'm not sure I know how, Mama. Can you send someone to guide me?"

I already did, the soft voice said.

Chapter Nine

The diner was quiet that Tuesday afternoon. The lunch rush hadn't been too bad with Vicky taking care of the kitchen and Jancy and Emily dividing the dining room duties. Vicky had just refilled her glass with ice and water with a slice of lemon and was on her way to a booth when the phone rang. She grabbed it, listened for a minute.

Her heart felt like a stone in her chest, and she thought she'd throw up. The room did half a dozen spins before the walls stopped moving. Her glass hit the floor.

"Mama?" Emily asked.

"It's Nettie. She's had a heart attack. She dropped in the waiting room of the doctor's office. They've admitted her." In her own ears, Vicky's voice sounded to her like it was coming from the depths of a deep barrel.

"Go. Both of you go. I'll manage the place by myself. I worked in fast food. I can make burger baskets," Jancy said.

"Hey, ladies." The bell above the door chimed, and there was Andy. "It's a hot one out there.

Thought I'd stop by for a tart . . ." He stopped with a puzzled look on his face. "Is something wrong, Vicky? You look like you just saw a ghost."

"It's Nettie. She's had a heart attack," Jancy said.

"Where is she?" Andy asked.

"Palestine," Vicky whispered.

He turned around and opened the door for her. "Come on. I'll take you."

Emily threw an arm around Vicky's shoulders and guided her outside. "That way you can bring Nettie's car home. We'll close early and be down there as soon as we can get out of here. Don't worry, Mama. Jancy and I can run the place. I'm less than thirty minutes or a phone call away, so . . ."

Andy opened his truck door, and Vicky crawled inside without arguing. What would she do without Nettie? And how did this happen?

"Has she been sick? Did the ambulance take her?" Andy asked.

"No and no," Vicky said. "She went in today for a regular checkup, and they called about the same time you walked into the diner. She's complained a few times with her arm but thought it was arthritis."

"Well, thank goodness she was at the medical center when it happened. They would have gotten her immediate help."

She wrapped her arms around her body and shivered.

Andy reached over and turned down the air-conditioning. "Don't go to the dark place unless it's absolutely necessary. There's always hope."

"It's Nettie. She's been like my mother for years. She's been a grandmother to Emily and my partner in business. That dark place you mentioned terrifies me. I don't know how I'd manage without Nettie," Vicky said.

"Did you ask them about the severity?"

She shook her head. "They said it was a mild heart attack and that she was asking for me."

"I've got a gut feelin' that it'll take more than a heart attack to get that woman down."

"Why would you say that?" Vicky cut her eyes around to glare at him.

"Hey, no offense meant. That was a compliment. The way she stood up to Carlton Wolfe at the town meeting and then at the picnic impressed the devil out of me." Andy smiled.

She stopped shivering. "She *is* a force, isn't she?"

"Yes, she is, and that means a lot. We're half-way there. Another few minutes and we'll be at the hospital. You might want to take your apron off," he said.

"Oh. My. Gosh!" She gasped. "This apron is the least of my worries. I didn't even bring my driver's license or money."

"The girls can bring your purse when they drive down here. I'll stay with you until they arrive, so you are in good shape except for the apron." He grinned.

She undid the ties at her waist, leaned forward and pulled the thing off. She glanced at him and he tilted his head toward the back seat of his crew-cab truck.

"Just toss it back there. I'll make sure it comes back home."

When she saw the blue hospital sign, the tension in her whole body eased up a little. He turned into the parking lot, and she took a deep breath. She'd have to be strong for Nettie. If it was bad news, like, God forbid, open-heart surgery, she couldn't break down and cry. This wasn't about her or her problems. It had to be about Nettie's well-being.

He stopped at the front entrance. She slid out of the truck, slammed the door, and hurried inside the hospital. The lady at the information desk told her what floor and how to get to the elevators. She was pushing the "Up" button for the fourth time when Andy walked up beside her.

"Open sesame," he whispered, and the doors opened immediately. "A little magic never hurts."

"Save some of that for Nettie," she said as she hit the right floor button.

She heard Nettie's familiar voice when she and Andy stepped out into the hallway and stopped in her tracks to catch her breath.

"I'm tellin' you that I'm not stayin' here all night. Put that damned thing in me right now and turn me loose. I've got work to do and . . ."

Vicky took off so fast that Andy had trouble keeping up. She marched through the open door with her finger already up and shaking toward the bed. "You will do exactly what this doctor says, and I'll hear no more of that tone from you."

"I'm the nurse, ma'am," the tall guy said. "The doctor has been in already."

"And?" Vicky asked.

The nurse looked at Nettie, who nodded and said, "Tell her. I already put her name on the list so that she can know everything about me."

"We've done a couple of tests," the nurse began. "She's on a heart monitor. We were able to get things going really fast, but most likely she will have a pacemaker put in toward the end of the week."

"I'll be home and in my diner kitchen tomorrow morning," Nettie declared.

"Put something in that IV to knock her out," Vicky said.

"You do and I'll jerk it out," Nettie said.

"Doctor has to order that kind of thing. Are you her granddaughter?" the nurse asked.

She read his name tag. "No, Eric. More like her daughter, but I will be sitting right there in that chair all night. She *will* behave."

"Says who?" Nettie growled.

Vicky plopped down in the chair. "I didn't even bring my phone. The girls will be worried sick."

"Here." Andy handed her his. "Use mine and let them talk to her."

"First tell me what the doctor said, Nettie."

"That I've had a mild heart attack and that a pacemaker is what I probably need, but they want to monitor me for two days and then put it in probably on Friday and I can go home on Saturday evening if all goes as planned."

"The forty hours after a heart attack is a critical period," Andy said. "That's why you have to stay. My dad was in here for the same thing about two years ago. They know what they're doing."

She shot him a go-to-hell look. "Do you know how much it costs for me to lie in this bed and how much I'm needed at the diner?"

"Not a dime," Vicky answered. "You've got good insurance and you've met your deductibles already this year. We can manage the diner until you get out of here."

"When was the last time you missed a day of work?" Andy pulled up the second chair and sat down.

"I only miss for funerals and for my twice-a-year doctor visits," she answered.

"I'm not ready to miss work for your funeral," Vicky told her.

"Okay, okay! You win, but you are not stayin' here with me. Someone has to help those two girls run the diner."

"How long did we run it by ourselves before Jancy got stranded?" Vicky asked.

"You got an answer for everything. I'm going to take a nap, and when I wake up, you better both be gone." She yawned and shut her eyes. "You tell Emily and Jancy what I said. I don't want to talk."

Jancy grabbed the phone on the first ring, said hello and put it on speaker so that she and Emily could both hear at the same time. Shane and Ryder left the booth and leaned on the other side of the counter.

"You've got me, Jancy, Ryder, and Shane here, Mama. Tell me she's going to be all right."

"It was a mild heart attack and they are probably going to put in a pacemaker. She's faking sleep," Vicky said.

"I am not," Nettie said.

"Putting it on speaker," Vicky said. "You've got me, Nettie, and Andy."

"What do we need to bring when we come down there?"

"If you need anything before they close the diner, I'll bring it to you," Ryder said.

"Thanks, but I'll be fine until then. It's only a few hours. Emily, pack a bag for me to stay until Friday, and don't forget my purse. Andy is going to stay with me until y'all get here."

"Don't you dare bring stuff down here to last until Friday." Nettie's eyes snapped open. "I'll be just fine and she's needed at the diner."

"Hey, I'll call Waynette to fill in the rest of the week. She'll be glad for the extra money and I'll do the cookin'. You know very well that between me and Jancy we can run this place. Where is the tart recipe?" Emily asked.

"In the cigar box in the safe," Vicky said.

"I thought it was in a lockbox at the bank," Jancy said.

"It is, but there's also one in the cigar box. I'll raise your classified status enough that you can see it, but if you even let Andy Butler catch a whiff of it, I'll fire both of you." Nettie raised her voice.

"If you don't behave in this hospital, I will go to the diner and steal it," Andy teased.

Nettie shook her fist at him. "Put a woman in a hospital gown and everyone thinks they can boss her around."

"Mama, do you want us to close up now?" Emily asked.

"Not necessary. I'll stay if Waynette will help out for the next few days," Vicky said. "See you in a little while."

"Love you," Emily said and put the receiver back on the stand.

It was on the tip of Jancy's tongue to add her "love you" before Emily hung up the phone, but she held it back. The way she'd worried and kept the tears at bay all morning made her feel like family, and she did love Vicky and Nettie.

"It could have been much w-worse," Shane stammered. "How about w-we all go together this evenin'? Ryder can take his truck so there's plenty of room. Vicky is stayin', so she w-won't need a ride home."

"That's sweet and yes, thank you," Emily said. "We'll be ready soon as we close the doors. I'll call Waynette right now, and even if she can't work, we can manage, can't we, Jancy?"

"We can," Jancy agreed. For Vicky and Nettie, she'd gladly go that extra mile. They'd sure enough done a lot for her, giving her room and board and a decent salary—taking her in and treating her like she was part of their family. She owed them a lot.

"M-me and Ryder can come in during lunch rush and help out."

"Then I don't even need to call Waynette." Emily smiled. "I'll take you up on that, Shane."

Ryder groaned. "You just volunteered us for a job that means Emily is my boss."

"It'll be good for you." Shane grinned. "I'd let Jancy boss me any day."

174

"I'll be easy." Emily smiled as she rounded the end of the counter and sank into a booth. "I'm so relieved that I could cry."

Ryder slid in beside her and draped an arm around her shoulders. "It's okay, honey. She's going to be fine, and me and Shane have been here so much that we know how to write up an order and pin it on that thing up there." He pointed toward the window into the kitchen.

"W-we might not be as fast as you girls, but everyone w-w-will understand," Shane said from across the room.

Woody pushed into the diner, his old eyes wide as saucers. "I just heard about Nettie. What can I do to help?"

"You could take Mama's purse to her. Her phone has already rung about twenty times. I'm sure folks will start callin' the diner soon," Emily said. "And if you'll follow me down to the house, I'll pack her and Nettie a bag."

"You go w-with her, Ryder," Shane said. "I'll help Jancy until y'all get back."

Emily and Ryder both stood up and headed for the door.

"I'll grab a cup of coffee and wait for you right here. Now, Jancy, tell me the truth. Is she having open-heart surgery?" Woody said.

"No, it wasn't that serious, but she'll probably have a pacemaker."

Woody swiped a hand across his forehead.

175

"Give me one of them tarts to go with my coffee. I got a pacemaker five years ago. That's not a big deal. This is the best bad news that we could have. If y'all need anything at all, you just call me. Don't matter how small or big it is. You will keep the diner open, right?"

"Ryder and Shane have offered to help with the lunch rush. Emily and I can manage it with that much help. We might be callin' on you if we need something else. Thank you, Woody," Jancy answered.

Woody took a deep breath and let it out in a whoosh. "We'll get through this. We folks here in Pick stick together in times like this."

Jancy put a tart on a plate while Shane poured a cup of coffee. Working together in such close quarters meant shoulders and hips constantly brushing against each other, creating heat. Big, beautiful, fiery sparks jacked her pulse up.

"Thank you," Woody said when they got him set. "I thought I'd better have one, since there's only four left and Nettie won't be able to make them for a few days."

"Jancy and Em-Em-Emily are going to try their hand at making them." Shane stammered even more than usual.

"Well, now, that'll be interesting." Woody picked up the tart with his fingers and took a bite. "Just take a word of advice, darlin', and don't get too good at it or Nettie won't feel needed. It might even be best if you fail and have to make something else like strawberry cupcakes so that her feelin's won't be hurt. This is her claim to fame."

Jancy gave him two thumbs-up. "You may have something there. I'll suggest that to Emily. We could make cupcakes or one of Nettie's lemon sheet cakes."

"Strawberry cupcakes," Woody said. "That'll be keepin' with the name of the diner just fine. Put a little heart-shaped candy on the top and all will be good. And wrap up two of what's left for me to take with me. If I can't get one for a few days, that might tide me over."

"You'll eat them both tonight," Shane laughed.

"Probably so, and I'll whine and carry on about not havin' any more. Here come the kids with the stuff." He polished off the rest of the tart and downed half a cup of coffee. "Y'all ain't to worry about one thing. I'll be by first thing in the mornin' to see what you need done."

"Thanks, Woody," Jancy said.

"And soon as I get that phone down there, I'll tell Vicky to check in with an update about every hour. See you later." He met Emily in the parking lot and put the duffel bag and purse into the passenger's seat of his truck.

"You okay? You look like you've been cryin'," Jancy asked Emily.

"I have, but I'm better. It just hit me hard that

life without Nettie would be so empty and . . ." She grabbed a napkin and dabbed the tears from her eyes. "I'm sorry. I need to be stronger. I was raised by the strongest women in the whole county. This is unacceptable."

Ryder drew her close for a hug. "It's okay. Cry if you want to."

She leaned into his chest and then took a step back. "Thank you for the hugs and for helping me at the house. I'll be fine—especially after I see her tonight. Y'all will be here at seven thirty, right?"

"On the button," Shane said. "We should get on back to the shop. I promised that feller that his car would be detailed and ready to pick up by five."

The diner seemed emptier than usual when they'd left. Jancy grabbed a broom and started sweeping. Emily began to spray the booth seats down, and then she dusted the mini blinds covering all the windows in the place.

"Where does Shane live these days?"

"In a little white house just north of the junk-yard and body shop."

"What was that old story about his folks?"

Emily sat down on a bar stool and twirled it around so she could lean against the counter. "Story is that his parents married young, and after he was born they decided they were going to join up with a commune up in Wyoming. His grandpa told them that they weren't takin' a two-year-old off like that, so they gave Shane to him to raise. Nettie thinks that the reason he stutters on *W* and *M* is because their names were Waylon and Melissa. They both died a couple of years after they left. Shane's grandpa says they got the flu and the people in the commune didn't believe in doctors or medicine. They were treating them with herbal stuff. Pneumonia was what was on the death certificates. They'd asked to be cremated like your mama was and for their ashes to be spread over the mountains."

"I remember part of that story but had forgotten about their names," Jancy said. "And Ryder? Where's his folks?"

"Both passed away a while back. His mama is buried in Dallas and his dad up in Montana. I think he still has cousins, but he never has much contact with them. He still lives with Shane when he's in town. They've always been like brothers," Emily answered. "What about you? Other than that cousin you were going to visit, you got any others?"

"Nope. You?"

"Some distant ones scattered around Texas but no one that we've kept up with other than cards at Christmas," Emily said.

Jancy finished sweeping, poured two glasses of sweet tea, and carried them to the booth. "I always wanted a brother or a sister."

"Me, too," Emily said. "I'm having half a dozen kids. Being an only child is lonely."

Jancy sighed. "You are preachin' to the choir, girlfriend."

Chapter Ten

Vicky hadn't had such nervous jitters since the day she and Creed told Nettie that she was pregnant and they wanted to get married. She'd barely settled down when Creed had died in the motorcycle wreck. She'd been disappointed when Emily told her that she wanted to finish college with online courses, but she didn't get the hollow feeling in the pit of her stomach that seeing Nettie hooked up with tubes brought about.

Andy laid a hand on her forearm. "I must've driven past your diner hundreds of times. It all started with a girl from Pick who came in for a wedding cake."

Making small talk wouldn't make the emptiness in her gut go away. Even so, his touch was comforting. It helped knowing that another person was there trying to soothe the vacuum that fear created.

He went on. "What she really wanted instead of a groom's cake was a fancy tiered stand with tarts from your diner on it, but it wasn't possible. When I asked her why, she told me the rule about only two going out the door. I thought she was crazy, but then a couple of my employees stopped just to see what the big deal was, and they came back raving about them. So I decided to see for myself."

Listening to his deep drawl kept Vicky from letting herself go into that dark place where pictures of Nettie in a casket flashed through her thoughts.

"And you are thinking of that, why?" she asked.

"If I hadn't, then I wouldn't have gotten a cravin' for them and I wouldn't be here today with you. There's no place I'd rather be," he said.

"In a hospital?"

Nettie chuckled, interrupting the moment. "Well, darlin', that's where you are. Why don't you two go on out of here for a spell? Get something to eat. Take a walk around the hospital grounds. Talk without a nosy old woman hearing every word you are sayin'."

"I'm not leavin' you alone," Vicky declared.

"And you are welcome to listen and even give advice if you want." Andy grinned. "I've never been very good with women. I'm not exactly a candidate for someone to take home to meet the parents. Can't y'all just hear a woman introducing me? 'Andy makes wedding cakes and cute little fancy cookies, Mama. Isn't he just the dreamiest?' "

Vicky giggled. "I know exactly how you feel. Can't you hear what a man would say if he took me home to meet Mama? 'She owns this old diner, works seven days a week, and has a twenty-two-year-old daughter. Yes, she's been a single mother for all those years and she's only been out of Texas a couple of times in her life.' "

"Menfolks do manly things like haul hay and stretch barbed wire," he argued.

"That girl who bought the cake from your place of business was Emily's friend. That cake you made was excellent; everyone at the wedding raved about it. I'd take you home to meet my mama and would be proud to introduce you. I think she might even like you," Vicky said.

"I know she would have, but she still wouldn't sell you our recipe for tarts," Nettie said.

He removed his hand, stood up, and walked around the room a couple of times before sitting back down. "Are you tellin' me that the bride who bought a cake from me was a dear friend and you still wouldn't cater the tarts for her wedding?"

Nettie hit the button to bring the head of the bed up higher. "Unless Emily gets married inside the diner, she don't even get tarts. Rules is rules and we do not break them. And thanks for staying with her, Andy."

"My pleasure, ma'am. Can I get you anything?" he asked.

"I can reach the water and I expect they'll bring me some supper here in a minute. I bet there's not a bit of bacon in it. And I'm tellin' you right now, if it's tofu, I'm going to throw it in the trash."

"I'll help you hide the evidence if that's what they bring in here," he laughed. "You'll be out of here in a few days and feelin' a lot better. Dad said that he had dizzy spells and sometimes his heart felt funny before they put in the pacemaker, but afterward he was fine."

"I won't be happy until I'm back in my kitchen at the diner," she said. "I'd be happy if Vicky would go on home and get some rest tonight."

"I wouldn't sleep a wink, so I'll just stay right here," Vicky said.

"And—" Andy started.

Nettie quickly butted in before he could finish. "You can't stay, Andy."

"I wasn't going to offer unless Vicky asked, but why can't I stay?"

"Because it's against the rules to have sleep-overs with strange men. You have to date for at least three months first." Nettie winked.

"That could be arranged, Nettie," Andy told her.

"Talk to her, not me. You could never keep up with an experienced woman like me." Nettie yawned.

"Ahhh." Andy sighed. "I had my heart set on you, since you are the one who makes those tarts."

"I'll teach her how to make them if you'll get serious and ask her out," Nettie teased.

Before he came back with another smart-ass remark, Emily led a pack of four into the room in a rush. Vicky had never been so glad to see a bunch of kids in her life.

"Nettie!" Emily bent over the bed and kissed her on the forehead.

"You scared the bejesus out of us." Jancy patted her on the shoulder.

Shane picked up her hand and kissed it. "W-we all been w-worried, Miz Nettie. Whole town m-misses you already."

Ryder hung back until they all stepped aside, and then he knelt at the side of the bed. "You've got to get well. Emily and Jancy can run the diner without you, but they need you, Nettie. It's not the same without you in the kitchen."

She patted him on the head. "I'll be there soon as they let me out of this joint. It's a shame that I had to pass out in the doctor's office and get hauled in here to get this kind of attention. If I'd known that, I would have done it years ago."

"Listen to her," Vicky scolded. "She was carryin' on somethin' awful when I got here, sayin' she was goin' to work in the mornin', and even told me I couldn't stay with her tonight. But y'all come in and she's sweet as molasses."

"I was not. I been the picture of a sweet little southern lady all day." Nettie's eyes twinkled.

"That true, Andy?" Emily asked.

"I plead the Fifth." Andy smiled.

"So who's going to make the tarts?" Nettie changed the subject.

"Neither of us. With only two of us to run the diner, we don't have time. And besides, making them is too scary. What if they aren't as good as what you make? We could lose customers." Emily sat down on the edge of the bed and took Nettie's hand in hers.

"So we're going to make strawberry cupcakes instead," Jancy said. "We found this amazing recipe online. We can use frozen strawberries and make a simple cream cheese frosting. It won't be your famous tarts, but it will keep the strawberry theme going until you can get home."

Emily shot a sly wink toward her mother. "When you feel up to it, you can make the tarts again. I bet the folks in Pick will line up all the way to Leonard's place to get one after they've had to do without for a few days."

Nettie shook her head slowly. "Never miss the water till the well runs dry. They'll have to make do with the cupcakes until I get home. It won't be but a week at the most. You'll tell them all, especially Woody, that I'm real sorry, won't you?"

"We will," Jancy said. "He took his two home with him just today."

"I should be going now," Andy said. "Walk me to the elevator, Vicky?"

"No hanky-panky or I'll get jealous." Nettie grinned.

The heart attack had definitely affected Nettie's ability to keep her mouth shut. She might as well put up a neon sign saying that Vicky was in bad need of a boyfriend, which she definitely was not. She had to straighten out her daughter about going to college for the final year. She did not have time for romance.

"Sorry about that," Vicky said when they were in the hallway.

"She's a hoot. I wish my dad had some of that humor. I wanted to make sure you have my number in your phone before I leave. If you need anything, no matter whether it's the middle of the night or early morning, call me." He took her phone from her hand and programmed his number into it.

"Thank you, but . . ."

"Friendship has no *but*s," he said as he pushed the "Down" button. "I'll check on you tomorrow afternoon."

"I'll look forward to it," Vicky said.

The doors slid open, and he stepped inside. "Good night, and if you can't sleep, call me."

After the doors closed, she backed up against the wall and sat down on the floor, pulled her knees up against her chest, and wrapped her arms around them. The last couple of days had been totally surreal. First Emily saying she wasn't going back to college and then this thing with Nettie. And finally the past three hours with Andy.

"Mama?" Emily whispered.

At first she thought she had imagined her daughter's voice, but then she felt a presence next to her, and Emily tucked her hand into hers. "Are you all right?" Emily's face had gone pale. "Do you know something that we don't?"

"No, I've been honest with you," Vicky said. "And I'm all right. A little tired and still worried about her, but I'm fine. Once the pacemaker is in place, I'll feel much better."

"I know what you are thinkin'," Emily said. "Folks say if they have a second heart attack it's pretty often fatal. But Nettie is strong, and she's in the hospital, not at home."

"Exactly. But that is why I'm still stayin' with her. If she so much as groans, I'll be there," Vicky said.

"Want me to stay as *your* support system? You and I are hers," Emily said.

"No, you and Jancy need to go home by bedtime and get some sleep. You are helping by keeping the diner open. Did you even get the recipe out for the tarts?"

"Busted!" Emily put her wrists together as if she was about to get cuffed. "Woody said that folks need to be needed and if we started making tarts Nettie would lose some of that. That got me to thinkin' about Jancy. She hasn't ever felt like folks needed her, but we do. How do we get that across to her?"

"By being there for her like she is for us right now." Vicky stood up and pulled Emily up with her. "We'd better get back in there. She's probably trying to talk Ryder and Shane into helping her escape."

Emily slung an arm around Vicky's shoulders. "I feel so much better since I've seen her and talked to you. You see why I have to be at home, Mama? What if this had happened during the school year?"

"One day at a time, my child. We've got all summer to discuss that," Vicky said.

When they were back at home that evening, Shane walked Jancy to the door, her hand tucked into his. He let it go and wrapped his arms around her in a lingering hug. "Don't w-w-worry. Nettie is goin' to be okay."

"I'll do my best, but no promises. I inherited the worry bug from my mother." She smiled.

"Your m-mama, Miz Elaine, w-was always good to m-me. I really did like her."

"Thank you, Shane." She forced herself to take a step back.

"Good night, Jancy," he said.

" 'Night," she whispered.

Ryder had been standing close to Emily, but

he took a step back. From the corner of her eye, Jancy noticed that their pinkie fingers were locked together. Maybe Ryder was the real reason that Emily didn't want to go back to school. If he was the reason she'd come sneaking in the house before dawn, Vicky would be the next one in the hospital with a heart attack.

Emily unlocked the door and lingered on the porch while Jancy went inside and flipped on the lights. It had been a whole week since she started to work at the diner. She had friends, a boyfriend, and folks accepted her, even considered her one of their own. Everything she'd always wanted. What would they all think of her if they knew about the trouble she'd been in?

"Tell me this didn't happen today," Emily moaned as she flopped down on the sofa.

"Wish I could." Jancy made another trip around the room. "I'm scared."

"Nettie looked good. She was teasing with us and she wasn't pale. Did you see something I didn't? You've been through the death of a loved one. I haven't. You'd tell me, right."

Jancy sat down in Vicky's recliner. "Nettie looked fine, and I'm tellin' you the truth."

"Then what on earth are you afraid of? We need you, Jancy. Please don't leave. I'm talkin' about long term, not just a few months," Emily said.

"Folks needin' me is a scary thing. What if I disappoint y'all, or what if Shane decides this whole thing is just a schoolboy crush that went on too long? I could go on and on." Jancy sighed. "I've never made friends this fast. When I left Amarillo, I swore I'd never trust anyone again, and here I am, falling right back into the same old ways and in even a shorter time."

"One week, twenty-four/seven. That would be close to a hundred and fifty hours you've spent with them and a lot of hours with me. You've been in the center of solving the drama with Carlton. You've got a boyfriend who really cares about you and respects you. And we are your friends, but you are also our friend, Jancy," Emily said. "Think about it. If you were making friends with someone and saw them once a week at, say, a yoga class or a Bible study, for three hours, this would be the equivalent of fifty weeks or almost a year. We're all just getting everything at warp rather than slow speed."

"That's a good point." Jancy threw the lever and stretched out in the chair. "But—"

"No *but*s. Besides, you didn't just fall into a foreign country. Your granny lived in Pick her whole life and you were here for two years. You're like the prodigal son who's come home. No, I'm the prodigal son and you are the wandering soul who's found his way back to where he belongs."

Jancy giggled. "I don't think either of us has the right equipment to be a son."

Emily tossed a throw pillow at her. "You know what I mean. You've simply come home, Jancy. It's like your destiny—own it."

She caught the pillow midair and hugged it close to her chest. "And you? Are you owning your destiny?"

"Tryin' to, but it's harder for me. I wish I was you."

"That's crazy talk." Jancy threw the pillow back at her.

Emily had never had to save tip money for days to start a bank account so she could get her service back for her cell phone. She'd never had her car burn up in front of her. And she'd never once wondered where her next meal would come from.

"It's the truth." Emily tucked the pillow under her head.

"Are you bat-shit crazy?" Jancy asked.

"Nope, just wishin' for the best of both worlds. I'd never want to have had to live like you did, Jancy. But I wish—oh, it doesn't matter." That Emily needed to get something off her chest was evident by the way she kept twisting a strand of her hair and staring off into space.

"What's his name?" Jancy asked.

"Who?" Emily asked without looking at Jancy.

"Only a man can make a woman act like you

do. So what's his name? Get it off your chest and you'll feel better."

"It's Ryder," Emily whispered.

"Sweet mother of God!" Jancy gasped even though she'd halfway expected it. "How long have you been dating? Vicky is going to throw a fit."

"We were going to tell Mama last Sunday, but I decided that telling her I wasn't going back to school was enough for one week. Now what do we do? I can't tell her about Ryder with Nettie sick. That's too much to put on her."

"Did this all start this past weekend?" Jancy flipped the lever, sending the chair into an upright position.

Emily shook her head. "Been dating him since last Christmas."

"Holy crap, Emily. How did you keep that a secret?"

Emily popped up from the sofa and started pacing around the room. "I was in school. He was out on the rig three weeks and then back home for two weeks, so it wasn't so hard to keep it quiet. But now that I'm home and he's not going back out—we just need to bring it out in the open."

"Does Shane know?" Jancy asked.

"He's the only one."

"Poor Shane. Knowing and protecting his friends but still feeling guilty because he loves Vicky and Nettie, right?"

"And now I've put you in that position, too. I have to talk to someone. I sure can't tell Waynette and my other friends about this. They'd freak out and beat a path straight to Mama. Ryder always had such a horrible reputation, but he's changed and he loves me. I have to make Mama see that. What am I going to do?"

"Give it time. Nettie will get well. This thing with Carlton Wolfe will disappear. When everything's settled down, then tell her. You don't have to be in a hurry. I'll keep your secret, because you need to be the one to tell her. But what's the big deal? Ryder has a good job. He's a sweet guy and he's homegrown."

Emily flopped back down on the sofa. "You do remember his reputation and you know how protective Mama is, right?"

"It's not a bit worse than mine," Jancy said.

"But I'm not marrying you," Emily groaned.

"Marry!" Jancy's voice went high and squeaky.

"June 24." Emily's tone left no room for argument.

"But that's only three weeks from now. How is Vicky supposed to manage a wedding with all this going on in only three weeks? And isn't the festival right near then?"

"June 17." Emily groaned again.

"Forget the baby step idea. You've got to tell your mama *now,* and then you've got to put the wedding off for at least a few months. You are her only daughter, and she's probably planned all kinds of fancy things for you."

"The baby is due on Christmas Day. I've been real lucky not to have had any morning sickness."

Jancy was absolutely speechless for several seconds. She opened her mouth, but words would not come out. Three weeks to plan a wedding and a baby on the way? Vicky might have a heart attack herself.

"I feel so much better just getting it off my chest. Thank you for listening and for keeping the secret until Sunday." Emily sat back down on the sofa.

"Ryder?" Jancy managed one word and then a couple more. "A father?"

"He's ecstatic and so ready to settle down. He's hated dating in secret. Oh, Jancy, he's the best thing that ever happened to me."

"Really?" Her head buzzed with jumbled possible scenarios.

Emily's phone rang, and she leaned forward enough to work it up from the hip pocket of her skinny jeans. "Hello, Mama. We are home safe. About to go to bed so we can get to the diner early in the morning and get started."

A moment of silence.

"I didn't call Waynette. Shane and Ryder offered to help us through the lunch rush. And, remember, you and Nettie ran this place by yourselves for weeks. We can do this. Don't worry."

If you only knew about what is coming, you'd think managing a diner was nothing. Jancy's thoughts began to form whole sentences. *You're about to have a son-in-law that you would have never picked out for your daughter and you're going to get a really big Christmas present.*

"Yes, I will call you after the morning rush. By then the doctor will have been in with whatever reports he has and you can tell me about that," Emily said. "Good night, Mama. Get as much rest as you can. Love you."

She put the phone on the coffee table when she finished talking. "Mama says to tell you thank you from the bottom of her heart."

"I should be thanking her. When Nettie comes home at the end of the week, you have to get this out in the open, Emily. How on earth are you going to get a wedding put together in such a short time?"

"It will be simple. We've rented chairs and an arch that will be set up in the parking lot at eight o'clock that night. The sun will be setting behind us at that time. The reception food will be on the counter in the diner. No cake, just Nettie's tarts and finger foods, which we'll have catered. I just have to hire someone to do the job, but that shouldn't be hard."

"You have to have a cake. Give your mama that much. And a dress and flowers," Jancy argued.

"Okay, then after we tell her, will you help me pick out a cake?"

"That's your mama's job. You could get Andy to do the cake. He could maybe even bring his book of cake pictures to the diner," Jancy said. "Where is your engagement ring? Are you hiding that, too?"

Emily hopped up, rounded the coffee table, and hugged Jancy. "I didn't want one. All I want is a wide gold band—very, very wide— and a matching one for Ryder so that all his old girlfriends and one-night stands will know he is taken. We've already picked them out and they're being engraved. They'll be ready a few days before the ceremony."

"Looks like the plans are coming along, even if Vicky is in the dark." Jancy yawned.

"Yes, they are, and maybe I can even sleep now that I've got a friend to talk to about all this. You know I was really worried when Mama said she'd hired you. I made her promise to lock her door at night."

"So that was you." Jancy started toward her bedroom. "I heard the click. Have to admit that I locked mine, too. Seems like years ago rather than a week, though."

"I'm going to call Ryder and tell him that I told you. He'll tell Shane, I'm sure. See you in the mornin', and thanks again, Jancy." Emily stopped by the recliner and gave Jancy a quick hug. "I'm glad you are here and I really hope that you don't ever leave." And then she was gone from the room.

Jancy couldn't get past the lump in her throat to talk. To process the whole day would take months, not thirty minutes. She couldn't possibly leave before the wedding. Besides—she almost smiled—Nettie had said she had to give them a six-month notice. Vicky and Nettie would need her that long, and then there was the baby. They'd need help during that time for sure. Simply sitting there, she could feel the roots sinking into the ground right there in Pick, Texas.

Chapter Eleven

On Wednesday morning, Emily fired up the oven, the range top, and the grill for breakfast while Jancy found the recipe for strawberry cupcakes. She whipped up four dozen and popped them into the oven. While they cooked, she made cream cheese frosting and set it in the refrigerator. Then she helped Emily by arranging biscuits on the baking sheets so they would be ready to go into the oven as soon as the cupcakes were finished.

"Fifteen minutes until time to open." Emily cracked two dozen eggs into a bowl and whipped them up.

Jancy pulled two trays out of the oven and slid two more pans in behind them. "We make a pretty good team."

"This ain't the first rodeo for either of us," Emily told her. "I talked to Ryder last night. Shane is so excited that someone else knows about everything. He's been about to explode because he has no one to talk to about it, so you'll get an earful today and again tonight when we go see Nettie."

"Do you think Vicky is going to get suspicious when we all four show up again?"

Emily stopped for a minute and stared out into space. "Maybe that would be good thing. We've decided to tell her and Nettie together on Sunday night after church. If she already suspects something, maybe it won't be such a shock." Emily nudged her shoulder. "Promise me you'll be there with me."

"That should be a private matter between you and your family."

"Then I'll adopt you and Shane both. If y'all are there, maybe it won't get crazy."

"What you better hope is that Ryder walks out of the house alive." Jancy's laugh held a nervous edge.

Emily giggled with her. "I'll protect him. Now if you will unlock the doors and turn on the lights, we'll prove that we can run this diner all by ourselves."

Vicky's smile was flagging by midafternoon, but she kept it pasted on through several more visitors. That was the least she could do when folks came to support Nettie. But after nearly no sleep the night before, all she wanted was a nap—even one of those twenty-minute power ones would be wonderful. Everyone finally cleared out, and Nettie glanced around the room.

"Is anyone hiding under the bed?" she whispered.

"Why would you ask that?"

"Because I'm going to take off this fake grin if they're all gone. This business of bein' sick is harder on a body than workin' at the diner all day," she said.

"Hello! We are here!" The four kids all piled into the room.

"Did you bring a file in a cupcake so I can escape this joint?" Nettie's smile quickly turned into something real that put a twinkle in her eyes.

"That's why they put you up on a high floor." Ryder pulled up a chair and motioned for Emily to sit down close to the bed. "Even if you figure out a way to saw through the window locks, you'd have to rappel down the side of the hospital. I don't think there's enough material in the sheets to get that done."

"Wh-what'd the doctor say?" Shane hung back, his arm around Jancy's shoulders.

"That he'll put the pacemaker in tomorrow evening and I can go home after twenty-four hours," Nettie said. "I'll be back at work on Saturday, and that's the day we all clean the cemetery, so . . ."

Shane's head went from side to side. "No, m-m-ma'am. W-we might let you sit in a lawn chair and boss us, but you ain't goin' to do a thing."

Nettie shook her finger at him. "You are not my boss."

"Nope, I'm not, but I'm the biggest one in this here room," Shane said.

Vicky yawned. "I'm goin' down to the cafeteria for a cup of coffee to keep me awake a little longer."

"Eat something while you are there," Nettie said. "Like maybe real food instead of vending machine chips and the cookies and fruit from those baskets."

"Wow, Nettie!" Emily exclaimed, seeming to notice the arrangements for the first time. "Folks must love you a lot."

"Y'all help yourselves. There's so much that it'll go bad before we can use it up," Vicky said as she headed out the door. "I'll be back in half an hour or less."

"Take your time," Ryder said. "We'll be right here until you get back."

Vicky's nerves were stretched out to the breaking point. Hospital time didn't run on a normal schedule. Some hours went by at warp speed. Others dragged on the tail end of a snail. If it was one or the other, it wouldn't be so tiring, but mix them up and it flat wore her out. She pushed the "Down" button, and the elevator doors opened right up. Grateful that it was empty, she touched the "G" to take her to the ground floor where the cafeteria was located. When the doors opened, there was Andy Butler standing right in front of her with two cups of coffee in his hands.

"Thought I'd bring you a cup." He grinned. "Great minds must think alike. How's Nettie this evening?"

She stepped out into the hallway. "She's been the queen and held court all day, but I think she's beginning to wear out. The kids are with her."

"Oh, okay. There's a little lounge area right around the corner. Want to sit for a spell or can I buy you supper in the cafeteria?"

"I'd rather go outside and get a breath of fresh air. I'm not hungry," she said.

"Then follow me. There's a place with a couple of benches right this way." He led them down a short hall.

Automatic doors opened for them, and she inhaled hot air that had the faint aroma of wild roses. He handed her a cup of coffee and waited for her to sit on one of the park benches. "I was going to come earlier, but I'm glad I waited if she's had company all day. The kids—as you call them—how long have they been friends and dating?"

"Jancy and Shane have only been on one date. He really does like her, but why would you think that Ryder and Emily are a couple? Not possible. He's not her type."

"Just the way that he looks at her and she at

him. Either they're in love or I've lost my ability to read people," Andy told her.

"Never. He's—"

"I know about Ryder Jensen. He dated one of my employees a couple of times. She cussed his name for weeks," Andy chuckled.

"My daughter is smarter than to ever get mixed up with him as anything more than a friend," Vicky declared. "You read that one wrong."

"Maybe so. I've been known to make mistakes before." He sat down beside her.

The noise of a helicopter above them meant someone was critical enough to be airlifted to the hospital. She looked up to see it hover overhead and then disappear to a landing pad. Her eyes snapped shut as she said a silent prayer of thanks that Nettie had been in the hospital when she'd collapsed. When she opened her eyes, Andy was staring at her. Their gazes locked for a long moment before she brought the coffee to her lips and sipped.

"Thank you for this. It's wonderful, but what's even better is getting out of that room for a little while. Though sayin' that makes me feel guilty."

"Don't let it. Everyone gets tired when time stands still. It's not natural." He drank his coffee and watched people come and go through the automatic doors without saying a word. The silence between them didn't need to be filled with words.

"Pretty sunset, isn't it?" he said.

"Gorgeous. They're putting the pacemaker in tomorrow just as planned."

"That's good news. She'll probably go home on Friday. I love the sunsets in Texas. I've seen dozens in many different states, but they can't compete with our sunsets. How are the girls doing at the diner?"

"I called Emily several times today to give her updates. They did fine. You might talk them out of their strawberry cupcake recipe. They sold every single one that they made."

Cupcakes. Sunsets. Pacemakers. All rolled up into one conversation. It should be strange—awkward, at the least—but it wasn't.

"Then take a little advice from a guy who's been there with an older relative. Take the weekend off and stay home with Nettie. Let the girls run the diner. It'll make them feel like you trust them," he said.

She caught his gaze and held it. He looked really smart, but that was the worst bit of advice she'd ever heard. It was going to be hard enough to keep Nettie out of the diner for a few days, but for her to stay at home would have Nettie pitching a first-class southern hissy. She didn't even like being laid up in a hospital bed and doing nothing. To have someone watching over her at home—that would go over like a dead rat in a punch bowl.

"I can see from your expression that's not an option." He took her empty cup from her hands and carried both to the nearest trash can. "She must be as bullheaded as my dad."

"You got that right." Vicky stood up. "I should be getting back in there."

"I'll go with you, but I'll only stay a few minutes. It's getting late." He picked up her hand and looped it into his arm. "So the thing with Shane and Jancy? I thought they'd been together for ages."

"They knew each other years ago. She lived in Pick for a spell when she was a teenager, but she only came back a little bit ago. Her car caught on fire in the diner parking lot. If you believe in fate, you can call it that. She was stranded with no family or place to live and we needed a waitress. She's been a lifesaver in more ways than just by working for us."

"I believe in fate," he said. "How else does anything make sense?"

They weren't so lucky as to have the elevator to themselves that time. It was packed so full that they had to wedge into the thing. Her back met his chest so tightly that she could feel his heartbeat. Sure and steady. She wondered if that was an indication of his whole outlook on life. The doors opened at their floor, and she felt as if the elevator spat them out.

"Whew! Good thing neither of us is claustro-phobic," he said.

"Who says I'm not?" she joked.

"You did pretty good if you are. I don't mind snug spaces." He guided her down the hall with his arm slung loosely around her shoulders.

"Well, look what Vicky drug up." Nettie grinned. "Did she tell you that I'm breakin' out of this joint on Friday evening? Thanks for the cookies you sent up here this morning."

"She did tell me, and you are very welcome. I just wanted to pop in for a minute. Since you've got a roomful, I'll be going. Good luck with the surgery. It doesn't take long and you'll sure feel better," Andy said.

He disappeared with a wave, and Vicky settled back into the recliner. "So, Shane, how'd you like being a waiter today?"

"W-we did just fine. Got us a free lunch for an hour's w-work and even got to eat with the ladies." Shane wiggled his thick eyebrows. "I'd do the w-work every day for that."

"Only one more day," Nettie said. "Then it'll be back to normal."

Ryder winked at Vicky. "We were thinkin' maybe you'd take a week off and get all rested up."

"Well, you were thinkin' wrong." Nettie raised her voice.

Sparks danced around the room, but Vicky

couldn't tell who or how many people were producing them. Vicky wouldn't try to figure out all that right then. She had a cranky old Nettie who needed every bit of her attention for the next few days.

"We'd better get out of here before she gets all worked up and they don't let her get her machinery tomorrow," Emily said.

"W-we're goin' to go get us an ice cream cone. You w-want a milk shake or a malt, Vicky?" Shane asked. "I'll be glad to bring one back up to you. Just say the w-word."

"Look at that window ledge. Folks have been bringin' in cookies, fruit, and all kinds of food all day. I appreciate the offer, but no, thanks, Shane."

"We'll wait for you by the elevator, Emily," Ryder said. "Take your time."

"Be there soon as I kiss these two tired girls good night." She smiled up at Ryder.

"Good night, Nettie." Emily bent down and planted half a dozen kisses on her forehead when the women were alone. "I miss you. Get well, and we'll fight about when you go back to the diner when you get home."

"There won't be any fights. My word is the law," Nettie protested.

Emily rounded the end of the bed and hugged Vicky. "Jancy and I are doing a good job, but we'll sure be glad to have you back in the diner.

The guys do what they can, but they aren't you."

"Thanks." Vicky smiled. "Send a text when you get home so I know y'all are safe."

"Will do, and call me soon as you know what time the surgery is going to happen. We'll drop everything and get down here if you need us. Good night, Mama."

" 'Night," Vicky said.

"Did you feel something strange goin' on?" Nettie asked as soon as the room was cleared.

"I don't know for sure."

"What are we goin' to do if she's got a thing for Ryder Jensen?"

"If she does, it's just happenin' now. She always had a good head on her shoulders. When we get home we'll ask her outright, but I don't think we have anything to worry about. Maybe the sparks were from Shane and Jancy. We could be imagining things."

"Maybe." Nettie sighed. "I'm so tired of this bed. I just want to go home. Promise me when it's my time to die, you'll let me do it at home."

"I don't want to talk about that."

"Promise or I won't even get the pacemaker. I'm already at the three score and ten and I've had a good life, but I do not want to step off into eternity in a place like this. I want you and Emily, and maybe even Jancy if we get to keep her, standing with me to support me when I breathe my last," Nettie said.

Vicky's voice cracked as she spoke. "I promise."

"Good. Now let's get some sleep."

The good-luck/bad-luck thing wasn't supposed to start until the first day of summer, not three weeks before. Vicky shut her eyes and pulled the hospital blanket up to her chin, but it didn't do a thing to warm the chill in her heart.

Shane and Jancy sat in the back seat of Ryder's truck. The ice cream had done nothing to cool her off. Her hand felt small in his big paw. She'd never known a guy like Shane. Most of the ones she'd dated wouldn't have been happy just to sit beside her and hold her hand.

Ryder turned on the radio to a classic country station, and every song seemed to reach right into her heart and deliver the message that she should stay in Pick, Texas, for a while.

"W-words to all the songs are talkin' right at us, aren't they?" Shane whispered just before his lips found hers in a steamy kiss.

"Shane, you deserve better."

"You let me be the judge of that." He pulled her close enough that she could lay her head on his shoulder.

"I Want to Be Loved Like That" by Shenandoah started, and Ryder sang along with the lyrics that said he was the high school rebel and she was the teenage queen. Emily touched his face and leaned over the console to kiss him.

When the song ended, he took Emily's hand in his. "I can't believe you are really goin' to marry this old sinner and we are going to have a beautiful baby together."

"I'm so glad she told you," Shane whispered to Jancy. "I thought it would be great to talk to someone about it, but wh-when I'm with you all I w-want to do is talk about us."

"Vicky is going to stroke out," Jancy whispered.

"Naw, she'll throw a fit, but she'll be all right when sees how much Ryder loves Emily. It's Nettie that I worry about," Shane said.

"I think Nettie has already figured out part of it," Jancy said.

"Good," Shane said.

Ryder pulled up in the driveway. "Home. It's late. We'll see y'all at noon tomorrow."

"I'll walk you to the door," Shane said.

"And I'll make out with Ryder on the tailgate until you get back, Shane." Emily giggled.

"Gladly," Ryder chuckled.

When Shane and Jancy made it to the door, he traced her cheek and tipped up her chin for a long, passionate kiss. If she hadn't had a wall to lean on, her legs would have buckled. The kiss ended, and she leaned in for a second one. She fought the urge to reach out and pull his arms around her again when he finally took a step back. Never in her life had she wanted to take a man's hand and lead him to her bedroom more than she did right then.

"I'll see you at noon tomorrow. I like w-workin' w-with you, Jancy. Maybe w-we missed our callin'. We should have gotten together right out of high school and put in a restaurant."

"Or I should have taken car repair with you at vo-tech and helped you work on vehicles," she said. "Good night, Shane."

He whistled back to the car, and in a few minutes Emily appeared out of the darkness, her hair all a mess and her lips bee-stung from so many kisses.

"It will be such a relief to get all this out in the open. I love Ryder so much, but I hate this secrecy," she said as she unlocked the door. "We've got to get you a key made, Jancy."

"You don't hate it a bit more than I do. I was glad that Vicky left the room for a little while. I felt guilty sitting there, knowing and not being able to tell her. She's liable to fire me when she finds out."

"She'll be so busy with wedding and baby that she won't even think about firing you. Besides we need you, Jancy." Emily fished her ringing phone out of her pocket. "Hello, Mama. Yes, we're home."

"I'll grab a shower while you talk and then you can have the bathroom. See you in the morning." Jancy could have sat down on the floor right there and wept out of pure jealousy. She would love to have still had a mother who cared enough to call her just to make sure she made it home safely. To be able to kiss her on the cheek and tell her good night or tell her all about her day, maybe to make macaroni and cheese out of a box and open a can of pork and beans to go with it.

But those days were gone, and crying or envying her new friends for their relationships couldn't bring them back. She had already started running a bath when her phone rang. Thinking it was probably Shane, she answered it without even checking the ID.

"Hey, Jancy, I just wanted to tell you good night and to say thanks for all you are doing," Vicky said. "God sure did bless us when he dropped you on our doorstep."

"Thank you," she said around the lump in her throat. "But I'm the one who got the blessing."

"Guess we both did. Get a good night's sleep and keep a watch on Emily. She's up to something. I can feel it in my bones. See y'all tomorrow. Good night."

The phone went dark before she could say a word, but the feeling inside her was so overwhelming that it brought tears to her eyes.

Chapter Twelve

Jancy had been in a dead rush all morning, but she hadn't worked a bit harder than Emily, who was cooking and keeping orders filled from the kitchen. They were about to see a little bit of daylight at the end of the breakfast-rush tunnel when Woody came into the diner and chose a bar stool not far from the cash register.

"Where's Ryder and Shane?" He removed his cap and laid it on the counter in front of him.

"They'll be here in about twenty minutes. Your favorite booth is open," Jancy said.

"Yeah, but there's two carloads of folks comin' inside. One has two little kids and the other is four older folks," Woody said. "I don't mind eating my dinner right here. I'm sure glad that you girls are goin' ahead with the blue-plate special today, because chicken-fried steak is my favorite thing that y'all make."

"No one can complain about Nettie's burgers or the desserts in this place." Leonard parked his tall, lanky frame beside Woody. "But I'm glad, too, that y'all are keepin' up with the program. I want the lunch special and a big glass of sweet tea."

The little bell above the door jingled, and Jancy glanced over her shoulder to see Shane and Ryder, plus the folks Woody had mentioned arriving right behind them. She finished drawing up two glasses of tea while Shane washed his hands and slung an apron around his waist. Ryder went straight to the kitchen and came out a few minutes later drying his hands on a bar rag.

"Hey, Shane." Woody waved. "You ain't as pretty as Vicky, but it's a good thing you guys are helpin' out while Nettie is laid up."

"Yeah, but I'm bigger than Vicky, so you better be nice," Shane teased.

"When do you go start to work up in Frankston?" Leonard asked Ryder. "I know you've told me but don't remember the exact day."

"July 5. The day after the holiday," Ryder said.

"Never pictured you as an inside guy," Leonard said.

"I get to be close to home, and I can help Shane out on Saturdays for my dose of physical labor." He looked to the pass-through for a moment. "Got to get busy. These women won't feed us lunch if we slack off on our duties."

"Order up!" Emily called as she slid two plates on the shelf.

Ryder grabbed them, checked the slips, and set one in front of Leonard and gave the other to

Woody. "Looks pretty good, guys. Holler if you need anything else."

"You got a woman, don't you?" Leonard eyed him carefully.

"Ain't a woman in these parts that he ain't already had," Woody chuckled.

"Naw, this one is serious. He's settlin' down to a job, and somebody told me he's done bought a trailer and he's puttin' it over by Shane's place," Leonard said.

"Rumors have wings. And old men gossip worse than old women," Ryder said and moved to the other end of the counter to take an order.

"Burgers and fries!" Two red plastic baskets appeared. Shane grabbed them and headed toward a booth.

Woody raised his voice. "If you really got a woman, I pity her."

"Hey, now!" Ryder protested. "Why would you say that?"

"She'll always wonder if she can really trust you not to go back to your old ways," Woody said.

"You was the Ryder of our day, and Irma settled you down but good," Leonard said. "Hey, tell Emily that this is some fine grub. Some man is going to get a really good woman when he lassoes that filly."

Jancy grabbed the next order that Emily shoved through the window. Shane moved in right behind her to get a couple of cupcakes and took time to squeeze her hand gently.

"Aww, W-Woody, wh-when old Ryder falls in the fountain of love, he'll go right in the deep end. He'll settle right down. His woman won't have a thing to worry about," Shane said.

"Oh, really, so he's already found someone?" Leonard asked.

"Maybe," Ryder said. "Maybe Shane is talkin' in poet's language, since he might be in that deep water, too."

"I'm ready and I can swim better than you can," Shane said.

Ryder nudged him with a shoulder. "Then do something about it. And this counter is my territory, so move on out."

Jancy's heart did a double thump in her chest. Shane had said that he was ready to dig in and settle down. How could things move so fast?

Vicky was glad that Emily and her friends were in the waiting room with her that evening when they rolled Nettie away for the surgery. The doctor had assured her that it was minor. But that didn't stop Vicky from worrying.

"Don't worry. It'll be over in less than an hour and our Nettie will be fine." She wasn't sure if she was trying to convince herself or comfort Emily, who had tears floating in her big blue eyes. Maybe it was both.

In that moment, she realized that she didn't want Emily to come to a crisis like this in her life and only have the support of one child. Her daughter should have a loving husband who'd be there for her in the difficult times, who'd give her a shoulder to cry on and who would hold her hand no matter what. And later in life, she needed children—more than one, because that put too much burden on the only child.

The second hand on the clock at the end of the waiting room slowly made one round and then another. Vicky felt as if she aged a year with each minute that ticked off. By the time an hour was up, she would be older than Nettie. Maybe they'd just throw her up on a bed and take her on back for a pacemaker, also.

"Leonard told m-me that the w-wolf had come sniffin' around his door again," Shane said. "I thought he'd give up since he ain't been around for a week now."

"That fool ain't ever givin' up," Jancy said. "Not until he's six feet in the ground. Zebras don't trade their stripes for bunny fur."

"Speakin' from experience?" Emily asked.

"Yes, I am. I've known a lot of people and . . ." She paused.

"What?" Vicky said.

"I'm thinkin' this through," Jancy said. "Let me start again. I've known a lot of folks who haven't changed, but it was because they had no desire to have a different life. Like my folks. Neither ever changed. Trouble is, I've got a little of both of them in me."

"But you have a choice in which one you let control your destiny," Emily told her.

"It looks to me like both of you have made the choice to settle into your mamas' ways," Ryder said.

"Not really," Emily said. "My dad was wild and stubborn. I might not have got the wild from him, but I sure got his stubborn streak."

"Amen to that," Vicky said.

"And my dad was a drunk and a wanderer. I didn't get his taste for alcohol, but I did get the wandering streak. When the going gets tough, my first impulse is to run away from it," Jancy said.

Vicky glanced at the clock. Thirty minutes had passed. Bless those kids' hearts. They'd taken her mind off the surgery for a little while. Her phone pinged, and she fetched it up out of her purse to find a message from Andy: **Thinking of you. See you this evening. If you need anything call.**

She typed back, **Thank you.**

The return was just a smiley face with one eye closed in a wink.

Shane and Ryder were in the middle of a story when she put the phone back in her purse.

"We tied a rope to the back of Shane's old truck and did some dry-land skiing," Ryder said.

"You did what?" Vicky gasped.

"On skateboards, until w-we burned the rubber off the wh-wheels." Shane grinned.

"We never get enough snow to ski, and we sure didn't have the money to go to Colorado like a bunch of rich kids," Ryder said.

"Shane got on one and Ryder got on the other and I drove the truck out on Cemetery Road," Emily confessed.

Vicky's eyes popped open so wide that they ached. "You didn't!"

"Yeah, Mama, I did," Emily laughed. "But that was back when I didn't have my driver's license. Waynette had hers, but she'd had two beers so I couldn't let her drive. I did let her sit on the hood and pretend to be a beauty queen."

"Sweet Lord!" Vicky whispered.

"I w-won!" Shane pumped his fist in the air. "Ryder fell off his board before I did."

"Every one of you could have been killed. Were you in on this thing, Jancy?"

"No, ma'am. I grew up with a drinking father and a religious mother. Never tasted the stuff until I was past eighteen. I was probably in church that night, which is kind of ironic considerin' what my recent past is compared to Emily's."

"And, Mama, just so you can breathe again, that was my only night of bein' a bad girl as a teenager. Waynette and I did sneak a bottle of her dad's whiskey to her bedroom one night, but it only took one taste to convince me that I didn't

220

like it. In college I developed a little taste for beer, but I'd rather have sweet tea. So now my confession is over. What is my penance?" Emily teased.

"You have to go to church on Sunday, promise to never drive the truck for two idiot boys who are bein' crazy, and—" Vicky stopped midsentence when Ryder nodded toward the newcomer in the doorway. She stood up and filled her lungs with air. Her hands broke out in sweat, and her pulse slowed to a snail's pace.

"Went fine," the doctor said. "She's a real strong woman, and I don't see any reason why she can't go home tomorrow. If you can keep her tied down for a few days, it would be great. Maybe let her do a little at the diner for an hour or two starting Monday. And now the other good news. There wasn't an actual heart attack, but what we call heralding pains. The next pain might have been a big one, so we got it in time. The pacemaker should fix things. Just make sure she follows the directions that we'll send home with her, which includes calling in once a month."

"Yes!" Shane said so loud that they all jumped.

"Any questions?" the doctor asked.

"When can we see her?" Emily stood up.

"Half an hour or so. A volunteer will come and get you to go into the recovery room to see her. She should be in her own room in an hour," the doctor said. "She's going to be fine. Just be sure she follows up with regular visits to her cardiologist. If you think of anything else, feel free to ask the nurse. I'll be around later this evening to check on her."

"Thank you," Vicky said and sank back down into her chair. Shane and Ryder both had their phones out and were texting so fast their thumbs were blurs. No doubt they'd tell Woody and Leonard and a couple of the ladies at the church, and the news would spread like wildfire.

"See, Mama, I told you she was a tough old bird." Emily's voice cracked.

"Prayers answered," Jancy whispered.

"Amen," Ryder said as he put his phone away.

"W-Woody says he'll spread the news. I'm going to the cafeteria and getting all of us coffee and doughnuts," Shane said. "Jancy, w-will you go w-with m-me and help carry?"

"Glad to," she answered.

Jancy had never prayed so hard or worried so much as she had in the past hour. She'd spent precious few hours of her life in a hospital waiting room. Her grandmother died at home, her mother simply dropped right in the kitchen while she was making dinner, and she hadn't been there when the cancer finally claimed the last hours of her father's life. Not her choice but his after that last fight they'd had over him moving again.

"Roots," Shane said as they headed down the hallway toward the cafeteria.

"What?" she asked.

"Wh-what you said back there about prayers answered. If you didn't care, you wouldn't pray for Nettie. That's the first sign of roots, Jancy."

"Maybe so." She smiled. "But I've seen huge trees dug up by the roots and transplanted."

"Yep, but those trees never ate one of Nettie's strawberry tarts, did they?" He slung an arm loosely around her shoulders. "I like the w-way we fit together, Jancy. I always felt like a big dummy around other girls. You m-make me feel like I'm special."

"Shane, you are very, very special, and just for the record, I've never felt like a dandelion in a bed of pretty pansies when I'm with you. You make me feel like . . ." She hesitated, looking for the right word.

He stopped in the hallway. "I know, darlin'. I know. The feelin' is m-mutual. Like I said, roots."

He bought four cups of coffee and half a dozen frosted doughnuts with sprinkles, and they made the trip back to the waiting room. Vicky took a cup of coffee, though she shook her head at the doughnut.

"Did you have supper?" Emily asked.

"I had an apple and two cupcakes. I promise I'll get a burger or something later," she said. "Got a text from Andy, and he said he'd wait to eat if I wanted to get out of the room for a little while."

"A date?" Emily took a doughnut from the bag and bit into it. "Sprinkles. I love you, Shane."

"I'm a lovable guy." He grinned.

"And he knows how much you like sprinkles," Ryder said.

How could Vicky not see the electricity between them? Jancy wondered. Must be worrying over Nettie that put the veil over her eyes, or else she didn't want to admit what was right in front of her.

A sweet little lady with slightly purple hair that kinked all over her head left the volunteer desk and asked if they were Henrietta Fields's family. "If you'd like to follow me, I'll take you to her, but only two at a time. The rest of you can wait in her room. Same one she was in before."

Vicky stood up quickly, and Emily followed her.

"No food or drinks," the lady said.

Vicky trashed her coffee cup, and Emily handed hers off to Ryder after she'd stuffed the last of the doughnut into her mouth. They disappeared out into the hallway.

"We've got a few minutes. Might as well finish our doughnuts here. Nettie might not be able to have food for a little while, and we wouldn't want to have to fight her for them," Ryder said.

"Henrietta?" Jancy frowned.

"You better not ever call her that. She hates it. I think it's got something to do with her ex-husband. He m-might have called her by her real name when he was angry," Shane said.

"Then Nettie it is." Jancy polished off the last bite of doughnut, downed the rest of her coffee, and threw away her trash. "Y'all about ready?"

"I am." Shane popped up.

Ryder did the same. "Me, too. Thanks, Shane. That was good, but not as good as tarts and cupcakes. Y'all should think about making them all the time, Jancy."

"No, sir!" she said. "Nettie is the tart queen. The cupcakes would steal part of her thunder. As soon as she's able, hopefully on Monday, she can come in and make tarts, and then we will only make cupcakes for picnics and church dinners."

Nettie's eyes were wide open when they arrived in the room. She was still hooked up to monitors and to an IV, but she looked right at Ryder. "Did you bring me a beer?"

"No, but if the doctor says you can have one, I'll go to the store right now," he said.

Her eyes fluttered shut, but she had a smile on her face.

"Is she okay?" Jancy whispered.

"The nurse said she'd be like this most of the evening," Emily answered. "She'll drift in and out and may fall off to sleep right in the middle of a sentence. It's pretty normal. She'll be fully awake come mornin'."

"I'm glad y'all were all here with me," Vicky said. "And I'm really happy that they did the surgery in the evening instead of early morning. Now she'll sleep through the night and . . ."

"Well, where did all y'all come from? Shane, I want a burrito with extra chili and cheese," Nettie said.

"If the doctor says you can have it, I'll go get one for you. W-want a beer to go with it?"

"No, I want a shot of tequila." Her eyes fluttered shut again.

"Forget about sleeping through the night," Emily whispered.

Vicky waved to include all of them. "Y'all can go on home now. It's late, and you've all got work to do tomorrow."

Despite Vicky's words, Jancy sat down in a chair beside the bed. "Could we have a welcome-home party for her?"

Nettie's eyes opened, and she looked straight at Jancy. "Yes, you can, and I'll make a sheet cake. No more than two tarts can walk out of the diner. I don't care if you are Jesus. Where's the party? If it's at our house, y'all better go home and get it ready." That time when she shut her eyes again, she began to snore.

"I think she's out for good this time," Vicky

said. "Give me a good-night hug, Emily, and scoot on out of here. She thinks she has to talk if she's awake. If no one is here and the lights are dimmed, she'll stay asleep."

"What about someone being here when Andy comes and y'all want to go out to get something to eat?" Ryder asked.

"Did I hear my name?" Andy said from the door. "I brought a couple of sandwiches and some bottled water in case Vicky didn't want to leave."

"Thank you," Emily said. "I don't think Mama has eaten anything all day but vending machine food or whatever is in those fruit baskets."

Andy handed Vicky the brown paper bag. "Fresh-made chicken salad straight from my kitchen."

"Sounds great." Vicky opened it up and sniffed. "Smells wonderful. I want hugs from all of you before you go. And thank you so much for all you've done."

"Good night. See you tomorrow evenin'," Jancy managed to get out after she'd hugged Vicky. "If you need us, call and we'll be here soon as we can."

"I know that," Vicky said. "You've been great, Jancy. I haven't even worried about Emily since I know you are there to support her through all this."

Hand in hand, Ryder and Emily went from the

hospital to his truck with Shane and Jancy behind them. Shane's arm was around her shoulders and her hand was tucked into his right above her right breast. When they were in the truck and on the way home, she leaned forward and air slapped Emily on the shoulder.

"What's that all about?" Emily asked.

"I'm mad at you. Why'd you tell me anything at all? Now I feel guilty because Vicky trusts me to support you and I'm keeping secrets from her."

"Only for three more days, and then it'll be out in the open. Please, Jancy, I know I've put you in a tough position, but I need a friend so badly," Emily begged.

Jancy had never expected to hear such sincerity in her voice when she said *friend*. She'd had friends, but they weren't the kind that lasted more than a few phone calls or texts after she'd left a place and moved on.

"I'm your friend?" Jancy whispered. "But what about Sarah and Waynette and Teresa?"

"I can have more than three friends," Emily answered. "I love my friends, but you are . . ." She hesitated.

Ryder finished the sentence. "More like a cousin to her. I'm told that siblings argue a lot but that cousins get along pretty good."

Related? The only kin Jancy had was Minnette in Louisiana, where she'd been going when she got stranded in Pick. She needed to call her in the next few days.

"If you don't tell on Sunday, I'm going to," Jancy said.

Emily stuck her little finger over the seat. "Pinkie swear."

Jancy locked her little finger with Emily's. Twenty minutes later they were home and Emily and Ryder had gone inside the house while Jancy and Shane stopped at the swing. If a month ago someone had told Jancy that she'd be sitting on the front porch with Shane Adams in Pick, Texas, she'd have thought they'd been hitting the bourbon bottle too hard.

And no one, not even Jesus, could have convinced her that she'd be as happy as she was right then, doing nothing but listening to Shane tell her all about some vintage car he was restoring. She squirmed in the porch swing and wished that she had the courage to tell Shane about her probation right then.

"So do you have anything for sale that wouldn't cost me a fortune?" she asked instead of speaking up about her past.

"Not right now," he said. "M-m-maybe not ever."

"Why?" she asked.

"Because if you have a car you'll leave." He draped an arm around her and drew her closer to his side. "I could get real used to this, Jancy."

"What?"

"Puttin' in a day at work and then sittin' on the porch w-w-with you every evening." He grinned.

Everything about him jacked up her pulse. His touch. His sweet smile. The way his eyes went all soft when he looked down at her.

"Don't you ever want something outside of Pick?" she asked.

Shane kissed her on the forehead. "Someday I'd like to travel to all fifty states. Maybe one a year, but I'll need someone to go w-w-with me to m-m-make it fun. All alone ain't no w-way to go."

"Amen." She snuggled deeper into his shoulder.

"But I'd always come home to Pick. Goin' w-w-would be fun, but home is where the heart is. I read that somewhere," he said.

"Me, too, and I thought it was a crock of bull until recently," she said.

"You like it here?" His tone went soft, and yet there was a touch of fear in it.

"More than I ever imagined," she answered. "Nettie and Vicky are good to me, and Emily— well, they're kind of like family."

"I can't imagine livin' nowhere else. Ryder's different than me. He's lived in Galveston and in Corpus Christi. I'm glad he's ready to hang up his w-wanderin' w-ways. Emily is really the one for him. She's sassy and m-makes him toe the line."

"Were you surprised when they started dating?" she asked.

Shane pulled her closer to his side. "I told him that Nettie would kill him and Vicky w-would help her dig the hole to bury him. I even showed him the two shovels out in that storage shed behind the diner. He w-wouldn't listen, and I'm glad he didn't. We'll get a baby to spoil." He paused. "Now let's talk about you."

"Not much to that story."

"Okay, then let's w-walk up to the diner and back."

Her radar spiked when he didn't pursue the subject of talking about her. Had Emily told Ryder about her past and he in turn told Shane?

"What did you want to know about me?" she asked.

"Anything you w-want to tell m-me, but only wh-what you w-want to tell m-me. So if you say there's not m-much to the story, then we'll take a w-walk."

"Why?"

"My legs need stretchin', and I like the way I feel wh-when you are beside me."

They stood up at the same time, and he shortened his pace to keep step with her. There was no lover's moon hanging in the sky. Only the stars and the security lights inside the diner provided any illumination at all, but that's all she needed to see into Shane's eyes. From the feelings in her heart, she figured he was seeing the same thing reflected in hers. She looped her arms around his neck and rolled up on her toes to kiss him right there in front of the dark diner.

He hugged her tightly and then backed up enough that he could tip her chin up with his big fist. She moistened her lips, but he held back from kissing her. His eyes bored into hers. Then he leaned back a little farther, and she got goose bumps as she gazed right into his soul.

"I could stand right here for the rest of my life and look at your beautiful face, Jancy. W-we've got us a second chance. Let's don't w-waste it."

She wasn't aware that there'd ever been a first chance, but whatever it was, she had no intention of letting it slip by her. A small flame of hope ignited that he wouldn't change his mind once he knew everything.

Chapter Thirteen

With Nettie through the surgery and snoring right beside her and nothing but time on her hands, scenarios of the past three days ran through Vicky's head. Some of them had to do with the budding friendship between her and Andy, but most centered on whatever was going on with Emily. Determined to get some answers, she hit the speed dial to Emily's phone.

"Hello, Mama. I wasn't expecting you to call tonight. Sorry it took"—her daughter's giggle did not escape Vicky's notice—"so long."

"Where are you?"

"I'm in the kitchen making a fresh pitcher of sweet tea so we can all have a glass before we go to bed," Emily said. "Is it important or can we talk later?"

"Do you have a boyfriend that you are keeping secret from me?" Vicky blurted out.

"What on earth makes you ask that?"

"A mother can tell when her daughter is lyin'. Something is going on," Vicky said.

"Okay, okay, I am seeing someone, but I don't

want to jinx it. I'll tell you all about him this weekend and maybe even introduce you to him," Emily said. "But only if you and Nettie promise to be nice."

"Did you meet him at college?"

"Kind of, but I'm not having this conversation on the phone. Good night, Mama," Emily said. "I will see you and Nettie tomorrow night."

The phone went dark, and Vicky laid it on the window ledge beside her.

"So?" Nettie asked.

Vicky shook a fist at the ceiling. "Kids can drive you crazy."

"What's goin' on?" Nettie asked. "Is the surgery over? Did I do okay?"

"It's over, and you did fine. If everything continues like it is, you can go home tomorrow night," Vicky told her.

"Hit the button to raise me up."

Vicky pushed one on the side of the bed and raised Nettie to a half-sitting position. "It's Emily. She admits she has a boyfriend, and I know that Ryder and Shane and probably Jancy already know the whole story. That's why there've been sparks flittin' around every time they're all in the room together. She says we might get to meet him this weekend. You ready for this, Nettie? Something down in deep in my gut says she's serious about this guy."

"Of course I'm ready," Nettie said. "I want a

234

drink of water. My mouth feels like it's got sand in it."

Vicky circled around the bed and poured a cup full of cold water, stuck a straw in it, and held it up to Nettie's mouth. After a couple of sips, she waved it away.

"I'm downright scared, Nettie. What if he's really rich and breaks her heart when he sees that she's from a little town like Pick and her mama runs a diner?"

"Didn't she tell us that she wanted to stay in Pick? I bet it's someone from our area, and besides, a boyfriend does not mean a wedding," Nettie said with a yawn.

Vicky groaned. "But she's a small-town girl, not a big-city one. And she is so trusting."

"Like Shane?"

Vicky fell back into the recliner. "Exactly, only without the stutter."

"She's a big girl. Let her make her own mistakes."

"She'll get her heart broken," Vicky said.

Nettie's eyes fluttered. "Maybe, but it's her heart and her decision. Just be here to catch her when she falls, like you've always been."

Vicky reached over the rail and patted Nettie on the arm. "I had the best example of that."

"She's five years older than you were when you started dating Creed and your mama was crazy with worry about you and that wild boy."

Nettie's eyes flew open. "I told Thelma then that you had a good head on your shoulders and to trust you. I'll tell you the same thing today about your daughter."

"I wanted a different kind of life for her. What if she has fallen for the wrong guy? She's worked so hard for her education, and she's so close to getting a degree."

"What you want and what she wants are two different things," Nettie said. "Stop worryin' about what might not even be happenin'. Now, let's talk about Jancy and Shane. We know that those two are definitely fallin' for each other. I ain't never seen that boy look at a girl the way he does her."

"You got that right." She sighed.

"Do you wish you'd found someone like Andy Butler instead of Creed Rawlins?" Nettie asked.

"No, because it would have changed the whole course of my life and I might not have Emily. She's been the biggest ray of sunshine a mother could ask for, even if I'm worried." Vicky reached for a cookie from a box on the window ledge.

"We can't none of us change the past. If we could, I wouldn't have ever married at all. I'd have just slept around and enjoyed the sex," Nettie said.

"Nettie Fields!" Vicky sputtered.

The old gal was fully awake now, without a

doubt. Her shoulders popped up in a shrug, and then she winced. "Ouch. Stitches. That kinda smarted. I always liked sex." She frowned. "Do you think anyone ever slapped Jancy around like my sorry-ass husband did me?"

"She's pretty skittish when it comes to trusting," Vicky said.

"Yes, but she's got nerves of steel, that one does. I'm surprised she didn't kill that boyfriend who was stealin' cars," Nettie chuckled. "Now, put my bed down. Ain't no use in either of us frettin' about what we don't even know. Let's get some sleep, and when we wake up, it'll be the day I get to go home. I'm glad you were here every time I opened my eyes. Only good things I ever did was buy the diner with Thelma and finish raisin' you and that sweet baby girl you produced. Y'all are my pride and joy," Nettie said.

"Thank you." Vicky patted her on the arm. "God only knows I would have been lost without you when I found out I was pregnant. I was glad Mama didn't ever know, because she would have been so disappointed in me."

Nettie's smile turned sad. "Not for long, honey. She adored the ground you walked on. Don't ever think that she would have lost an ounce of love for you. And she would have spoiled Emily even worse than I did."

"Ain't possible." Vicky laughed, breaking the

heavy emotional moment. "Just flat ain't possible. Do you think we'll keep Jancy past the end of summer when she's got enough money saved for a car and traveling?"

"If we spoil her enough," Nettie answered. "She's easy to love. Kind of like a little puppy that's been kicked around and needs real love. And she's a damn fine waitress. Don't know that we've ever had any better."

"Wouldn't be a hard job to spoil her, but she don't take to it. After the first couple of days, I offered her an advance so she could get her cell phone service back, but she refused."

"Kind of like Emily." Nettie yawned. "Trust her and don't push her too hard, or she might shut you out. Give her the right to grow up and make her own way. She'll always be your daughter, but time is coming when she'll also be your friend, like Jancy is proving to be."

"It's not easy." Vicky sighed.

"Never is, but it's for the best," Nettie said. "Now good night for the last time."

"Good night," Vicky said.

Vicky hit the button to lower Nettie's bed and then pulled the lever to throw the recliner into a horizontal position. But it was a long time before she drifted off to sleep.

Jancy went into the house that evening to find Emily sitting in Vicky's recliner. "I can't ever remember a time when I spent the night in this house without Mama and Nettie being here."

"And you are going to live in that trailer that Ryder is setting up, right?" Jancy lay on the buttery-soft leather sofa with her head on the arm. "Is it going to be ready by wedding time?"

"It will be by the time we get back from our honeymoon. Oh!" Emily gasped. "You won't leave before I get back from the honeymoon—promise me. Mama and Nettie need you at the diner."

"I hadn't planned on it." Jancy smiled. "Where are y'all goin'?"

"He's booked us a seven-day Caribbean cruise out of Houston. I can't even imagine a whole week with Ryder all by ourselves." Emily sighed. "And now for the next thing I want to ask you before we talk to Mama and Nettie. Will you be one of my bridesmaids at the wedding? As soon as we tell Mama and Nettie, I'll ask Sarah, Teresa, and Waynette to be the others. I'm not having a maid of honor because it would be too hard to pick among all four of you."

"Are you sure? I could just sit at the guest book or maybe serve cake." Jancy could scarcely believe that Emily would even ask.

"You've been here with me through this tough time. I want you to stand up with me, and I really want you to be here with me when I have this baby. I need your strength to get me through it."

Jancy wiped a tear from her cheek. "Okay, I'll be a bridesmaid, but I can't make promises about staying all the way until Christmas."

"Please, Jancy. Mama is going to need you. She'll freak out worse than I will when I go into labor. And Nettie's liable to have another heart attack if Mama goes into a full-fledged panic attack. Please?"

"Emily, Waynette and your other friends will be there. Besides, your mother had you, so she understands labor," Jancy said.

"You have a calming effect on Mama. You just have to stay," Emily said.

"Okay, I'll stick around until then," Jancy agreed.

"Shane is going to be the godfather, and I'd like for you to be the baby's godmother," Emily pressed.

"Hey, now, that's a big decision. You think on it until after the wedding and then we'll talk about that," Jancy said.

"Deal. So now you know all my secrets," Emily said. "Did you ever get married?"

Jancy nodded. "I was married, but my husband already had a wife that he had not divorced. I threw a fit, and he ripped off his belt and hit me twice before I yanked it out of his hands and knocked him out cold with my fist."

"How did you get into a situation like that?" Emily frowned.

"We had gotten our marriage license at the courthouse and gone to a preacher's house for the marriage. He told the preacher he'd take it back to the courthouse the next morning and file it. Only he didn't because he hadn't divorced or even left his wife, and I didn't find out about it for two months. And he had two kids."

Emily's voice came out high and squeaky. "You should have shot him dead while he was passed out. How'd you find out?"

"I wanted a copy of the marriage license to put in a pretty frame. Went to the courthouse and they said there was a record of it being bought, but it had never been filed. When I confronted him, he got angry."

"When did all this happen?"

"After the time the one boyfriend got put in jail, and the one that wanted to turn me into a hooker. Trust isn't so easy anymore. Not always in people but in my own judgment."

Emily was on the edge of her chair. "Why on earth did you trust us?"

"Didn't have a choice at the time," she answered. "Now, it seems like we've been friends for years."

"Jancy, I'm so sorry you've had all these bad experiences in your life. You didn't deserve that kind of thing."

"Experiences, good or bad, are what made me who I am. The only regret I have is that I'll have to tell Shane my story, and when I do, he's never going to look at me the same again."

"Don't be so sure, my friend. He's got broad shoulders and a big heart."

"It'll take both," Jancy said. "Why didn't you ever date Shane?"

"He's like a big brother to me," Emily answered.

"Try to make sure, when you tell Vicky, that she doesn't get prejudiced or mean against Ryder. She just desperately wants you to have a better life than she did," Jancy said.

"I know," Emily whispered. "And I will have that with Ryder. If I didn't believe it with my whole heart, I wouldn't be marrying him."

Chapter Fourteen

Jancy heard the van coming up the lane and yelled through the screen door. "They're here, Emily. Turn on the lights."

Nettie was out of the vehicle the second that it stopped, a big smile on her face at the sight of twinkling lights flashing around the porch posts. Emily and Ryder came outside to join Jancy and Shane.

"Welcome home!" Emily held out a hand to help, but Nettie refused it.

"I do not need mollycoddlin'. I do need a glass of decent sweet tea, and the swing belongs to me for the next half an hour," she said.

"We've got the kitchen table set up with finger foods and cupcakes," Emily said.

"Those two big strappin' boys can bring it out here to the porch. I'm sick of being inside. I need fresh air." Nettie settled in on the swing.

"We can do that." Ryder and Shane headed inside with Emily right behind them.

"I hope you got meat loaf sandwiches on that table," Nettie yelled.

"Of course we do." Emily's voice floated through the screen door. "With mustard."

"Welcome home, Vicky." Jancy picked up two green plants from the van and set them on the porch.

"Thank you. Are you any good with plants and flowers?" Nettie asked.

"Yes, ma'am," Jancy answered. "Mama passed on her green thumb to me. They'll be fine on the porch tonight. Tomorrow mornin' I'll get them inside. Right now I'll take the rest of this baggage to your room. If you need help later unpacking it all, just holler."

She'd set the bags on the floor beside Nettie's rocking chair and was crossing the kitchen floor when her phone rang. She pulled it out of the hip pocket of her jeans and smiled.

"Hello, Minnette. I've been meanin' to call you all week," she said.

"You are a hard person to catch up with. I've been trying to call you for weeks," her cousin said.

"I'll get into it later over beignets and coffee," Jancy said.

"About that. We are actually leaving Louisiana. Donald enlisted in the army six months ago. He's gotten his orders to go to Germany for two years, so we have to leave next weekend. Just wanted to let you know, so you wouldn't make the long trip down here."

Jancy felt as if a virtual door slammed so hard that it rattled her mind.

Emily laid a hand on her arm. "Are you okay?"

"Who is that?" Minnette asked.

"A friend. I'm in Pick, Texas," Jancy said.

"I remember when y'all lived there. How'd you end up back there? I thought you were in Amarillo," Minnette said.

"I was on my way to Louisiana, and my car burned up right here in Pick," Jancy said.

"Well, *chère*, you know what our maw-maw used to say—in the end, things work like they should. Who'd have thought I'd be headed to Germany and you'd be right back where your mama grew up? I'll call when we get settled and give you a contact number and address. If all else fails, where can I send you a letter?"

"Just send it in care of the Strawberry Hearts Diner, Pick, Texas," Jancy answered. "And even though we don't see each other very often, I'll miss talking to you."

"Then come see me."

Jancy laughed. "Yeah, right!"

They said their good-byes, and Jancy stuck the phone back in her pocket. Was this an omen? Was she supposed to stay in Pick? She'd moved to a town many times without having a friend or a relative living there.

"Are you okay?" Emily asked. "And pardon my nosiness, but what's coming in the mail? If you'll take the lemonade, I'll carry out the sweet tea."

"That was my cousin in Louisiana. I told her where she could send mail if she couldn't reach me by phone. Remember when I told y'all I was on my way to Louisiana to see my cousin when my car broke down? Well, she called me. Her husband joined the army, and they're going to Germany for two years. End of story."

"Or the beginning of one," Vicky said. "Maybe fate closed that door for a purpose."

"You have to put your hand in God's and tell him to lead," Nettie said as she entered the kitchen. She picked up a sandwich and bit into it. "Lord, this tastes good. Know why folks work so hard to get well in a hospital? So they can go home and eat good food."

"Did you ever put your hand in God's?" Jancy asked.

"Every single mornin' since my divorce," Nettie answered. "And he ain't led me wrong a single time. Let's go on back outside. Fresh night air is wonderful."

They followed her to the porch, where she sat on the swing, polished off the sandwich, and picked up a cupcake, bit into it, and smiled. "I bet the folks really liked these. They're good."

"They'll do for a substitute, but everyone misses your tarts," Emily said.

Jancy sipped her glass of tea and listened to the discussion of what was happening over the upcoming weekend. Cleaning the cemetery the next day. Church on Sunday.

Then the bomb would explode. She had to grip the tea to keep from dropping it as she imagined all the emotions, the disappointments, the fears, and the anger that would be in the house. It would be so different than the festive feeling wrapped around them that evening.

"Where's your head, Jancy?" Nettie asked.

A couple of fast blinks brought her back into the conversation. "Thinking about how things work out, I guess."

"For the best." Vicky smiled.

Hopefully, she'd remember those three words on Sunday night.

Vicky stumbled into the kitchen on Saturday morning to find Nettie, a cup of coffee in one hand, dressed for work. "Oh, no! The doctor said you are going to rest for the weekend and maybe you can work an hour or two on Monday."

"You got a choice. You can let me go to the diner and sit in a booth or on a stool in the kitchen, or I'll stay home and run the vacuum, dust, and clean all day," Nettie said. "I'll abide by whatever decision you make."

"Nettie! You were supposed to sleep until noon and then watch movies all afternoon." Jancy stopped in the middle of the floor.

"Or maybe talk to your church ladies all day."

Emily came to an abrupt stop right behind Jancy.

"I can talk to people at the diner. I hate phone conversations. How on earth y'all keep those cell phones glued to your hands is a total mystery to me," Nettie said. "So do I get out the vacuum, or are you going to let me walk to the diner with y'all this mornin', Vicky?"

"I'll stay home and watch her," Emily said.

"You do and I'll make you clean out all the cabinets. That means washing all the dishes, putting in new shelf paper, and—"

"Okay, okay." Vicky's palms shot up. "You win. But you aren't lifting a single finger to do one thing. You can't even fill a tea glass. I don't care if it's your glass. You can sit and visit."

"I could sit on a stool and run the cash register. That wouldn't hurt anything, now would it?" Nettie poured the rest of the coffee in the sink, rinsed the cup, and put it in the dishwasher.

"For what my opinion is worth, I think that would be a great job. It would help us out so much if we didn't have to stop and tally up the bills," Jancy said.

"I agree." Emily nodded. "Now let's get on up to the diner. We've got cupcakes to make. And no tarts, Nettie, not until Monday. If you even look like you are going to do anything other than take money today, I'll handcuff you to the sofa and make you watch animated cartoons all day."

"I can make tarts sitting on a stool, and it's no

more trouble than taking money," Nettie argued.

"Baby steps." Jancy slipped an arm around Nettie's shoulders. "Little bitty steps, and by this time next week, you'll be right back in your rut."

"Y'all are bein' almighty difficult," Nettie grumbled.

"It's for your own good." Jancy shortened her stride to keep up with Nettie's as they left the house. "Just like it was for my own good when my car burned up in the diner parking lot. You can't fight fate, Miz Nettie."

"You'd do well to remember that," Nettie said.

Vicky chuckled. They'd come a long way since that first day when things were so awkward. Whether it was bad luck or good settling in for the summer, nothing had been boring.

"Maybe it's all in how you look at it whether it's bad or good," she reflected under her breath.

"What did you say, Mama?" Emily asked.

"Just muttering to myself," she said and then quickly changed the subject. "Everyone is going to be so glad to see Nettie. Get ready for a busy day."

"Feels like I've been gone a month," Nettie said.

"Yes, it does." Vicky opened the back door and switched on the kitchen lights.

Nettie stepped inside and inhaled deeply. "Ahhh, my sweet, sweet diner. I hope I never leave you again. Now let's get busy."

Vicky pulled up a stool. "This is as busy as you get until the doors open. Then you can move to the cash register."

"Run, Jancy! Get out of here in a hurry. You are working for a tyrant," Nettie joked.

"I'm not going anywhere until you are one hundred percent well," Jancy said. "I'll start the sausage gravy, Emily, if you'll do the cupcakes this morning."

"Nettie is supposed to start a heart-healthy diet today," Vicky said. "We'll make her an egg-white omelet with mushrooms and tomatoes."

"You will get shot if you do. I will eat what I want and die when I'm supposed to. I want a sausage-and-egg biscuit. And the whole egg, not just the white," Nettie declared. "I have my family, my church family, and my food. That's my holy trinity, and I'm not giving up any of it."

It was going to be an uphill battle.

The aromas of breakfast foods and smoked turkey had filled the diner half an hour later when Vicky went to the front to turn on the lights and unlock the doors.

Nettie was home. There was light at the end of the tunnel. In two weeks, max, things would be totally back to normal. Get up and go to work. Go home to a few hours with her girls, Emily and Jancy, and start all over the next day.

The future looked great right up until she saw Carlton Wolfe coming toward the diner. His toothy smile did not light up the place when he pushed his way inside.

"Coffee, please. No menu."

The whole time that Vicky filled the cup, she wished she could lace it with arsenic. "What brings you out this mornin'?"

"I came to offer my condolences on your partner. I understand that she's no longer able to work," Carlton said.

"You heard bull crap," Nettie called from the back room. "I'm working today."

Carlton's smile faded, and he lowered his voice. "Are you sure her coming back here in her weakened condition is wise? I came to make a final offer for your land and this diner. Someone"—he pointed toward the ceiling—"could be sending you a message."

"Someone"—Vicky rolled her eyes upward—"would probably tell me to dig a hole six feet down and put you in the bottom before he told me to leave Pick, Texas. I'm not interested in your offers, no matter what they are. You might as well take your business elsewhere."

"You will be sorry in ten years," he said. "You'll never get another offer like I'm making you. My final offer is a quarter of a million dollars. Here's another of my business cards with my number on it. You have one week to change your mind. Your town can't go on forever. Take advantage of what is before you. And that offer for dinner is still on the table, Victoria."

She shot a mean look his way. "My name is—"

He butted in quickly. "I know you like to be called Vicky, but Victoria suits you so much better. It's regal, like you are."

The bell above the door let her know that someone had arrived. She'd never been so glad to see Ryder in her entire life. He popped a hip up on a stool right beside Carlton. "Mornin', Mr. Wolfe. What brings you to Pick at the crack of dawn?"

"Just here to do a little business with Victoria. I'm going down to see Leonard and then I'll be on my way." Carlton pulled out two dollars and laid them on the counter.

"Don't go yet," Ryder said.

"You got property to sell me?" Carlton spun the stool around to face him.

"No, sir, I do not own property in Pick. At least not yet. But I've got a question to ask. Have you ever been to a cemetery cleanup?" Ryder asked.

Vicky's hands clenched into fists. What on earth was Ryder thinking? The man was on his way out of the diner. Let him go.

"Of course not. It sounds horrible." Carlton shuddered.

"Well, we're goin' to have one tonight. We all gather up at the cemetery and we bring a tailgate supper. We share the food and the duties, and even the little kids work to help get it in top-notch shape once a year. While we work we

252

remember the stories that we've heard about the folks who are buried there. We remember that Jancy's grandma made the best lemon pie in the whole state and always brought one to the church dinners. And we talk about how Vicky's mama never lived long enough to see Emily. It's a time of cleanin', yes, and when we get done, it'll look right nice for the folks comin' in for the festival."

"What's that got to do with me?"

"Exactly," Ryder said. "It has nothing to do with you or with the people who would buy your fancy houses. It has to do with the people who live in Pick now, the ones who will be buried out there in that cemetery someday and who know that their graves will be cleaned up before festival day. This isn't just a chunk of dirt to us. It's our heritage and our lives. And that's not for sale at any price."

"Everything is for sale. It's just a matter of price and time," Carlton snapped.

"You have my deepest sympathy," Ryder said.

Vicky could have hugged Ryder. The younger generation was stepping up to the plate and realizing their responsibilities toward keeping their community intact.

Carlton jerked his head around to glare at Ryder. "Why would you feel sorry for me?"

"Because you have nothing of value if everything you have has a price tag on it. Just between me and you, you will not talk anyone out of their land here in Pick. You have a nice day now," Ryder said. "Miz Vicky, I'd like a tall glass of milk and whatever breakfast special is on the menu today. And welcome home, Miz Nettie. It's good to have you back even if they won't let you do much today."

"You have my offer, Victoria." Carlton slid off the bar stool.

Ryder picked up the two bills and shoved them back into the pocket of Carlton's snowy-white shirt. "Put his coffee on my tab, Miz Vicky. I'll pay for the last cup he ever gets in this diner."

Carlton stormed out, gunned his fancy little car enough to sling gravel against the metal siding, and left at least six months of rubber on the highway.

"I think that went very well." Ryder grinned.

"That went amazingly wonderful." Emily backed out of the swinging doors and set a big platter of food in front of him. "And this is on the house. We heard every word you said, and no one could have done better."

"Thank you. I was just speakin' from the heart. Folks like Carlton don't know about the way we do things here in Pick. It probably went in one ear and out the other, but hopefully he doesn't have a Teflon brain."

Emily giggled, and Vicky frowned.

"Nothing sticks, Mama," Emily explained.

It started with a giggle then went into laughter,

and finally Vicky was grabbing napkins from the nearest dispenser to wipe the tears flowing down her cheeks. "I don't imagine"—she hiccupped—"that we've seen the last of him, but you earned your breakfast. You ever think of goin' into politics, Ryder?"

"No, ma'am. I'll be happy to pitch a tent right here in Pick and work out of the office in Frankston until I'm old enough to retire."

"Well, if you"—another hiccup—"ever change your mind, I'll be your campaign manager." Vicky poured a glass of water and took seven sips without coming up for air. Just like her mother always said, it stopped hiccups. If only she could make Carlton Wolfe disappear the same way.

The day went fast for Nettie, and that evening Vicky relegated her to sitting in a lawn chair. It was the first time that she hadn't made her way through the cemetery helping a little here and there and bossing everywhere. She should be glad to be above the ground and not under it.

Nothing had changed in the more than sixty years she'd been coming to the cemetery cleanup day. Compliments of a group of FFA boys back in the forties, a metal sign above the entrance said **PICK CEMETERY**. Most of those guys now had tombstones in the newer section toward the back. One central road led past the oldest tombstones.

Halfway to the back side, a road cut across the main thoroughfare. A water faucet was located at each of the four corners of that road, and hoses were stretched out every which way. Tomorrow morning every tombstone would be cleaned and shining, and there wouldn't be a weed in sight.

Woody set a chair beside her and eased his lanky frame down into it. "Glad to see you here. Wouldn't be the same without you."

"Or you. We're the old folks now. Remember when our parents were the ones who sat in chairs and watched the young folks work?" Nettie sighed.

"Yep," Woody agreed. "But we ain't ready to turn up our toes just yet. Right now we got to save our strength for that wolf that's still knockin' on our door. Sorry son of a gun can't take no for an answer. He was in town again today."

"Ryder put him in his place," Nettie said. "Hey, Jancy, your granny's grave looks good. Elaine would be right proud of you takin' care of it on cleanup day."

Jancy pulled up a dandelion. Then she stood up and took a couple of long strides, sitting down on the grass beside Nettie. "I can feel Mama's spirit. Does that sound crazy?"

"Not a bit. We all feel that way on this day," Woody answered. "It brings back memories, and that's a good thing, not a crazy one. And when the folks come home for the festival and visit their departed loved ones, they'll have the same feeling."

"I wish Mama and I could have participated in this when we were here, but Granny was in the hospital that day and we spent it with her. I remember that she fussed and said we should be here instead of there, but they thought she wouldn't make it through the day. She lived almost another year, though," Jancy said.

Nettie laid a hand on Jancy's shoulder. The child had been through too much for a kid her age. She needed to shed those wandering wings and let love surround her right there in Pick.

"It wasn't time and she was determined not to leave this world except in her house. I'm glad that Elaine could be with her during those months," Nettie said.

"Hey, girl," Vicky yelled from fifty yards away. "If you are done there, I can use some help this way."

Jancy popped up on her feet and jogged in that direction, her ponytail whipping back and forth.

"Oh, to be able to do that again." Woody sighed.

"What? Grow enough hair to make a ponytail?" Nettie teased.

"No, woman! Hop up like that and then run. My bones would threaten to break if I took a step, and if I took off in a run, I'd sprawl out flat on my face," Woody said.

"Maybe we are ready for these chairs," Nettie said.

"Speak for yourself, Nettie Fields." Woody grinned. "Want a cold orange soda pop?"

"Love one," Nettie said.

He pulled two cans from a small cooler beside his chair, popped the top on one, and handed it to her. "Just like when we were kids."

"Wouldn't be the same without it or getting to drink it with you." Nettie clicked her can with his. "I miss Irma today. The three of us kids couldn't wait until snack time so we could get one of the ones our mothers brought." She held the can up to get a better look at it. "Only in those days it came in bottles."

"Memories." He smiled.

Chapter Fifteen

Jancy could feel Emily's edginess that Sunday morning when they opened up the diner and got ready for the breakfast run. The energy in the place was off—not bad, not good, just eerily strange. But then, Jancy could understand it. She'd never been in that exact position, but there had been times like that in her life. Like when she testified against her crazy boyfriend for stealing cars and the friends she'd made at the fast-food place kept their distance. Anxiety affected folks the same.

The normal pre-church breakfast rush was over, and the four of them sat at the counter and ate breakfast together. The lunch rush hit about fifteen minutes after the last amen at both churches in town, and when it was over, everyone fixed a plate except Jancy. She opted for a double meat and bacon burger with extra cheese and an order of tater tots.

They hadn't seen Ryder or Shane all day. Jancy figured Ryder was lying low, building his courage for that evening. But she hadn't even gotten a text from Shane, and that was odd since he normally fired off half a dozen by noon.

She'd finished the last bite of her burger when she saw Ryder's truck pull into the parking lot. He got out, shook the legs of his jeans down over his boots, and headed toward the diner. Then the back door opened, and Shane crawled out, jogged around the back of the truck, and opened the door.

Jancy recognized Shane's grandfather, Hank, right away. His hair had gotten grayer, his back a little more bent, and his walk slower. He still wore bibbed overalls and a plaid shirt, but his scuffed-up old work boots had been replaced with running shoes. Shane popped open a walker and helped Hank push it across the gravel parking lot.

"Well, look who Shane is bringing for a visit." Nettie went to the door and opened it wide. "Hank Adams! It's good to see you," she said as they entered the diner.

He smiled. "It's good to see all y'all, Nettie. Even though I've made a lot of friends in the center, I miss this place. You still makin' those tarts?"

"Most of the time, but I had a little visit in the hospital last week. We've got some almighty good strawberry cupcakes that the girls whipped up. You want one?"

"Yes, with a cup of your nice strong coffee," he answered. "Now where is this girl that Shane brought me to see? I hear that she's Lucy Wilson's granddaughter. I always liked Lucy."

"You still take it with two sugars and double cream?"

"Yes, I do, and two teaspoons of instant coffee stirred into it to give it some kick. They won't let me have that much caffeine in the center. I tell them that my innards are fine. It's just my bones that have failed me." His head went up and down like a bobblehead doll.

"Gramps, sit right here." Shane helped him get settled into a booth. "Jancy, come say hello."

Hank smiled when he caught sight of Jancy. "I swear, it's like lookin' at Lucy when she was a young girl. Tell me again how you got back to Pick after all these years."

Shane wrapped his big hand around Jancy's and led her to the booth. "Gramps, I told you about her car catchin' on fire and how she's working here at the diner."

"Yes, but I want to hear her voice and see if she sounds like Lucy." Hank smiled.

Jancy took a step forward. "It's like this, Mr. Hank. I had no intentions of even stoppin' in town. I went to the cemetery to see my granny's grave, but fate had another plan. My car caught on fire right out there about where Ryder has parked his truck. And there was a sign in the window that said these folks needed some help."

"You sound more like your mother than your

grandmother. Elaine always had a sweet, soft voice. Honey, it wasn't fate that dropped you where you need to be. It was God sending Shane the girl he's always had a thing for." Hank winked.

Crimson filled Shane's cheeks. "Gramps!"

Hank chuckled. "Don't fight heaven. You'll lose every time. Now, where are them cupcakes? Nettie, sit down right here and let's visit."

"We miss you around here," Vicky said.

The older man looked around. "I miss this, too, but I'm in a good place. Shane is runnin' the business and doin' a good job. I've got new friends and some fine domino partners. And I like the look of this woman Shane is going to marry."

"Gramps!" Shane blushed again.

"Just callin' it like I see it, son."

Jancy tucked her hand in Shane's. "Shane, will you help me in the kitchen?"

"Sure thing." He hopped up, giving Nettie his place.

When they reached the kitchen, he wrapped her into his arms, tipped up her chin, and kissed her so passionately that she could feel happiness filling the void in her heart. Had her grandmother really sent her straight to Shane to find what was missing in her life?

Sweet little shivers traced up her spine as she stepped back and locked gazes with Shane.

"That's so sweet of you to bring him to meet me and to visit with Nettie."

"I've w-wanted him to m-meet you ever since you got back in town, but he's asleep by the time you get off w-work. When the doctor told him that he had the worst kind of arthritis, he put his affairs in order and checked into the care center. I hated it, Jancy. I could take care of him."

"He knows you love him, and he's proud of you." Jancy rolled up on her tiptoes and kissed him on the cheek. "Do you remember he sat on the pew behind me and Mama at church? You were always there with him," she said.

"I remember, believe m-me." Shane kept her in his embrace as he looked out through the serving window. "There are folks at the care center who can't leave their beds. I'm glad that he's out with us."

"Me, too," Jancy said. "Is Ryder nervous about tonight?"

"Not so m-much. He just needs it to be over," Shane whispered. "W-we'll only be here a little bit. All right if I pick you up for church?"

She leaned into his shoulder. "Of course. Maybe we ought to sit up closer to the front with the family. Emily might need my support tonight."

"I promised Ryder I'd be there when the stuff hits the fan. Is Nettie going to be all right w-with it?"

"She already suspects," Jancy whispered.

"Really?" Shane gasped.

"Not much gets by Nettie. She thought that Emily might be falling in love with you at first," Jancy answered.

"I've had m-my eye on another girl for a long time. I'm just glad that she decided to come on back home," Shane said.

Something strange was in the air. Emily was as nervous as a hooker in a tent revival. Nettie was antsy, too, but that could be attributed to the fact that she was worried that she'd lost her touch with the tarts. Something was slightly off with Jancy, even. Yet no one was complaining.

When Andy dropped by an hour before closing, Vicky filled two glasses with sweet tea, put the last two cupcakes on a plate, and joined him at his booth.

"On the house," she said.

He peeled the paper from a cupcake. "Needin' company?"

"Needin' something. I'm not sure what it is. I'm not clairvoyant, but there's something in the air today."

"It's probably that Nettie is home and fidgetin' to get back to work. That her adrenaline rush is settling will create all kinds of crazy feelings," he said. "Dad was like that the first few days. He wanted to be on his horse and rounding up cattle for a branding day. Mother and I hovered over him, which was something we'd never done. The atmosphere was strained, to say the least."

"Could be, but I don't think so," she answered.

"You're still sleep deprived," Andy said. "It'll all be fine tomorrow, and if it's not, you can cross the bridge then. No use in worryin' about it today. That's my mother's advice, not mine. You should take an afternoon off sometime and come out to the ranch and meet my folks. Or maybe I'll bring them by here for a tart."

"Not without warning." She smiled.

"Fair enough," he said. "I dropped by to check on you and Nettie but also to bring some news. Carlton has staked out another town. He's selling them the same con that he's tried to pass off on y'all."

"It's a wonder the seat of his expensive britches don't catch on fire."

"What?" Andy asked.

"Liar, liar, pants on fire." She laughed.

Andy chuckled. "The folks over in Troup are listenin' to him a little better than y'all did, so maybe he'll move away from Pick."

"Well, bless their hearts. If they get taken in by that fake smile, they'll need all the blessings they can get," she said.

"You got that right," Andy said as he finished off the last of his cupcake. "Thanks for the treat, and I'll see you again real soon."

"You are very welcome. Thanks for stopping by and for the news."

"My pleasure." He tipped an imaginary hat as he left the diner.

Nettie had seen all of her circle of friends from her church group in the diner over the weekend, but it was wonderful to be back in church that Sunday evening. It had been a downright weird day at the diner, and she needed that peace. She thought about those poor folks in the care facility where Hank lived. It would be tough seeing them day after day in that condition—seeing their loved ones come and go. If she had a choice between his affliction and dropping with a fatal heart attack, she'd take the latter any day. She'd rather be dead than have her precious memories start leakin' out.

Her favorite hymn, "Leaning on the Everlasting Arms," began.

When she'd dropped in the doctor's office, there wasn't a light beckoning to her or a voice from God asking her if she was weary with life and living. One minute she'd been standing in front of the check-in desk, the next she was being rushed to the hospital emergency room. But the experience had created a need to renew her vow to lean on God—to put her troubles in his pocket.

She silently hummed the song all the way home

that evening. Vicky parked between Ryder's new truck and Shane's older one. Nettie laid a hand on her arm before she could get out.

"Give me five minutes. I've got something to say."

"I know, Nettie. You don't have to say the words," Vicky said.

"Yes, I do. You and Emily were my salvation that year after I got a divorce, and you have been every day since. I'm making a will next week. Everything I own will go to you, but my half of the diner is Emily's. That said, I still hope I live to be a hundred and drop dead in the diner after a sixteen-hour shift."

"Nettie . . . ," Vicky started.

"No *if*s, *but*s, or *maybe*s. That's the way it is. I ain't one much for tellin' folks how I feel—I just had to get it done. Now, let's go sit with the kids for a spell."

Ryder and Emily had been sitting on the swing. When Nettie arrived, they both stood up and gave it to her. Shane and Jancy rested on the steps. His arm curved around her, drawing her head to his chest. A nice picture, but the aura wasn't peaceful. Whatever spirit had been in the diner and was now on the porch was about to speak its mind.

Nettie settled into the swing. "So what did y'all think of the sermon tonight?"

"Didn't hear a word of it," Ryder admitted.

"Why's that?" Vicky joined Nettie on the swing.

"Because we've got something to say and we were both worried about it," Emily said.

"Well, spit it out," Nettie said.

Ryder took Emily's hand in his.

Vicky gasped.

Shane and Jancy both smiled.

"We've been dating since Christmas," Ryder said.

"No!" Vicky clamped a hand over her mouth.

Emily leaned into him. "We are in love, Mama."

Vicky felt her whole world slip out from under her. "How long has this been going on? When did it start?" she sputtered and then went on. "Is this a joke? Why didn't you tell me?"

"Because at first we were just flirting and then it got serious. I wanted to tell you," Ryder said. "But, well, you know me, Vicky. You know my reputation and you know that I'm not good enough for Emily. But I love her and I've changed. I'll do right by her, I promise."

"It's been going on since Christmas and it's not a joke," Emily said.

"Then this is you asking me for permission to date my child right out in the open?" Vicky stared at Ryder as if he had an extra eyeball right in the middle of his forehead. God Almighty! Had Emily lost her mind?

Ryder took a deep breath. "This is me asking for your blessing on our marriage."

"Sweet Lord!" Vicky whispered. Surely she'd heard him wrong. Had it gone that far without her knowing? She threw a hand over her eyes.

Nettie patted her on the arm. "Take a breath."

Dating was hard enough, but marriage? Vicky was glad that she was sitting down. She caught Emily's gaze, begging her to understand, pleading with her to accept Ryder. She wanted to refuse, to take Emily away to a faraway place and keep her there until she came to her senses. A picture of a convent even flashed across her mind. But she knew it would be wrong to interfere, no matter how much she wanted to. A wedding—she'd need six months to plan it. Maybe a Christmas affair with red velvet bridesmaid dresses and poinsettias all over the church.

"This is a lot to sling at me all at once," Vicky said.

"Mama, please." Emily crossed the porch and knelt in front of Vicky, throwing her arms around her. "I need this. I don't just want it. I need for you to be on board with us. Not with me, but with us."

"Okay," Vicky said slowly as she hugged her daughter. "Ryder, you've got a year to prove yourself to me. You can be engaged to my daughter, but—"

"Not a year, Mama. We're getting married

269

three weeks from yesterday. June 24," Emily said.

"I cannot get things ready in that . . ." Vicky grabbed her heart. "Weddings take time and planning and . . ."

"Whoa! Time for another breath," Nettie said. "Why June 24, Ryder?"

"Because I start to work at the office in Frankston soon after that. I've booked a week-long cruise for a honeymoon, and that will give us time to get moved into the trailer and get settled and . . ." He paused and looked like a fish floundering around out of water.

Nettie stood up, and Shane did the same.

"I'll get you a chair," Shane said as he raced into the house.

"Bring two. Emily and Ryder need the swing more than we do," Nettie said.

Vicky was glad to let Nettie take control, because her mind was whipping around in circles. Ryder? Emily? How in the devil would she get a wedding ready in less than three weeks? She stood up and let Shane guide her to a kitchen chair, where she plopped down. Surely this was a nightmare. She'd wake up any minute and find out that it was the result of sleep deprivation, like Andy said.

"What trailer?"

"They're moving one in beside my house tomorrow m-mornin'," Shane answered. "It's real nice, even if it is a used one. That w-way they don't have to pay rent and can save up their m-money for a down payment on some land and a house."

"But three weeks?" Vicky put her head in her hands.

"Don't worry, Mama. We've already got plans in motion. We're getting married in the parking lot of the diner at eight o'clock. The sun should be setting about then," Emily said.

"I see you've been thinkin' about this for a while." Vicky's voice sounded all high and squeaky even to her ears.

"Yes, ma'am, we have," Ryder said. "Vicky, please give me a chance. I love her more than anything in this world."

"Parking lot?" Vicky grimaced.

"We can't take out more than two tarts. It's the first rule." Emily's smile was weak, but her eyes shone with love. "And I want tarts on the counter right along with a wedding cake. Think Andy will take care of that for us?"

"Dress, flowers, invitations?" Vicky floundered at the enormity of it all.

"Public invitation at church. Flowers can be ordered. Nothing fancy. I'd be happy with wild-flowers picked from the side of the road. The dress is something I saved for me and you to do together. Of course, we'll need Nettie and Jancy to go with us, and Sarah, Teresa, and Waynette, because they're going to be bridesmaids, too.

Maybe we'll close up early next Sunday and go shopping."

"But why so fast? Can't we . . . ," Vicky started.

"The baby is due Christmas Day, Mama."

"But I proposed long before we got pregnant," Ryder said quickly.

Chapter Sixteen

T hat is a lot to spring on a woman in one night," Nettie scolded.

"I'm going to be a grandmother?" Vicky whispered.

"Yes, you are, and Nettie is going to be a great-grandmother," Emily said.

Vicky's head swam with information overkill. Nettie was speechless. Emily looked as if she was about to burst into tears. Ryder's nervousness filled the whole area. Something had to be done to ease the emotions, to get things going in the right direction rather than stalling out on the worries of putting together a wedding.

Jancy squeezed Shane's hand and said, "I'm butting in where it's none of my business, but there's going to be a wedding and a baby. Might as well get the first over with so we can all look forward to the second. Emily and Ryder have things under control, Vicky. Everyone in town will attend the wedding, and every chair will be filled. Folks can park their cars over on the north forty." She grinned. "I've always wanted to use that phrase. One church couldn't hold everyone, anyway. Ryder has promised to be a good husband and father, and if he's not, I'll take care of his dead body. Nettie will help me dig."

"Yes, I will," Nettie said with a nod.

Jancy put her hand on Shane's shoulder. "Let's take a walk, Shane, and let the family have some alone time."

They were all the way to the diner when Shane stopped and drew her into his arms. "That w-was brilliant, darlin'."

"Women need to talk things through, Shane. It's the way we're made. Sometimes it's best to boil it down to a few words that can be easily digested and then move on."

"I love that you see things so clear." He sank his face into her hair. "And I love the smell of your hair. Coconut, right?"

"That's right." Her hands flattened out on his wide, muscular chest.

His thick lashes fluttered and then rested on his high cheekbones. She barely had time to moisten her lips before his met them. Everything that was going on back at the house faded away. When he took a step back, she leaned into him so hard that she had to rush to right herself.

"I like the way you fit in my arms," he chuckled and then got serious. "You have a big heart that doesn't even hear m-my stutter. Your beauty comes from the light inside you. It's brighter than that m-moon hangin' up there in the sky."

Jancy's eyes filled, and she had to blink fast to keep them from spilling over. There wasn't a pickup line in the world that was more romantic than what Shane had said. She'd thought that she was in love before, but those relationships couldn't even compare to what was slowly developing with Shane.

Maybe that was the secret to happiness—patience and waiting instead of jumping in with both feet and immediately having regrets.

Nettie had gone to the church to meet with her ladies' group that Wednesday evening. The discussion on the agenda was who would donate what to the church bazaar that fall. That would take about three minutes, because each of them donated the same thing every year. The next hour would be dedicated to the newest gossip—the upcoming wedding.

Ryder and Shane had picked Jancy and Emily up at the diner as soon as it closed that evening at eight o'clock. With Nettie gone, Vicky had the too-big, too-quiet house to herself. So she carried a bottle of water to the front porch and sat down in the swing.

Back when Emily was first born and wouldn't sleep at night, she'd spent hours on that swing, hoping that the motion would make her baby sleepy. Then when she was a little girl, they'd talked out all kinds of problems to the squeak of the old chains. As a teenager Emily and her friends giggled about boys, makeup, and clothes in the same old red swing. And now Vicky had it all to herself with nothing but memories.

The ringing of her phone brought her back to the present with a jar. She grabbed it up from beside her on the swing, saw that it was Andy, and answered on the third ring.

"Hey, how's Nettie? Been meanin' to call all day but got tied up in Frankston with a new oven that we're having put in," he said.

Vicky's heart did a little flutter when she heard his deep drawl. Nettie had teased about her dating him—the timing was all wrong with this wedding business and a new baby on the way. It was still too much for Vicky to take in, but his voice brought a little calm into her world.

"She's pretty much back to normal. We're letting her make tarts, but I'm helping so that she doesn't overdo." Looking back, it had been like that in the hospital, too. When he was in the room, she wasn't nearly so anxious about Nettie.

"I'm about half a mile from Pick. Want to get an ice cream at that convenience store down the road from you?"

"Not really, but you could sit on the porch with me if you've got time. I could use a friend tonight." It wasn't an all-consuming thing like she'd felt when she and Creed were together, so maybe it wasn't anything but friendship after all.

"Be there in a few minutes."

He was gone before she could ask if he wanted a glass of tea or a beer, so she took a chance on the latter. She'd just set a pair on the porch rail when she heard tires crunching on gravel as Andy's truck slowly moved from the diner toward the house. She squinted against the setting sun to see Andy's broad shoulders. In a few long strides he was at the bottom of the porch steps.

"Evenin'," Andy said. "I could hear worry in your voice on the phone. Want to talk about it?"

She patted the space beside her and pointed to the beer. "Yes, I do. There's a lot going on, and I'm not doing so good at processing it."

He twisted the top off the beer and sat down. "Nettie's okay?"

Just like in the hospital and when she heard his voice, his presence put peace into her heart and soul. Was this what an adult relationship was like?

"She's the least of my worries." She went on to tell him about Emily's upcoming marriage and pregnancy. "I'm going to be a grandmother," she said.

"How do you feel about that?" he chuckled.

"Happy. Worried. It's not funny. Ryder is the father, and they want to get married in less than three weeks. That's what I'm having trouble processing," she said.

"The only thing that can change a person is

love. They'll be all right. I would have come on over sooner if I'd known you needed a shoulder."

"I needed some time to wrap my mind around all this before I talked to anyone. The shock still hasn't worn off," she told him.

"Can you change any of it?"

"Not a thing," she answered.

He sipped his beer for a few moments and then said, "Nice evenin', isn't it? We won't get too many more of these. I bet this old swing could tell some stories if it could talk."

"You are changing the subject," she said.

"That I am. Fretting is not good for the soul."

A friend would worry with her, let her talk circles around the whole thing, even if they couldn't fix the problem. A best friend would help her to move past the problem and focus on something else to keep from going crazy. Andy had just proven to be the latter.

"Okay, you changed the subject, so what are we going to talk about?" Vicky took another drink from the bottle and then set it back on the porch railing.

"You." Andy grinned, and her pulse jacked up a notch. "It's crazy that our paths have never crossed before now. And to think it was all because of a strawberry tart."

Vicky took a sip of her beer and set it back down. "True, even with our rival high schools. I was born and raised right here in Pick. My grandparents owned this house, and when they died they left it to my mother. I can remember my grandpa telling me stories about Pick while we ate red Popsicles out here on this swing. Then he passed away and my dad and mama moved in here when I was four. I've lived in this house ever since," she said. "Lots of mileage on this swing, for sure."

"Didn't you move out when you got married and had your daughter?"

She shook her head. "My new husband and I were going to rent a place of our own, but we stayed here with Nettie to save some money. He died six weeks after the wedding."

His long arm stretched across the distance and patted her shoulder. "I'm so sorry. That must have been tough. So Nettie is your grandmother?"

She didn't see stars or hear bells and whistles, but she did like the way his hand felt. And there was a little spark there, but she attributed that to the nerves about this whole marriage and baby thing.

"No, Nettie was my mama's distant cousin and friend. When she divorced the summer that I was seventeen, she moved in with us. Thank God! I don't know what I'd have done without her then or now."

"How long had she been here when your mama died?"

"A month. Nettie moved in with us in June.

Mama died in June, too, leaving me this house and half ownership of the diner. I found out I was pregnant in August and was a widow by the end of September."

"That's too much for anyone to endure, especially a teenager." He took her hand in his and held it on the swing between them.

It was a simple gesture, but it felt right and good. Maybe she would go out with him if he asked.

"That which does not kill us, and all that . . ." She smiled.

"You should be able to shoulder a full-grown longhorn steer if that's the case." He held his bottle toward her. She retrieved hers and touched it to his.

"To nothing but good luck in the future," he said.

"I agree."

"Okay, then, looking toward the future. Will you go to dinner with me on Friday night after you get off work?"

Had she heard him right? She'd just been thinking about going out with him and then, less than a minute later, he asked. Could he read her mind?

"We are about to get knee-deep in wedding stuff. A rain check?" She needed a little more time to think, even if she had already let the idea flutter through her mind.

"After the wedding, we'll celebrate getting through it all by going to dinner, then. We won't get many more pleasant evenings like this. Pretty soon even the nights won't drop below the nineties and it will be too hot to sit out here."

"This old swing has seen me work out problems in the heat, too."

"Then here's to lots of evenings on this swing." He smiled. "I really like spending time with you, Vicky."

"Likewise," she said.

"Good, that's a step in the right direction."

"For what?"

"Hopefully, a relationship when things settle down, but a friendship until then," he answered.

"I'd like that." She nodded.

He stood up and brushed a kiss across her forehead. "I should be going now. Please, call me if you want to talk or if you want me to drive up here. I'll be on my way."

"Thanks, Andy." She smiled for the first time, and it lightened her whole attitude.

Shane wrapped his hand over Jancy's in the middle of the wide bench seat in the 1958 Chevrolet he'd been restoring for years. He'd put the top down and they were both leaning back, looking at the twinkling stars circling around the faintest sliver of the moon.

"If they gave out crowns for the luckiest girl in

the whole world, I'd be wearing it tonight," she said.

"And if there w-was one—" he started.

She put her fingers over his lips. "You'd already have it."

He captured her fingers in his hand and kissed each one. "Ryder says I don't have m-much self-esteem, but wh-when I'm w-with you, I feel like I'm on top of the w-world."

"Amen." She grinned. "Me, too, when I'm with you. Can we leave the top down when we go?" she asked.

"Anything you want," he told her.

With wrecked cars all around her and a sky full of stars above her, Jancy's future had never looked so amazing. "I guess it's time to take you home," he finally said. "I don't want Vicky or Nettie to get the wrong idea."

"Which is?" She locked gazes with him.

"I respect you, Jancy, and I want to do things right by you." He was as serious as a sinner on judgment day.

A man who treated Jancy Wilson with kid gloves. Well, that was sure the first in all her twenty-two years. "You are one of a kind, Shane." She scooted across the seat and kissed him.

With one hand on the back of her head to brace it firmly and the other around her shoulders, he spun one kiss into another, each one getting hotter and hotter until they were both panting.

Finally, he pulled back and traced her jawline with his finger. "I think I just tasted heaven."

"As hot as that was, darlin', I believe maybe we've been singed by the fires of hell," she laughed.

He chuckled down deep in his chest. "You got that right. Now let's leave our limo and go get in the pickup so I can take you home."

He said "our," not "mine," not "this" limo but "our," she thought.

Nettie came in the kitchen door. One of her church friends had given her a ride home that evening. The kitchen light was on and a couple of empty beer bottles plus a dirty plate rested on the counter, which said at least two folks had been drinking. Probably Jancy and Shane had come home early and Vicky had let him have those last two tarts left over from the diner.

She poured a cup of cold coffee and heated it in the microwave. Carrying it through the living room and outside to the porch, she found Vicky on the swing and Jancy sitting on the porch with her back against a post.

Vicky motioned with a wave of her hand. "Have a seat. How did your meeting go?"

"Same-O, same-O," Nettie said. "I'll send half a dozen sheet cakes to the bazaar. They'll cut them up in squares to sell for a dollar a piece.

We decided to hold it after church on the first Sunday in September. Folks will stop by and buy on their way home, and we could make more for our scholarship fund that way. Everyone wanted to fuss over me like I was on death's door. I was glad to see the evening end."

"And the newest gossip?" Vicky asked.

"You know without askin' that it's all about the wedding. Haven't seen this much juicy rumor stuff in years. Folks is wondering how you are doing with all this—her marryin' Ryder and you bein' a grandma." Where had the time gone, anyway? It was only yesterday that Emily started kindergarten. In another six years, her child would be getting ready for his or her first days of school. Suddenly Nettie felt very old. "Then there's the stuff with Jancy and Shane to top it off."

"Me and Shane?" Jancy asked.

"Shane is the town sweetheart. Don't hurt him or you'll suffer the wrath of all the old ladies in town," Nettie said. "Where is Emily?"

"With Ryder," Vicky said.

"Andy came tonight," Jancy said.

Nettie gave the swing another push with her foot. "So spit it out. What did Andy want?"

"To go out to dinner sometime after the wedding," Vicky answered.

"And?" Nettie asked.

"We're friends right now," Vicky said.

284

"But he kissed her on the forehead before he left," Jancy tattled.

Vicky rolled her eyes toward the sky. "Friends can give each other a peck on the check or the forehead. That's all it was. Friends can go out to dinner together," Vicky said. "I don't have time for romance, Nettie. Besides, who wants a relationship with a grandmother?"

"You look like a bag lady. Please tell me that you changed into that after he left," Nettie said, ignoring the question altogether.

"He caught me sittin' in the swing just like this. Barefoot, shorts, and hair in braids. I couldn't very well jump up and go change into a ball gown, could I?"

Nettie got so tickled that she nearly shot coffee out her nose. "I don't imagine your senior prom dress would have impressed him any more than those skimpy shorts." She wiped at the coffee stains on her shirt with a hankie that she pulled from the pocket of her jeans. "Jancy, tell me about your date with Shane."

"We sat in that '58 Chevrolet he is restoring and he put the top down. There's not much moon, but we looked at the stars and made out like a couple of high schoolers on a back road. And then—" Jancy could feel the heat traveling from the back of her neck all the way to her cheeks. "He said that he respected me and wanted to do things right. Which I guess means that he doesn't want to fall into bed with me until later."

"Like I said, he's the town sweetheart. You won't find no better, Jancy," Nettie said on a yawn.

"That's the gospel truth, Nettie. He said that I've helped his self-esteem, but I feel like he's bringin' stuff home for me, too," she said.

"You are welcome," Nettie said.

"I'm going to claim the bathroom first this evening. Good night." Vicky stood up, stretched the kinks out of her neck, and headed inside.

"I'm worried about her," Nettie said in a low voice.

"Why?"

Nettie sighed loudly. "She's worrying too much about Emily. That's what happens when a mama only has one chick in the nest. She puts all her energy and love into that one little baby and then spends the rest of her time trying to make life perfect for her."

"And what is perfect for the mama ain't always the same for the chick, right?"

"Pretty good thinkin' for a kid your age. Vicky is on the way to total acceptance, but she needs a little more time. Getting involved with the wedding plans is going to help a lot," Nettie said.

Jancy patted Nettie on the shoulder as she headed into the house. "You are so wise. I wish my car would have burned up in the parking lot about four years ago."

"Timing might not have been right then," Nettie said.

"Have I told you that I adore you, Nettie?" Jancy stopped long enough to give her a gentle hug and then disappeared into the house.

Nettie kept the swing going for a while longer. All alone on the porch with nothing but years' worth of memories, she could feel a change in the air. It didn't have anything to do with the weather, the mosquitoes buzzing around her ears, or even the bad or good luck of the summer. It went deeper than that. She could only hope that it brought peace to Vicky and happiness to Emily—and maybe even more self-confidence to Jancy, who'd sure put a smile on her face with that compliment.

Chapter Seventeen

Shane poked his head in the door at exactly eight o'clock that Thursday evening and smiled at Jancy. "You ready to go, or do you need to go change clothes?"

"Do I need to get all dolled up?" Jancy asked Emily.

"Heck, no! I'm wearing what I've got on. We're going to be cleaning a trailer, not walking down a fashion runway," Emily told her.

"We'll meet y'all there soon as we get finished making the tart shells for tomorrow," Nettie said.

"Ryder's finishing up doing the last of the underpinning before y'all get here," Shane said as he led the way to his truck. "He's pretty scared that it ain't good enough for you, Emily, but he's most w-worried about Vicky."

"I'm so excited that I can hardly sit still. I don't care what it looks like. I get to live there with Ryder," she said as she crawled into the truck.

A tiny streak of jealousy shot through Jancy at the idea that things still weren't completely settled in her life.

It was cramped with three of them in the front

seat, but that just meant Jancy got to sit real close to Shane, and that was fine by her. She snuggled close to enjoy the ride.

A picket fence encircled a little white frame house with a wide front porch. Thirty yards off to the north, a white trailer house faced the road. It looked to Jancy like it had just rolled off the assembly line. She'd lived in trailers most of her life, and none of them had looked a thing like that.

"Oh! It's beautiful," Emily said as she hurried out of the truck.

"That thing's really used?" Jancy asked.

"It's four years old, but it was lived in by an elderly lady who had it parked next to her son's place down south of Palestine. They sold it wh-when she died," Shane explained.

"Did she die in the trailer?" Jancy asked.

"No, in the yard w-workin' in her flower beds. I w-would love for Gramps to die in our house. I hate the idea of him leavin' this w-world in that care center."

"I'm surprised that he's in one," Jancy said.

"Me, too, but it w-was his idea not m-mine. It ain't easy." Shane's voice cracked as he walked with Jancy to the trailer.

Shane knocked on the trailer door, and Emily threw it open. "Come in, come in! Ryder and Shane have already cleaned this from top to bottom and it smells brand-new. Jancy, you have to see the room where we are putting the nursery."

"We'll have a real porch by the time we get married. For now those tacky old concrete steps will have to do." Ryder waved at Nettie and Vicky, who were walking across the grass toward the trailer. "Come inside. We have lemonade and doughnuts. The other furniture won't arrive until next week."

Vicky came inside with Nettie behind her and clapped her hands. "It's a lovely little starter place. Your father and I would have been glad to have something like this. Now show me the nursery so we can start planning where we'll put the crib. And you'll have to have one of those monitor things and a bassinet that will roll around to whatever room you are in at the time."

"You mean to take to the diner?" Emily laughed.

Ryder heaved a sigh of relief that only Jancy caught sight of. She shot a wink his way, and a smile covered his face.

"See," Shane whispered, "I told you that wh-when Vicky got her m-mind wrapped around a new baby, she w-would be fine."

"We want all y'all to go with us when we pick out stuff for that room." Emily slipped her arm around Ryder's waist and leaned on his shoulder. "We bought bedroom stuff and a big old comfortable sectional for the living room. That's enough to get us started."

"We got a bar and two cheap stools." Ryder slipped his arm around Emily. "What do you think, Vicky?"

Jancy shared Emily's happiness at that moment and wondered if Ryder was right when he said that they were like cousins. With both of them having ancestors in Pick, maybe somewhere back in the history books they did share an ancestor or two.

"You could have parked it next to our house and then the new baby would be close to her grandma," she answered.

"But," Shane quickly said, "he w-wouldn't be close to his uncle Shane."

"His?" Nettie asked. "Do you know that it's a boy?"

"Not yet," Ryder said. "We aren't sure we want to know."

In her mind's eye, Jancy could see a beautiful baby girl with Ryder's dark hair and Emily's big blue eyes. The baby was dressed in a cute little pink smocked dress and was wrapped in a hand-stitched quilt. Yet when she blinked, a boy with a mop of blond hair toddled along behind Shane and Ryder. Both visions were so vivid that she wished the children belonged to her.

"I'll have a swing on the front porch by the

end of next week." Ryder led the way down the hall to show them the nursery and their bedroom. "Emily says we have to have a swing in case the baby has colic. She's been researching all kinds of things."

A porch swing had always been at the top of Jancy's wish list when her dad went looking for a place. Rental property seldom had anything special like that, so she'd never gotten one. Someday—she promised herself—she would have a swing and at least two children.

Nettie settled into a lawn chair. "My baby gift will be a good sturdy rocking chair. You can't swing a baby in December. Poor little thing will catch pneumonia. Pass me one of those chocolate-covered doughnuts."

Ryder handed Nettie a paper napkin and opened the box to give Nettie first choice. "Right there at the end of the box. Emily's been craving chocolate ones, too, and thank you for the offer of a rocking chair."

"Did these come from Andy's?" Nettie asked.

"Yes, they did. You said that he brought some to the hospital and you liked them." Emily poured lemonade into red plastic cups for everyone. "Can you believe that I'm a hostess in my own house for all y'all? When we get back from the honeymoon, we'll have real glasses and plates when y'all come over."

Lemonade and doughnuts might not constitute

a party in some people's eyes, but Jancy thought it was the best one she'd ever been to.

The world spun around Vicky too fast as she headed down the hallway toward the bathroom. Holding on to the vanity and staring at herself in the mirror, she held back the tears. She wanted to throw a two-year-old's tantrum or smash her hand into the mirror to destroy the image staring back at her. From the time the doctor laid that precious baby girl in her arms, she'd had a plan for Emily's life. In no way did it involve living in Pick in a trailer house. She had to accept it because she couldn't change it—but dear God, if she could, she would. She'd put on a happy face for Emily, but all she wanted to do was cry.

She pasted on a grin and stepped out into the hallway to find Jancy sitting on the floor, her back against the wall and her knees drawn up under her chin. She eased down beside her and stretched out her legs.

"You waitin' on the bathroom?" she asked.

Jancy shook her head. "Came to see about you. You looked like you were about to cry when you asked if the plumbin' was workin'."

"I'm fine," Vicky whispered.

"You can fool Emily, because she wants you to be okay with all this, but not me." Jancy took Vicky's hand in hers and squeezed. "You're doin' a fine job of coverin' up what's inside."

293

"I hope so. I want this to be a happy time for her, but Jancy, I had such big plans for her," Vicky's voice broke.

"When you read a good book and reach the end, how do you feel?" Jancy asked.

"What's that got to do with right now? Are you trying to take my mind off my disappointment?" Vicky couldn't begin to understand where that question came from.

"Just answer it. The end. Now tell me, if there was one more chapter, what would you want?"

"To know that the hero and heroine would live happy ever after and that all the other characters would support them." Her eyes grew wide.

"Now you've got it. This is not the end. There's at least one more chapter. Support them and pretty soon, all that disappointment will disappear. In less than a year, you'll wonder why you ever felt the way you do today." Jancy smiled. "Emily is a lucky woman."

Emily wasn't a woman. She was still a girl. Just yesterday she'd taken her first steps with wispy blonde hair finding its way out of her two-inch braids. How could she have grown up so fast?

Jancy squeezed her hand and then let go. "It's a lot like the steps you go through when you lose someone. First there's denial, then shock and then anger. After that is acceptance, and then you move forward. This, too, shall pass."

"I am so mad that I'd like to kick something

or shoot Ryder for getting my daughter pregnant. I wish you or someone would make this pass faster," Vicky said.

"It takes two to make a baby, Vicky. Emily's halo might not be as tarnished as mine, but it's definitely got a few dings. I am here for you if you need to talk," Jancy said.

"Talk about what?" Emily sat down on the floor with them. "Ryder and Shane have gone outside with Nettie. They're trying to decide whether to put the deck on the front or the back of the trailer."

"We need to talk about what kind of wedding dress you want," Jancy said quickly. "If you want a long one, we'll have to rent a length of carpet. You can't have a train draggin' on the gravel parking lot."

Bless Jancy's heart for such quick thinking, but Vicky had always envisioned her daughter with a train that went halfway down the center aisle at the church.

"Mama, can I wear Granny's wedding dress? It'll fit me, I know it will. I've always loved that portrait collar. And I'd like to wear the pearls that she and you both wore."

"But we were going shopping for a fancy dress," Vicky sputtered.

Emily slung an arm around her mother. "You can pick out the veil, but nothing over my face. And you and Nettie and all four of my bridesmaids need dresses. Plus, we need to figure out how big my bouquet of roses needs to be."

"Roses?" Vicky managed a weak smile.

"Red, like you carried. Can I borrow your wedding ring to tie into the bouquet for good luck?"

"Who's going to walk you down the aisle . . . I mean, across the parking lot?"

Emily hugged her tightly. "You are, Mama."

If that didn't melt Vicky's anger, nothing ever would. Jancy could feel the tension turning into sweet love right there in the narrow hallway.

"I don't have to wear a tux, do I?" Vicky smiled.

Emily giggled. "I'm thinking that something in red would be nice."

"The same color as the glaze on top of the strawberry tarts?" Jancy asked.

"Yes! Now let's go outside. I can't believe those guys did all the cleaning for us. Ryder said it was because I didn't need to inhale fumes. He's so protective of me and the baby." Emily got up and offered her hand to Vicky.

Jancy followed them into the living room and out to the backyard, where Nettie, Shane, and Ryder were pointing and talking. It was a perfect spot for a deck, right off the kitchen door, over-looking nothing but a wooded area. She could picture sitting on a swing and watching the sun set every evening.

Shane slipped an arm around her and drew her close to his side. "This is all pretty awesome, huh? I didn't get to spend as m-much time w-with you as I w-wanted these past few days, but I had to help Ryder get it all cleaned and aired out for Emily. Do you think that she w-was surprised?"

Jancy nodded. "Definitely, and very happy."

Two emotions battled inside Jancy. She loved these people. They were great folks, and every one of them deserved happiness. But a touch of sadness mixed with the joy, because she really had to talk to Shane. His opinion could change things. Not that she would leave Pick before the baby came—she'd promised Emily that much. But if this beautiful bubble that she and Shane were floating inside burst? She didn't want to think about that now.

Shane squeezed her shoulder. "W-would you like to see m-my place?"

No, put it off a little longer, the voice in her head said.

"W-we're here and—"

"Yes!" She cut him off midsentence. She was taking total control of her life and what she did. She refused to be influenced by other people's thoughts or her own insecurity. She slipped her hand into his and smiled up at him.

Easier said than done, that irritating voice whispered.

Maybe so, but I've got some really good examples around me, she argued.

"Hey, w-we'll see y'all later," Shane yelled. "I'm goin' to show Jancy m-my place. I'll have her home by m-midnight, Nettie."

"If you don't, your truck will turn into a pumpkin," Nettie told him.

"W-will you m-make pies out of it if that happens?"

"No, but Jancy might."

He didn't let go of her hand when he opened the gate leading into the yard. The back porch couldn't be called a deck by any stretch of the imagination. There wasn't room for a swing, but it held two old wide-armed rockers with deep seats and comfortable-looking cushions. Red roses trailed up the porch railing, and impatiens supplied splashes of color in the flower beds.

"I use the back door m-more than the front. Gramps liked to sit out here and w-watch the sunset at the end of the day. He said he was too busy gettin' things done to see it come up, but when evenin' rolled around—w-well, that was his reward for puttin' in an honest day's w-work."

Two rocking chairs might be every bit as good as a swing, especially if they drew them up close enough together that they could hold hands in front of that screen door.

"I always thought it would be great to have an old wooden door like this. We lived mostly in trailers, and they have storm doors that close quietly. A kid needs a good loud door to slam when she's upset," Jancy said.

He opened it and stood to one side. "Wh-when you leave you can slam it as hard as you w-want. Or I'll be right glad to see how m-much noise I can m-make right now. I sure got in lots of trouble for that back when."

"That's all right." She smiled. "Oh, look, a big country-type kitchen. My mama would have loved all this room."

Square with cabinets along one side, a table with six chairs surrounding it, and a hutch filled with antique dishes, to Jancy the room looked like something out of a magazine. Her grandmother had had a shelf full of cream pitchers, most of which were carnival glass. When they'd sold the trailer, her mother had wanted to keep them all, but there wasn't room for a box full of useless items like that, so they'd been sold with the trailer. Jancy hadn't ever thought she'd have a house to put them in.

"Livin' room is through here." He tugged on her hand. "And down that hall is a bathroom and three bedrooms."

The living room was about the same size as the kitchen. East windows would let in the morning sun. Hardwood floors gleamed when he flipped on the light. He sank onto an oversize leather sofa and pulled her down into his lap. With his arms around her, she snuggled against his chest.

"It's just like I imagined it would be," he said.

"What?"

"Holding you in m-my living room."

"Me, too, Shane," she said.

Then his lips found hers, and it didn't matter if they were in a tent out in the middle of a forest or on the fortieth floor of a fancy hotel. All she wanted was to stay in his arms forever. She wrapped her arms around his neck, and he stood up, carrying her as gently as if she was a child.

"Wait," she said breathlessly. "Sit back down on the sofa with me, Shane. I can't do this until we've talked."

"About?" he asked.

She'd never felt compelled to tell anyone in her previous relationships about her past, but this burden had weighed on her soul for so long.

"My mama died," she said.

"I know that." He kept her in his lap when he eased back down onto the sofa.

"She was my best friend and the glue that held the family together. I didn't want her to be cremated. I wanted her to be buried in Pick by Granny, but—"

She went on to truly open up about her feelings. Then, step by step, she told him the rest—about how her life had taken a dark turn since that day four years ago when her dad called her workplace and told her that her mama was dead.

When she finished, she expected him to push her off his lap and tell her to go. But he tipped up her chin and looked deep into her teary eyes.

"Is that all or is there m-more?" he asked.

"That pretty much covers it." She'd stopped short of telling him that she'd been on probation for a year for her part in the car theft. Later, she promised herself, she would come clean about that part of her life.

"W-well, then, that's not so bad." He grinned. "You m-made some bad choices, but then, all of us have. It's the decisions we m-make going forward that are important, Jancy."

This, too, shall pass. She'd said those words to Vicky, not realizing that Shane would be willing to erase her past. Tears flowed down her cheeks and left wet dots on her bright-red T-shirt. She started to swipe at them, but Shane covered her hand with his and kissed away the tears.

"I can't stand to see you cry." His warm breath sent waves of desire through her body. "I promise to never, ever hurt you, Jancy. I'll always be here for you, and you can tell me anything."

"Okay, then, please pick me up and take me down that hallway to your bedroom," she said.

He cupped her face in his big hands and kissed her—long and hard—with so much passion that the whole world stopped moving. She felt as if she floated from the living room to his bedroom, where he laid her ever so gently on a chenille bedspread that covered a king-size bed and then kicked the door shut with his boot.

Jancy awoke with a start and sat straight up in bed when an alarm went off. Shane said something in his sleep, and she heard someone mumbling in the hallway. She quickly jerked her clothing on and slipped out, feeling her way down the dark hallway. When she reached the living room, someone stood up from the sofa.

"Emily!" She wasn't aware that she could squeal in a whisper.

"Jancy!" Emily gasped.

"What are—" she started.

"Same thing you are, I imagine," Emily butted in. "Now it's time to go home and sneak into our bedrooms. I hate this, but it's Pick and I don't want—"

"I understand." It was Jancy's turn to interrupt. The only regret she had about the amazing night before was that she couldn't slam the back door. "Where's your car?"

"Parked at home. We cross the street, stay on the path through the vacant forty acres, come up behind the house, and go in the back door," Emily said. "It is what it is, but my sneaking days are over in a couple of weeks. What are you going to do about yours?"

"I don't know." Jancy was double stepping to keep up with Emily's long-legged stride.

"First thing you have to do is set an alarm." Emily giggled. "And then you have to make yourself get out of that bed and go home. The second part is the hardest. I can't wait until I can stay in bed with Ryder right up until it's time to get ready to go to the diner."

"Aren't you going to miss walking from the house with Nettie and Vicky?"

"You give up something for every benefit," Emily said. "Shhh . . . gettin' to the bedroom without wakin' up Mama is the hardest part."

Jancy held her breath all the way from the kitchen to her bedroom and let it out in a whoosh when she eased the door shut. She hurriedly threw off her clothing and jerked on a nightshirt, then turned on her bedside lamp. Pulling the stack of letters from the nightstand, she picked out the one near the top of the already-read stack.

Dear Jancy,

We've had the sex talk, and you know about the consequences of playing big-people games with no protection. So when the time comes that you want to do those things, promise me that you won't until you've gone to the clinic and gotten

303

birth control. Babies are wonderful, but even more so if they are planned. I've always felt as if I trapped your father into a relationship that he'd rather not have had.

I want you to find a true Prince Charming. That's what I want for you more than anything. To find happiness, love, and stability. Be sure that when you make your choice, you like the man you'll be sharing life with as much as you love him—enjoy talking to him, spending time with him, like the way that he makes you feel. Sometimes love blinds a person to like, and although love is important, like is just as much so. There have been many times over the years when I have not liked your father, though I still loved him. Friendship with love is a precious thing. If you find it, hold on to it and never let it go . . .

She finished the letter and tucked it back into the envelope before putting it back into the stack. "I wish you were here, Mama. I don't know that I could tell you how I feel in person without turning crimson. I slept with Shane last night, and it was amazing. Thank God I'm on the pill. I never quite understood your letter until now. I like Shane. He's my friend as well as . . . I'm not sure if I should call him my boyfriend. He sure wants things to go that way. After all of this, I think I'm fine with that, even if it's here in Pick. I never wanted to leave that bedroom."

Chapter Eighteen

Why don't you just move in with Shane? We could walk to work together every single morning," Emily whispered as they checked the front of the diner for stray crickets that Friday morning.

"For the same reason you don't move in with Ryder. You want your daughter to hear that you lived with him before you were married?"

Emily sighed. "The folks here live by a different set of rules. It's okay if I'm pregnant, but I'd better not move in until after the wedding."

Jancy shrugged. "You got that right. Besides, what makes you think Shane is ready to ask me to move in with him? He's only really known me a few weeks. That is a big, big step," Jancy said.

"He won't ask you," Emily said. "He's too afraid that you'll say no. When the time comes, you'll probably have to propose to him. 'Will you marry me' has two *M*s and a *W* in the four words."

Jancy hip bumped Emily. "Don't make fun of my feller."

"Just statin' facts, ma'am." Emily giggled.

"Facts about what?" Vicky came from the back room, tucking her dark ponytail through a hole in the back of a cap.

"About whether she should put a few white roses in her bouquet or use all red," Jancy said.

Hey, it had to be all right to protect both of her friends. She'd gotten Vicky out of a difficult and emotional spot the night before. It was only fair to give Emily the same consideration.

"All red roses," Vicky said. "What do you think, Nettie?"

"Maybe a few sprigs of white baby's breath," she called out. "How many tarts do you think we need for that day? I'm going to make the shells ahead of time and freeze them."

"Eight million," Jancy said.

"Give or take a dozen," Emily laughed. "I can't give you a number, Nettie. Make however many you can or want to and they will be eaten."

"Shane's job will be to be sure no one walks out the front door with more than two hidden in their pockets," Jancy said.

"One hundred," Nettie said. "That's what I'm going to make. When are we going to Andy's to pick out a cake?"

"Tonight after work," Emily said. "I called him last evening after y'all left and he offered to open up for us. Thank you, Mama."

"For what?" Vicky asked.

Jancy started arranging tarts on the cake stands.

"Darlin' Vicky, Andy really likes you, and that's the reason she's sayin' thank you."

"But . . . ," Vicky stammered.

"Hello." Woody pushed into the diner early. "Couldn't sleep. Coffee brewin' yet?"

"It'll be ready in about two minutes," Jancy answered. "Want a tart while you wait on Nettie to get your breakfast ready?"

"That would be great," Woody said.

"You and Mama both need to open your eyes." Emily took time to hug Nettie.

"How would you feel about her dating Andy?" Jancy asked.

"Wonderful. She needs someone in her life. Has for years," Emily said. "And so do you, Jancy."

"Maybe, but . . ."

Emily shushed her with a shake of the head. "When things are right, there won't be any *but*s."

"But"—Jancy emphasized the word with a smile—"we've got to get y'all two ridin' off into the sunset before we think about our future."

"Then it's a good thing that my wedding is comin' up fast."

"Yep, now let's get busy." Jancy hugged Emily.

Andy waited at a table with a big book of wedding cakes in front of him when they arrived that evening. He stood up, shook the legs of his jeans down over his boots, and motioned them inside the well-lit shop. The place smelled like a mixture of freshly baked cookies and Andy's cologne. He smiled as they entered the store, but his eyes locked on Vicky's and held for several moments before he winked.

"I've got coffee and iced tea and cookies for y'all while you choose a cake," Andy said. "Help yourselves. You and Ryder sit down and flip through the pictures, Emily. Tell me if you see something that you like, or we can design one special if you don't."

Ryder opened the book and waited until Emily told him she was ready before he turned to the next page. Part of the anger fell away from Vicky's heart as she looked at big old tough Ryder watching Emily's expressions rather than the pictures. If she liked it, then he was going to be fine with it. That said a lot about him.

"We can make adjustments to the size of the cake, but we will need to know how many folks it will need to feed," Andy said. "How many from your family, Ryder?"

"You're lookin' at it. And Shane," Ryder said.

"Just think about most of the people in Pick and add in a few friends that we'll invite from our colleges and workplaces. Probably not more than twenty combined, right?" Emily looked at Ryder.

"That's about right. Our family and friends kind of get all tangled up together." He grinned.

"Let me show you around while they pick out something." Andy took Vicky by the arm and led her into the kitchen area. "What's wrong?"

"I didn't think about outsiders coming to Pick for the wedding, Andy."

"And now you are worried about what they'll think, right?"

She gulped. Was it that obvious?

"It's Emily's wedding. If she wants to get married in a cow pasture with everyone sitting on bales of hay while country music blares in the background and beer cools in cattle watering tanks, that's what she should have," Andy said.

"How can you know exactly what to say?"

"I say what I think. I'm glad that it's the right thing tonight. If I'd had a daughter, I'd have wanted one like Emily, who knows what she wants."

With that attitude, Andy would have made a terrific father. "So do you regret—"

He put his finger over her lips. "Not in the least. I married my career. Sometimes it's been a lonely partner. Here lately, a little more than ever. I like having you for a friend, Vicky. Shall we go see what those kids have picked out?"

"You mean what Emily chose. Ryder's so much in love that she could ask for an armadillo cake and he'd love it," Vicky said.

"This one, Mama." Emily's sunny voice interrupted them. "It's heart shaped, like the tarts.

Hearts and roses is going to be the theme of our wedding. Look, there's even a groom's cake in that shape."

"That wedding cake will feed about a hundred and fifty. If you're going to have tarts also, that might be enough, but how about I throw in fifty heart-shaped cupcakes in case you need them?" Andy picked up a notebook. "I'd suggest an all-white cake with a tiny replica of your bouquet on the top. Maybe with ribbon streamers flowing down the front."

Vicky stood to the side and listened to Emily and Andy discuss the details and wondered what life would have been like if Andy had been Emily's father. It was insane to even think like that, because at the time Emily was conceived, Vicky wouldn't have given a man who wanted to grow up and be a pastry chef a second glance. Still, he and her daughter were popping ideas around like fireworks. He was writing in his notebook so fast that his hand had to ache.

Arms folded over his chest and wearing a big grin, Ryder's eyes twinkled at her excitement. Each time she realized how much he really did love Emily, a little piece of her disappointment fell away from Vicky's heart and soul.

"It's going to be a beautiful wedding," Andy said right at her elbow.

Vicky frowned. "I'd rather the wedding was in a church."

"There's more room in the parking lot, and we get tarts for the reception. We can bring tables from the church and set them up between the diner and the house so folks can take their cake and tarts around there. How does that sound?" Ryder asked.

Emily nodded. "We could put candles in fruit jars to light up the place. It will be so romantic."

"Why not set up a big white tent in that space? I can do that for you. My company can provide the tables, linens, centerpieces, and even air-conditioning so your guests will be cool," Andy said.

"On such short notice?" Vicky asked.

"Sure." Andy flashed a brilliant smile. "I've got a crew that can take care of it with no problem."

"Yes!" Emily said. "I'd love that. Mama?"

"What other ideas do you have, Andy?"

"Look at this." He flipped open a different book and showed her a picture of an outdoor wedding. "We could transform the parking lot to look like this if you'd like. I understand that you have already gotten an arch and chairs. I know that company, and we can work with them. I can supply everything else to turn that parking lot into a magical fairyland. A carpet from the front of the diner so that your dress won't drag on gravel and twinkling lights."

"Oh, Ryder," she squealed. "Andy, you are a genius."

"And we can shop for a dress?" Vicky asked.

Emily smiled. "You win, Mama. I want a wedding that looks like this."

Jancy and Shane were sitting on the back porch when Ryder and Emily brought pictures they'd taken with their phones to share with them.

"And look at the twinkle lights leading from the diner to the tent." Emily's excitement was contagious. "And Andy's crew will set everything up for us and it's going to be beautiful."

"Like a fairy tale, but, honey, you need to look for a big fancy dress to go with this wedding," Jancy said.

"I already told Mama that we'd go shopping for one. Do you think she's comin' around, Jancy?" Emily sat down on the porch and pulled Ryder down beside her.

"Yep." Jancy nodded.

She loved the pretty pictures, but she didn't want anything as elaborate as this wedding was turning into. But then, why was she thinking about a wedding? Shane was the only man in the world that she'd even consider trusting enough for that step, and it was way too soon to think about marriage.

But all little girls thought about their wedding day, so why couldn't a twenty-two-year-old? Jancy wanted a simple wedding with only a few dear friends in the room and then maybe a reception with cake and punch. Maybe a pretty dress, too. Then a lovely honeymoon in this little white house with two rocking chairs on the back porch.

If it never came true, she could still have the lovely dream.

"Jancy, where are you?" Emily singsonged.

"Daydreaming, I guess. What did you say?"

"I asked what you thought about silver bridesmaids' dresses?"

"With red rose bouquets, that would be beautiful. And I'm so glad that you took all those pictures to share with us," Jancy answered. "Andy is pretty great for getting this all done in two weeks."

"Yes, he is," Ryder said. "And Vicky was so excited about the dress. I don't think she wanted Emily to wear the vintage one."

"Me, either," Emily said. "We're going over to our trailer now. See you in the morning, Jancy."

"Bright and early." Jancy slipped her hand into Shane's.

"When you get married, what kind of wedding do you want?" he asked.

"Small and simple. What about you? Something big and fancy?"

"No, m-ma'am. I'd stutter so bad the cerem-mony w-would take hours." He grinned. "So small and simple?"

She shook her head. "My only living relative is

about to be in Germany. I'd have no one on my side."

"I'll always be on your side, Jancy." He brought her fingers to his lips and kissed the tips of each one.

Chapter Nineteen

S unday had always been Vicky's favorite day of the week, though the hymns usually touched her soul more than the sermons. She could hear all the voices on her pew as they blended together. A few weeks ago there had been three of them—Nettie, Vicky, and Emily—but their little family had doubled when they'd added Ryder, Shane, and Jancy. It made for a full pew and really nice singing.

According to the sermon that night, God worked things out. Whether folks liked it or not was up to them. They could be bitter or they could be better. Bitter had the letter *I* in it, and every single time people put themselves first, it became a problem that created a bitter attitude.

That part about bitter and better hit Vicky so hard between the eyes that it almost gave her a headache. She glanced to her right at Emily and Ryder holding hands in church. Even with his past, she couldn't very well ask for more than a man who adored her child and who went to church with her.

There were a few doubts still lingering in her

heart, but she'd gotten past that anger business last night at Andy's cake shop. Looking back, she realized that she'd gone through the same steps when her mother and Creed both died. She'd barely gotten past the denial and shock of the first when her husband of six weeks died. Two funerals that year, and she'd walked away from the last one with nothing but bitter anger in her heart. Nettie, with her love and patience, had helped her through those times. Here it was more than twenty years later and Nettie was helping her again.

It had been the birth of her precious daughter that had brought her out into the light again. Nodding when the preacher talked about how much a person's attitude affects those folks around them, she decided that the wedding was going to be just what Andy said—the most magical one Pick had ever seen.

She glanced at her daughter, sitting beside Ryder. From the stars in her eyes, she wasn't listening to a word the preacher was saying. No doubt the wedding and honeymoon were on her mind. Happiness was what she should have wanted for Emily all along—not a fancy job in a big city. Sweet peace filled her soul as she let go of all the doubts. Emily and Ryder would make it, and she'd be there for both of them.

And she's going to look beautiful in that

Cinderella wedding gown I picture her in. Vicky got a gorgeous vision of Emily getting married with the setting sun behind her.

Emily must have felt her mother staring at her, because she turned and their gazes locked. Vicky nodded and sent up a silent prayer that she got a granddaughter—a pretty little blonde-haired girl who looked exactly like Emily—so that she could watch her grow up to be the confident, determined woman Emily had become.

Emily laid her hand on her flat stomach. In a couple of months, there would be a bump. It would be awesome if she had the baby on Christmas. A picture of Ryder holding his daughter for the first time popped into Vicky's head, and if there was a tiny thread of doubt in her mind about him, that picture erased it.

Vicky had known Ryder's folks in their wild days—when they'd partied every weekend. And then they'd suddenly gotten religion and his life had done a 180-degree turnaround. No wonder he'd turned out to be a smooth-talking womanizer—he'd grown up in a party world until he was in his teens. Then, boom! His folks insisted that he go to church. Letting him stay behind when they left was probably the best thing that happened to Ryder, because he got a taste of stability from Shane and his grandpa. Hank always insisted the boys go to church on Sunday evening. He'd told Vicky once that he understood most of the time they weren't fit for morning services after their Saturday night fun, but according to him, they needed a little blood of the lamb washed over them.

With his wild ways, Vicky wouldn't have been surprised if Ryder had left Emily high and dry when she got pregnant, but instead of being terrified, he was on top of the world. It sure looked like old Hank's influence had come through really well.

Vicky's thoughts went to Shane and Jancy. They were headed toward marriage. Maybe not by the end of the year, but it was going to happen. Shane knew Jancy belonged in Pick, and he was a patient man. In the past few weeks, Jancy had blossomed from a girl who'd felt unworthy of even a decent meal to a young woman who was taking charge of her life.

Whether she realized it or not, her roots were growing deep into the ground in Pick. She hadn't even mentioned leaving in the past few days. Vicky wondered if maybe Emily hadn't made her promise to stay until the baby was born.

God or fate or destiny—whatever a person wanted to call it—had been in charge that day when Jancy's car burned up. Vicky saw Shane slip an arm across the back of the pew and rest his hand on her shoulder. Oh, yes, life was good for everyone that Sunday evening.

"Before I ask Ryder to give the benediction, I have an announcement to make," the preacher said.

Vicky sat up a little straighter.

"On, June 24 at eight o'clock, Ryder Jensen and Emily Rawlins will be married. The ceremony will take place in the Strawberry Hearts Diner parking lot with the reception starting in the diner and spilling over to a tent in the backyard. All friends and family are invited to the ceremony and to the reception. But Nettie says that the same rule stands about taking more than two tarts out of the diner."

There were a few giggles and chuckles, but they quieted down real soon when Ryder stood, bowed his head, and thanked God for all his gifts. Vicky didn't need a dictionary to get the underlying meaning of what he was saying, because she felt the exact same way.

Emily and Ryder were getting all kinds of congratulatory pats and hugs on the way out of church. Lots of folks were texting friends who hadn't made it to Sunday night services to tell them the good news. It took quite a while for the six members of Vicky's family to reach the back of the church.

The preacher grabbed Ryder's hand and shook it firmly. "Congratulations, son. I'm happy for you and Miz Emily." He finally let go and hugged Emily. "I've watched you grow up from a little girl. It's going to be such an honor to preside over your wedding." He lowered his voice. "Nettie already made arrangements."

"I'm going to get the truck, darlin'. I'll pick you up right outside the door." Ryder kissed her on the cheek.

Vicky was right behind Emily when they left the cool church and stepped out into the hot night air. The ragged gasp that came from Emily sent chills down Jancy's spine. She thought for sure something had happened with the baby until she looked across the parking lot to see a brunette with her legs wrapped around Ryder's waist and her hands tangled up in his hair.

An eerie hot wind blew up from the south as if telling everyone in the parking lot that there was fixing to be hell to pay in Pick, Texas. Jancy let go of Shane's hand and started across the gravel with Emily right behind her.

"Don't kill him. Let him explain," Nettie yelled.

They were almost to the truck when the brunette dragged poor old Ryder's lips to hers and ground against them as if she was trying to eat him alive right there before God and all the people pouring out of the church.

Emily peeled her away from Ryder like removing bubblegum from a shoe, set her on the ground, and leaned down until she was nose to nose with the woman. "I don't know who you are, who you think you are, or what you think you are doing, but I'm engaged to Ryder Jensen. And you are in the church parking lot. Have some kind of respect."

"Bullshit!" the hussy said as she looped her arm into Ryder's. "This big old guy is my favorite booty call. When I'm in Texas, I don't even have to call anymore. I saw his truck here, so this is where I'm meeting him. I don't give a damn where it is. You don't tell me what to do."

"And when was the last time you had one of these booty calls?" Emily asked.

Ryder pushed her back. "It was way before we started dating, Emily. I'm so sorry about this."

"Halloween, last year." She glared at Emily. "He'd never ask someone like you to marry him! He's not the marryin' type. Wake up, girl. He's a player."

Jancy took a step forward. "And why wouldn't he ask Emily to marry him?"

"He likes short brunettes with a lot of fire, not dowdy Sunday-school teachers."

"Whoa!" Ryder said.

"What did you say?" Jancy's hands knotted into fists.

"You heard me. Who are you? The piano player?" The woman took a step forward.

That was her first mistake.

The second was when she reached out and pushed Jancy.

Jancy came back with a right hook straight into the woman's eye. She squealed and grabbed Jancy's hair, pulling her to the ground with her as she fell. That was her third mistake, because Jancy was a scrapper. She didn't pull hair or mouth off useless words. She slapped the woman twice and then doubled up her fists to really do some damage to that smug face.

She took a couple of hits, but she was giving as good as she got right up until Shane and Vicky pulled them apart. She hadn't said a word from the time that she landed that first hit. The brunette jumped up and started to swing at her, but Jancy pulled up both legs and kicked her back into the dirt.

"I'll file assault charges on you," the woman said as she got up and ran to her little red convertible.

"I've got no problem with a few days in jail," Jancy said through clenched teeth. "Put me down, Shane. I don't think she's had enough."

Emily marched up to Ryder, pointed her finger under his nose, and said, "We'll discuss this later. You better let me cool off an hour or two before you even call and I'll be going home with Mama."

"And you can put me down, Shane." Jancy wiggled free of his embrace. "And next time I'm teachin' someone a lesson, you better stand back and leave me alone until I get finished. And I'm going home with Vicky, too."

"Let me explain," Ryder said.

"After I get through bein' mad. I don't care if it wasn't your fault. You are a big man. You could have thrown her off into the dirt instead of just standin' there like a statue," Emily said.

Vicky pulled up in the van, and both girls crawled inside. "Jancy, you're going to have a shiner tomorrow."

"Won't be the first one."

"Holy smoke, Jancy!" Emily said. "You didn't give her a warnin' or nothing."

"Found out a long time ago that you land the first punch and every one after that if you're goin' to win a fight. She shouldn't have pushed me." Jancy touched her eye and flinched. "She had no business insultin' you."

Nettie giggled, then laughter bubbled out of her, echoing off the walls of the van as she wiped away the tears with the back of her hand. "I ain't seen so many people with gaping mouths in years. Lord, that was fun. Can we go back and do it again?"

"The wedding is off," Emily said. "I can't do this."

Vicky glanced up in the rearview mirror. "You knew what Ryder was when you started dating him. Behind my back, I might add. And you could see very well that he wasn't holding her on his body. She sure was hangin' on like a monkey, though, wasn't she?"

"All she needed was a long tail to wrap around him," Jancy said. "And she did have a face like a monkey. Why would he have ever let her use him for booty calls? Maybe that's why there's so many paper bags at Shane's house."

Vicky frowned. "What?"

A faint giggle escaped Emily's mouth. "Thank you, Jancy."

"Paper bags?" Vicky asked.

"Got to have something to cover up a face like that," Jancy told her.

Nettie got tickled all over again. "I can't believe that you are takin' up for Ryder, Vicky. This is your chance to talk her out of the wedding."

"Not for this reason. She should have been the one to beat the crap out of that bimbo," Vicky said. "But I do appreciate you takin' care of it, Jancy."

"That foolish woman knew better than to push Emily. She'd have gotten her butt handed to the devil on a silver platter. She thought that she had a chance with me. She learned different." Jancy's pulse was still racing. "And you are welcome. Friends take care of friends. Emily would do the same for me if I got crossways with a six-foot woman."

"Yes, I would, but Mama, how can I live with all the women in his past comin' around? Oh.

My. Gosh!" She covered her eyes. "Everyone will be talkin' about it."

"How you goin' to handle it?" Vicky asked.

"Well, she's not goin' to tuck tail and run," Jancy answered.

"I'm goin' to go home and sit on the swing for an hour until I calm down, and then I'll call Ryder and we'll have a talk."

Jancy poked her and whispered, "Makeup sex tonight?"

"Shhh!" Emily shot a dirty look her way. "How are you goin' to handle it, Jancy? You weren't real happy with Shane, either."

"I wasn't finished. He had no business jerking me away from her like that." Jancy would do the same thing that Emily planned on doing, but she probably wouldn't wait a whole hour.

"I thought you were shy." Emily took her hands away from her eyes. "Where'd you learn to fight like that?"

"Bullies at one of the schools. I came home every day upset, and Mama finally told me to either stop whining or to take care of it. I told her they'd expel me if I started a fight and she said that if they tried, call my daddy."

"And?" Vicky asked.

"One of those mean girls pushed me into the edge of my locker door and bloodied my nose. When I got finished with her, the principal did have to call my daddy. I didn't get expelled, though she spent a couple of days at home. She still had two black eyes and a cute little crook in her nose when she came back to school. Everyone left me alone from then on. Nobody was my friend, but they didn't bully me no more," Jancy said.

"The many layers of Jancy." Nettie got out of the van and headed toward the porch.

"I don't like fightin', but no one is going to push me around or my friends, either," Jancy said.

"Or pull you away once you get started?" Emily hit the button to open the wide back doors.

Jancy hopped out of the vehicle and went straight to the bathroom, where she washed her face and picked the leaves from her hair.

Vicky watched her from the doorway. "Hope that black eye is healed by the wedding."

"At least the bride won't have a black eye." She grinned.

As Vicky went on down the hall toward the living room, Jancy's phone pinged in the pocket of her flowing skirt. When she reached for it, she realized there was a long tear in the gauze, and upon closer inspection, a big hole yawned in the shoulder of the matching bright-orange shirt. If that sorry broad showed up in Pick again, Jancy was going to finish the job she'd started—her favorite outfit was ruined.

"Hello," she said coldly.

"Guess it's too early to call?" Shane sounded miserable.

"My skirt and shirt are ruined," she said.

"And your eye is black."

"I can see in the mirror."

"I never knew you had a temper."

Jancy stripped out of the skirt and shirt and carried them to her bedroom. They weren't even fixable. She put the phone on speaker and dug out a pair of cutoff jeans and a tank top from the closet. "Shane, I learned a long time ago that people only push you around if you let them. I'll be over my mad spell in an hour if you want to drop by."

"Wh-why don't you come over here?" he said.

"Not tonight, darlin'. I'm not leavin' Emily."

"It wasn't Ryder's fault," Shane said.

"Yes, it was. He could have thrown that girl out in the yard."

She got dressed and fell back on the bed, the adrenaline leaving her body as fast as it had filled her veins. Now she was exhausted. "One hour, Shane. If you want to see me, be here at nine o'clock. I'll be the one with the black eye on the porch."

"Can I bring Ryder with me?"

"If Emily says it's okay. See you then." She hung up and pulled a letter from the night-stand.

My dearest Jancy,

This isn't going to be an easy letter to write, because if I don't get the words just right, you might get the wrong idea. But I want to talk to you about letting people run over you. I have not been a good role model in this area. The time to fix something is when it's first broken, not when it's shattered in so many pieces that there's not enough glue in the world to put it back together again. I love your father, but neither of us has been the type of parent that you deserve. With his wanderlust and my inability to stand up to him, life has not been good to you.

Don't ever be the bully that those mean girls were to you in Beaumont, Texas, but when someone is ugly, take care of it like you did then. Your daddy was so proud of you that day. He said that you were finally showing a little of his blood. Truth was, I was glad you stood up to that girl, but I worried that you might get a taste for that kind of thing. It would be easy to approach ugly situations with anger, but my advice is not to stand there with empty threats. Just get the job done and kick off the dust. Don't let your temper define who you are . . .

"But I did just that today, Mama. That bitch made me so mad when she insulted Emily and then pushed me. I'd already hit her before I realized what I was doing, and then I had to keep on or she'd have blacked both my eyes."

A soft knock sounded on the door, and then Vicky pushed it open. "You okay, Jancy?"

"I was just reading a letter from Mama," she said as she put it back into the envelope. "She had letters from my grandmother, and they were a comfort to her. I don't know that she had a premonition about her life, but she wrote me a stack of letters and left birthday cards for me. When things get tough, I get them out and read them, and she's right—they are a comfort."

"Oh, Jancy." Vicky sat down beside her on the bed and wrapped her up in her arms. "I'm so glad that you are here. What you did for Emily was . . . There are no words."

"Couldn't have her in jail because she killed that trash." Jancy smiled. "Ouch!"

"It's goin' to hurt worse tomorrow. Let's go get some ice to put on it."

"Guess I destroyed any idea that I was doing my best to be a good person, didn't I? Brawlin' in the church parking lot like that." Jancy groaned.

"You are you, Jancy. What anyone thinks of you isn't as important as what you think of yourself. Would you tie into that girl again?"

Without hesitation she said, "Yes, I would. She shouldn't have pushed me."

"Then your conscience is clear. I'm glad that you know how to take up for yourself, but then, I should have known that . . ." The sentence hung in the air like a big white elephant.

"That I've lived a tough life," Jancy finished for her.

"I was going to say that you didn't have anyone to do it for you, but I really liked Elaine and didn't want . . ."

Jancy hugged her. "It's okay, Vicky. I understand. Now about that ice?"

Vicky led the way to the kitchen. "I wish my mother would have written me letters. There were so many times I wanted to hear her voice."

"Hey, are you all right?" Emily handed Jancy a bag of frozen peas. "We don't have a steak, but maybe this will help."

"Thanks." The cold felt good against Jancy's eye and cheek.

"How do you know about steak and peas?" Vicky filled four glasses with ice and poured sweet tea into them.

Emily slung an arm around Vicky. "I lived in a dorm, Mama. Some of those girls had pretty wicked tempers."

"Vicky thought that a dorm was all popcorn and giggles?" Jancy grinned.

"If you're all right with it, I'm going over to

Shane's to forgive Ryder. This wasn't his fault, and I overreacted. If I'd gotten out of the church two minutes later, he would have peeled that woman off his body," Emily said.

"I'm fine. Go take care of this. Never go to sleep on an argument. Either get it settled and make up or fight all night," Jancy said.

Emily smiled. "Who said that?"

"An eighty-year-old woman who was still cookin' in a little café where I worked," Jancy answered. "Put these peas back in the fridge. I'll go with you. Shane and I need to talk, too."

"Take them with you," Vicky said. "So the wedding is still on?"

Emily hugged Vicky. "It couldn't have been easy to take up for Ryder—I appreciate it. I love Ryder and I'm going to marry him even if I have to plow through dozens of his old booty calls. And I'm sure glad that our wedding bands are those wide ones you can see a mile off."

"Amen!" Jancy said. "Let's walk over there. It'll give us a little while longer to get our makeup speeches ready."

"Great idea," Emily said.

Chapter Twenty

Ryder and Shane were sitting in the rocking chairs, each with a can of beer and both looking miserable when Jancy and Emily rounded the end of the house. Ryder stood up immediately, met them in the middle of the backyard, and opened his arms.

Emily picked up her pace and walked right into them. "Are we okay?"

"I am so sorry, darlin', and we are definitely okay."

"Let's go to our home and talk," she said.

They disappeared into the darkness. Jancy wasn't sure at that point whether to knock on the porch post to ask permission to enter or to turn around and go back home. Shane hadn't met her with open arms. He hadn't moved an inch from his rocking chair, and his head was hanging like he couldn't even look at her.

She'd been so afraid that she'd ruined everything with her past, but it was the present that had shot holes in their relationship. He could deal with her spotty relationships, but making a spectacle out of herself in front of all his friends—well, that was a different matter. She might as well face it and get the breakup over with now as worry about it all night. She marched up on the porch and sat down in the empty rocking chair.

"Some shiner," he finally said.

"I hope it's gone by the wedding."

"I've never been in any kind of relationship that lasted long enough to have a fight. M-mostly it was only for one night, a w-weekend at the m-most. Are w-we breaking up?"

She tossed the bag of peas on the porch and moved from the chair to his lap. "Do you want to break up? You've got good reason. I embarrassed you in front of the whole church."

His arms went around her. "Embarrassed, hell! I w-was proud of you, Jancy. I just didn't w-want Nicole to black your other eye. You are a scrapper, and I'm not m-mad at you one bit. I thought you w-were upset with m-me. I'm not good with w-women. Never had one in the house. Granny w-was gone wh-when I was born. Don't remember m-my m-mother."

She cupped his face in her hands and looked deep into his eyes. "Shane, darlin', I've had to fend for myself for a long time, and bullies make me so mad." She went on to tell him about her experience in the first days of her junior year of high school.

"Now you've got m-me to take up for you if

things get too deep." He leaned forward and kissed her eye before moving on to her lips. Then he looped an arm around her shoulders and the other under her knees and carried her into the house and straight to the bedroom.

Jancy was dreaming about a little dark-haired girl toddling around in the backyard chasing a bunch of kittens. She and Shane watched from the rocking chairs, and his face was a picture of contentment. She didn't want to wake up, but someone was knocking on the door and whispering her name.

She sat up with a start, and Shane mumbled something in his sleep. She eased out of bed and peeked out the door, still thinking maybe it was all part of the dream. But there was Emily, wearing a big smile.

"Rise and shine. We've barely got time to get home before Nettie's alarm goes off."

"Give me two minutes to get dressed. Meet you on the back porch."

She couldn't find her panties, so she pulled up her denim shorts without any. She had to hunt down one sandal, eating up the rest of the two minutes. When she got there, Emily was rocking as if she didn't have a care in the world.

"I didn't hear your alarm and I left my phone at home."

"Ryder and I thought we wanted to spend our first night in the trailer as a married couple, but after yesterday—well, it just seemed right to stay there last night. We slept on the floor in our bedroom. I guess you and Shane got things straightened out?" She stood up and started off in long strides.

Jancy practically jogged to keep up. "I thought he was embarrassed by me acting like, well, you know. And he says he doesn't have much experience in fighting in a relationship. I don't imagine that Ryder does, either. They've both lived in a love 'em, leave 'em world."

In only a few weeks I've found friends, gotten drawn into secrets, and could be falling in love.

"Well, that world is gone, and it's time for both Shane and Ryder to enter the real world of grown-ups," Emily said.

"You've known Ryder your whole life, so you do realize that his past is going to rise up sometimes, right?"

"Of course. I just didn't think it would be in the church parking lot."

"Exactly where did your relationship with him start, Emily?" Jancy asked as they rounded the end of the house. "Couldn't have been in college, because y'all went to different ones."

A shy grin covered her face. "Walmart."

"You are kiddin' me. Does that mean you can take him back for a full refund if he doesn't perform to your satisfaction?" Jancy asked.

Emily's giggles broke through the darkness. "I've teased him about that many times. It's kind of crazy and I've never told anyone this. I had to make a tampon run and that was the only thing in my cart." She blushed scarlet. "And the only thing in his cart was a box of condoms. Our carts had a fender bender as we both came around the same corner. We both looked down to check the damage before we realized that we knew each other, and then we got tickled."

"And he saw a skirt to chase?"

Emily shook her head. "It's hard to believe, but he didn't act like that with me. Not even at the beginning. We went for coffee and talked for hours that first day. I actually had to chase him. He didn't think he was good enough for me."

Jancy understood that feeling perfectly well. "So when did you go on your first date?"

"We met six times for coffee or for lunch and then it was Christmas and I was home for a month. He'd come into the diner and we'd flirt, but he wouldn't ask me out. Finally, when I went back to college, I called him and asked him for a date. We went out in the middle of January, and he was so nervous that it was cute. He brought a red rose to the dorm and took me to a fancy place."

"I feel his pain," Jancy whispered.

"Why would you feel his pain?"

Jancy collected her thoughts carefully. "I'm kind of like Ryder. I've lived with men, been disappointed by them, was almost married to a man who already had a wife. And here's Shane in my life. I don't feel like I'm good enough for him, either."

"I guess I'm like Shane, then," Emily said. "I'm in love, and the past doesn't matter to me, only the future. He may have had lots of women, but as long as I'm the last one ever, then I'm okay with that."

"But you don't want to see any of those women making passes at him, right?" Jancy lowered her voice as they quietly made their way into the kitchen.

"Good morning," Nettie said. "Coffee before you go to your rooms and get ready for work? I'm assuming that the wedding is still on and the makeup sex was good?"

"Nettie!" Emily's voice went all squeaky.

"Well?" Nettie asked.

"The wedding is going to happen, and good mornin' to you, too. I don't need coffee just yet, but I do need to change clothes. We'll be leaving at five thirty, right?" Jancy said as she headed down the hallway.

"On the dot," Nettie chuckled.

"Lord, I wish I was you." Emily trailed along behind her. "You are fearless."

"Sometimes that's a good thing. Sometimes,

not so much." Jancy grinned. "I need a fast shower. How about you?"

"Oh, yeah!"

"I'll be out in five minutes and you can have it. We'll still be ready in time to go to the diner."

Nettie made an announcement as soon as they opened up the diner that morning. "Jancy will be working with me in the kitchen today. Emily and Vicky can run the front."

"I don't care if anyone sees my black eye," Jancy said.

"It's like this—everyone who was at church and saw the fight is going to want to talk about it. Those who only got the story through the gossip vine are going to want to know details. If you don't stop and talk, they'll get their feelings hurt. If you do, it'll slow down the work. So you are cookin' today and those two are running the front," Nettie declared.

"I'm not lookin' forward to all the questions I'll get asked," Emily said. "I need Jancy for support."

"Too bad. Get out there and take up for yourself, your man, and your upcoming marriage. Let them folks know that you will fight for what is yours," Nettie said. "Well, look at that—Andy Butler is our first customer. He even beat Woody this morning."

Vicky tied an apron around her waist and

pushed open the door separating the kitchen from the front of the diner at the same time Andy entered the place. "Good mornin'. What brings you out so early?"

"Have to check on some stuff in Frankston before the Palestine store opens," he answered. "I'd like a tall stack of pancakes with sausage on the side and a cup of coffee. How's the wedding plans coming along?"

Back in the kitchen, Nettie threw an arm around Emily. "I think he likes your mama—a lot. How do you feel about it?"

"To be honest, I'm jealous. I'm not so sure I want to share her with anyone," Emily answered.

"Now you know how she feels," Jancy said.

"Never thought of it like that. Looks like we've got a lot of jealousy going on here at the Strawberry Hearts Diner. We're all a little green except Nettie."

"Don't think I'm not jealous of the whole lot of you. I'd love to be as young as you again and get to live in the world you do. Where folks don't judge like they did in my day. Which means if and when you want to move in with Shane, that's fine by me, Jancy."

"And I can move in with Ryder?"

"Hell, no!" Nettie said. "It's less than two weeks until your wedding. You can wait."

"Then why can Jancy?" Emily crossed her arms over her chest.

"Because I'm already a bad girl and you aren't," Jancy said.

"Bullshit!" Nettie growled. "It's because Emily needs to learn patience. Let me tell you something, girl, you've got to learn to love yourself or no one else can. Shane sees a fine young woman when he looks at you. Don't destroy that picture with your own self-doubt."

"Yes, ma'am." Jancy draped an arm around Nettie's shoulders. "That's the best advice I've had in years."

"But . . . ," Emily started.

Nettie shot a look her way. "It's six months until she and Shane get married. You've had your six months with Ryder."

"Six months?" Jancy stammered.

"Or less. Now let's get to work," Nettie said.

"Fine, then. Last night when the preacher was talkin' "—Emily stepped away and tied an apron around her waist—"I wasn't listenin' to a word he said. I was all up in thoughts of how perfect everything was. I got my wake-up call real fast when I saw that woman all wrapped around Ryder. I have to accept the fact that it could happen again and that I'll have to deal with it like an adult when it does."

"Not if Jancy is around," Nettie laughed. "Put that pan of biscuits in the oven while I make Andy's pancakes. I'm deliberately stalling so they'll talk longer."

"You are amazing, Nettie." Emily picked up the pan. "And I love Jancy for what she did, but I'm going to step up to the plate the next time around."

"Good for you." Jancy opened the oven door for her.

Nettie was a prophet, plain and simple. By the end of that Monday, Jancy was sick of hearing anything about the fight. Emily was threatening to poison the food of the next person that even mentioned it. When they got home that evening, Nettie and Vicky sank down on the swing and Jancy and Emily sat on the steps.

"First rule of the night is no talk of fights or black eyes or Nicole. After I say this, the subject is closed for good. I will never name a daughter Nicole or Nicky or any form of that name," Emily said.

"You better get Ryder to make you a list if that's the rule. And you'd better make a list of your old boyfriends so he knows not to use those names," Jancy said.

"You got a point. I hear a truck—Ryder and Shane are on their way. Why don't we just let them sleep in our bedrooms tonight, Jancy? That way we won't have to walk home tomorrow mornin'."

"Short answer to that question is no," Nettie said. "Long answer is hell, no."

"Hi, darlin'," Ryder said on his way from the truck to the porch. "We got busy today and didn't get to come by the diner. Shane is pouting because he didn't get a tart."

"Yes, I am," Shane agreed. "And since I didn't, I thought w-we m-might walk down to Leonard's place and get an ice cream. It won't be as good as a tart, but it'll have to do."

Emily jumped up and looped her arm in Ryder's. "Let's go. I'm starving for a Fudgsicle. Let's take our ice cream to the park and swing."

"Us guys could push you girls on the m-merry-go-round," Shane suggested.

"It's been years since I've been on a merry-go-round. That sounds like fun," Jancy agreed.

"You goin' to be m-my girlfriend from now on?" Shane whispered as they fell in behind Ryder and Emily, who walked faster than they did.

"I thought I already had that title. After all, I've been spending nights in your bed," she answered.

He stopped and kissed her right underneath a streetlamp. "You do, but I w-wanted to be sure that you knew that you had it."

"I love being your girlfriend and yes, from now on." She rolled up on her toes and kissed him on the cheek.

"And you'll stay in Pick?" he asked.

"Until the baby is born at the very least." A picture of her getting into a used car and leaving

Pick with Shane waving good-bye flashed through her mind, and her chest tightened. If she had that kind of pain at the thought, she'd never be able to drive away from him—not ever.

"That's a start." He took her hand in his and continued walking, keeping his steps short so that she didn't have to do double time to keep up.

"Lookin' back, I had a crush on you in high school, but I really fell for you when I saw you sittin' over there on your things wh-when your car was burnin' up. You were so beautiful and you . . ."

"I what?"

His stopped, and his eyes fluttered shut. Heavy lashes rested on his high cheekbones as his mouth zeroed in on hers. "You've always made me feel important, like I was somebody," he whispered when the kiss ended.

"You are, Shane."

"W-with you, I am," he said.

"Hey, you two. Y'all goin' to get ice cream with us or make out all evenin'?" Ryder yelled over his shoulder.

"Forget the ice cream if that's our choices," Shane hollered back.

"I want both. Get us three ice-cream bars, and we'll meet y'all at the park."

Shane sat down on a park table and pulled her down onto his lap. "All I got for us is a junkyard, Jancy, and I w-wouldn't have got through high school if Ryder hadn't helped me—a lot. I'm not smart."

"You know everything about cars and how to fix them. You have a job and you are honest. That's smart," she argued. "And don't you ever say bad things like that about Shane Adams again or you'll have me to fight."

"Exactly wh-what I was sayin'. You make me feel good about m-myself. That's wh-wh-why I fell in love with you right over that burning car." He grinned.

"Love," Jancy stammered.

"Yes, love. I don't expect you to say it right now, but I love you, Jancy Wilson. And like Gramps said, I am goin' to m-marry you. It don't m-matter when. That's for you to decide. Just know that I am and that I do love you."

She saw herself through his eyes, and she liked that woman. "I love you, too, but that marriage thing has to wait awhile," she said.

His smile lit up the whole universe. "I'm patient. Besides, Emily and Ryder need to be the center of attention right now."

Chapter Twenty-One

Jancy heaved a sigh of relief on Friday when the sun rose in a pale-blue sky without a single cloud floating around. The weatherman had said that that the weekend would be hot and dry, but he didn't always call it right. Even with all the excitement of the past few days—and nights—of being with Shane, something wasn't right. What went up had to come down, and all the euphoria surrounding Jancy couldn't last forever without the other shoe dropping—life had taught her that.

Vicky had mentioned the bad-luck/good-luck stuff that occurred in her life during the summers. At first Jancy had thought that the bad-luck devil had visited when her car burned, but lately she'd come to realize that maybe it was that pretty good-luck lady who'd waved a magic wand over her life that day.

"The day after the wedding is going to be like the day after Christmas around here." She pulled a basket of fries up out of the hot grease.

Nettie put a burger together and passed it over to Jancy to add fries to the basket. "No, you can get ready for a very busy week. We'll be gettin' last-minute things done to help Emily with the wedding and honeymoon packing right along with runnin' this place. And believe me, the day after Christmas is one of our busiest days. Everyone is tired of cooking and they want to get out and talk to the folks about their holiday stuff, so they show up here. We're always packed. And we will be the day after the wedding, so you are right, it will be exactly as crazy as the day after Christmas. If we had a lick of sense, we'd close for the day, but then where would the folks go?"

"I'm going to miss Emily living at the house," Jancy said. "I can't believe I was afraid that things would change when she got here."

"Got to admit—I had a little worry about how things would go with you two and with Vicky. It's the first time that we've had a fourth person in the mix. Look at that." Nettie pointed to the carousel where Vicky and Emily pinned up the orders. "One more is all we got, and we might have fifteen minutes before the noon rush starts to prop up our feet."

"Nettie, I told Shane about—well, you know—but I didn't tell him about my probation thing, and my conscience is killin' me," she said.

"Hey, Vicky!" Shane's deep drawl floated through the window. "I just come in for a cup of coffee and to see Jancy a m-minute."

She took a deep breath and peeked out the

window into the dining area. "Give me some advice, Nettie."

"Where is that girl who kicks butt and takes names? I like her better than one that cowers in the corner. Shake off the fear and tell him tonight. You are a good person, and remember what I told you about loving yourself."

Her back suddenly felt as if it had a rod of steel. She pushed through the doors and made her way behind the counter. "Hi, darlin'. Cup of coffee comin' right up."

"And a tart, please," Shane said and then lowered his voice. "That's the first time you've called m-me *darlin'* right out in public."

"I've thought it lots of times." She set the glass and tart in front of him. "So do you like it or does it embarrass you?"

"Love it." He wrapped her hand up in his. "I could sit right here all day and w-wait for you to say it again."

"Darlin'." She grinned. "We've both got work to do, but tonight I promise I'll say it a hundred times."

"I can't w-wait." He gently squeezed her hand.

"Order up!" Nettie called as she slid a plate and a basket onto the shelf.

Vicky grabbed it. "There's a tour bus parked out there. Looks like we'll be really busy for the next hour or so."

"Y'all need m-me to m-man the drink machine

for you?" Shane asked. "I've got an hour to spare."

"That would be wonderful," Vicky said.

"Looks like a senior citizens' group. That means lots of blue-plate specials and not so many burger baskets," Jancy said.

Emily gave Jancy a hip bump. "Nettie has sent me to the front and says she needs Mama in the kitchen." She turned to face Shane. "Did y'all get the deck started before he got called up to Frankston?"

"Not yet, but we've got all next week," Shane answered. "Ryder will need something to keep him busy so he's not so nervous about sayin' his vows at the w-wedding."

The door opened and people began to file inside, filling every booth and bar stool in the diner. Emily worked one side and Jancy the other while Shane took care of filling and helping serve the drink orders.

Jancy was all the way to the end of the diner when an old guy with a twinkle in his eye said, "Is that waitress on the other end kin to Katherine Heigl?"

"Not that I know of," Jancy said.

"Well, shoot. I was going to get her autograph. Guess it ain't my lucky day," he said.

"Two sweet teas, a lemonade, and a Pepsi." Shane set drinks down in front of the two elderly guys. "Wh-where y'all headed?"

"Vegas or bust." The other one pumped his fist into the air. "And I'm going to win one of them big million-dollar pots and get my picture in the newspaper. And, honey, you can get me a double cheeseburger basket with a double order of sweet potato fries. Cholesterol be damned. We're on vacation from the nursing home."

Jancy wrote on the order pad. "Well, good luck and have a great time."

"Would have been better luck if we'd gotten an autograph. Come to think of it, are you kin to Reese Witherspoon? You look a lot like her when she played June Carter in the Johnny Cash movie."

"She's prettier than that, but she can sing a lot like June." Shane patted the old guy on the shoulder.

The place was hopping for a solid hour, and then, presto, the bus was gone and everything was quiet again. Jancy sat down in a booth and pointed to the place across from her. "Dinner is on the house for helping us, right Emily?"

"Yes, sir. I'll put in our orders and help get them ready. Burgers or lunch special?" she asked.

"Burger for me," Jancy said.

"Same here, only I want sweet potato fries instead of regular ones," Shane told her.

"Sure thing," she said.

Shane got up and made his way behind the counter, where he drew up two glasses of sweet tea. "That was fun. I love old people. W-wish they could have stayed longer and told us stories about their past. It would be nice if m-my grandpa could go on trips like that. They have those kinds of things at his place, but he says sitting that long hurts him. It took him two days to get over comin' up here to the diner that day."

Emily brought their dinner and set it on the table, then disappeared back into the kitchen. "I loved seeing him, but next time let's go to him so he's not in pain. And I've got something I really want to tell you . . ."

"Hey, y'all!" Sarah, Teresa, and Waynette pushed into the diner.

"Hey!" Shane waved. "Wh-what are y'all doin' out today?"

"Lunch," Waynette said. "Hey, Emily, can we come back in the kitchen for burger baskets and talk wedding stuff?"

"Sure thing. I'll throw three more patties on the grill. I was just making mine," she said.

"That m-means I'm about to lose you since you're a bridesm-maid," Shane stammered.

"No, darlin', I'm going to sit right here with you until we finish our lunch," she told him. "Besides, I've got something to say. This might not be the time or the place, but it's eatin' me up so . . ."

"Then I guess you'd better spit it out," Shane said. "But first, I love you, Jancy."

She reached across the table and held his hands in hers. "Remember that old boyfriend who went to jail that I told you about?"

"Is he out? Please don't tell me that you are going back to him." Shane's gaze met hers across the table.

"No, darlin'," she said quickly. "But—"

"We brought our burgers out here." Waynette pushed through the kitchen door, and Emily and the rest of the girls claimed the booth right behind Shane and Jancy.

"That way we can talk about wedding stuff with you, Jancy," Sarah said.

"Tonight. You can tell m-me then, right?" Shane said.

Jancy nodded.

Shane finished his dinner, kissed her on the forehead, and headed toward the door. "Y'all enjoy your w-weddin' plans. I'll get on back to the shop now. Thanks for dinner."

"Thanks for helpin' out." Jancy nodded and slid back in the booth so that she could see the other ladies.

"No problem," he said as he shut the door behind him.

"So when are y'all announcin' something?" Sarah asked. "You have to promise us that you won't shock us like Emily did. Lord, we all about stroked out when she called late Sunday night and told us we were going to be bridesmaids."

"And we hadn't even got our minds wrapped around that before she unloaded the baby bomb," Teresa said.

"So?" Emily raised an eyebrow toward Jancy.

"What?"

"Announcing something like an engagement?" Waynette asked.

"I'll announce this much—I'm his girlfriend," Jancy answered.

"That's a good runnin' start," Waynette said.

Vicky and Nettie slid into the same booth with Jancy.

"Yes, it is, but I was wonderin' if we might get double use out of the bridesmaids' dresses?" Vicky asked.

Jancy shook her head. "Afraid not. When and if I get married, it'll be a tiny little ceremony with maybe a nice reception afterward."

"Why?" Waynette asked. "Weddings are such fun."

"Y'all are closing up shop on the day before the weddin', aren't you?" Teresa asked.

"I think that would be a great idea," Vicky said. "How about you, Jancy? You think we should shut up the diner for two days?"

"I get a vote?" Jancy asked.

"Of course you do. Aren't you plannin' on bein' here another year?" Vicky asked.

Jancy finally smiled. "At least until after Christmas. And my vote is yes, so that we can all pamper Emily the day before and the day of the wedding."

"We need to do nails and facials the day before," Sarah said.

"Speaking of making new rules," Nettie said. "Let's close up on the day before and Thanksgiving, too."

"Easter Sunday so I can wear my pretty new dress to morning services that day and dress the baby up all fancy," Emily chimed in. "What about closing early on New Year's Eve and bein' closed on New Year's? Think the budget would handle it?"

"We might have to cinch in our belts," Vicky teased.

Jancy picked the last two fries in her basket. "If that's the case, I'd better not waste this food."

"Well, crap!" Vicky sighed.

"What?" Jancy asked.

"The wolf is on his way to the sheep pen." Vicky picked up her empty plate to take to the kitchen. "Y'all don't rush. I'll wait on him. He won't eat anything anyway."

"Have a seat anywhere," she called out when the bell dinged announcing a new customer. "Oh, hello, Mr. Wolfe. What brings you to Pick today?"

"I have good news to share, and I'm not giving up on taking you out. I have trouble accepting the word *no*. The folks who own the twenty acres north of your land are talking seriously about selling it to me. I told them it was contingent upon you selling your place so that I could get enough land to get my project started."

"I thought you'd given up on us and gone on over to Troup," Vicky said.

He sat down at a booth without brushing it off, but from the pinched look on his face it wasn't easy. "I would like one of the tarts that everyone in town talks about and a cup of coffee. Do you have Jamaican?"

"We have decaf and plain coffee," Vicky said.

That the Robertson kids would be interested in getting rid of their land didn't surprise her. Both their parents had gone to a Frankston nursing home last fall and the two daughters lived in Florida these days. The Robertsons had grown strawberries on that place back when Nettie's grandparents had farmed the forty acres adjoining it.

"Okay." He sighed. "Just a tart then and what-ever coffee you have made."

She set his order on the table and laid the ticket on the edge. "No hurry, but I'm havin' a quick lunch with my daughter and her girlfriends."

"Knife?" He rolled his eyes.

She went back to the counter and brought out an oversize steak knife. "This do? Most folks just pick the tarts up or else use a fork to cut them."

"I'm not a redneck," he grumbled.

"No, sir, you are not," she said in a sugary-sweet tone. "And I'm still not selling my land or my diner. You might check north of the Robertson place, since I don't think you'll have much luck with anything south of there. We've all made up our minds to keep what we've got. I've told you that a dozen times. Like I asked before, why aren't you in Troup?"

"I'm lookin' into both places. Pick is my first choice, but . . ." He cut off a piece of the tart and put it in his mouth. "Not bad. Pretty good."

Emily shot a go-to-hell look across the room meant to fry the man into nothing but a big toothy skull and fancy shoes right there on the spot. "That, sir, goes beyond pretty good. Nettie's tarts are amazing."

"And you would be the daughter, right? I remember you from the picnic." Carlton broke out his smile and threw a few dollar bills on the table as he stood to his feet. "Keep the change." With all his usual fanfare, he strutted out of the diner.

Vicky picked up the money and snorted. "The change is exactly two cents."

"Can't expect anything better from a cheap con man," Emily said. "Next time he comes in here, Nettie, I want you to get out the magic potion and put it in his coffee."

"Magic?" Jancy asked.

"That would be the stuff they give folks who

overdose to make them throw up," Emily said.

"He sent that good-lookin' cowboy that was at the picnic to my folks' place," Waynette said. "He tried his best to make them sign a preliminary agreement that they wouldn't sell to anyone else."

"What happened?" Jancy asked.

"Mama brought out her shotgun and ran him off the place. He left the paper on the table and Daddy had the lawyer take a look at it. Preliminary, my butt! It was a contract to buy the property for a fraction of what it is worth," Waynette said.

Sarah raised a hand. "Same at my house, but it was Daddy who ran him off."

"We should have cornered him right here in the diner. Between the seven of us we could have done a number on him," Teresa laughed.

"Heck, we wouldn't all need to let our burgers get cold. Jancy could have wiped up the floor with that fool," Nettie laughed with her.

"Y'all are the best." Jancy stood up and started toward the kitchen.

The girls left, but it wasn't long until several cars pulled into the parking lot. Nettie hustled back to the kitchen, where she removed several steaks that had been marinating in an egg and milk mixture and coated them with flour. She'd made chicken-fried steaks every week for so long that she could do it in her sleep—her mind went to other things while she worked. Maybe when the baby was born, she would stay home a couple of days a week and babysit. After all, Emily had said that she'd be the great-grandma—that's what they did. Semiretirement would take some serious thought, but if Jancy would stay it might be a possibility.

"What's your secret on those chicken-fried steaks?" Jancy asked as she joined Nettie in the kitchen.

"Double breading. Dip them in the milk mixture, then in flour, then repeat the process. And get the grease very hot. Overcooking toughens the meat, and grease that's not hot enough makes for soggy bread on the outside. Plus, I put two tablespoons of cornmeal in the flour," Nettie told her. "Watch me do these two. You can do the next couple, and I'll watch to make sure you do it right. Like good bread making, it's technique as much as recipe. What's goin' on up front that you are back here?"

Jancy did not take her eyes off the process, and when it was her turn, she did it exactly like Nettie did. "I volunteered. Seemed like Vicky and Emily needed some more time together."

"You are a quick study, and I mean in more than just cookin', girl. You can do the rest," Nettie said. "And tomorrow morning you're doin' the hot rolls. I'm thinkin' that maybe when the baby is born I'll trade a few days a week in the diner for rockin' the little one up at the house, but keep that under your hat. I'm not ready to announce it just yet."

"You got it." Jancy smiled.

That evening when they closed up the diner and headed to the house, there was not a single tart left on the cake stands. Nettie had made crusts and had them ready to go for the next day. Cream cheese was set out to soften to speed up the filling process, and the strawberries' glaze had been made.

"How long has it been since someone hid an engagement ring in a tart at the diner?" Emily asked as they walked four abreast on the path from the diner to the house.

"Must have been last Valentine's Day," Nettie answered. "Eddie Don Anderson proposed to Melanie Drumright that day. He put her ring right in the top. It was so pretty that I took a picture of it."

"We should have taken a picture every time and kept a scrapbook," Emily said. "So Jancy, you want Shane to propose that way?"

"Hey!" Jancy threw up both palms. "I'm not rushing into anything. If the past has taught me anything at all, it's to slow down and think about things."

Nettie crossed the porch and sat down in the swing. "One of you young'uns bring out some good cold lemonade. That breeze feels like it's comin' from a bake oven."

"I'll do it." Jancy disappeared into the house.

Vicky sat down on the top porch step, and Emily joined Nettie in the swing.

"I love this time of evening when we can get some fresh air." Nettie sighed.

"Something that don't smell like grease or strawberries?" Vicky asked.

"Never thought I'd hear either of you say something like that." Emily kicked off her shoes and rolled up the legs of her jeans.

"Never thought I'd say it," Vicky said. "What time is Ryder picking you up this evening?"

"In half an hour. I've got time to grab a quick shower and get dressed," she answered. "All four of us are going up to the lake for a swim."

"Not a very exciting date," Vicky said.

"The excitement isn't where you go, Mama. It's who you go with. And you should encourage Andy a little. He gets stars in his eyes when he looks at you."

"Listen to her," Nettie said. "She's a smart kid."

"Amen." Vicky's head bobbed up and down several times. "She really is smart, but I've got too much on my plate for romance. Besides, those stars in your eyes are because you are so in love right now."

"What's this 'right now' business? I'm going

to be in love with Ryder until we die at the same minute, and then we'll hold hands and go to heaven together."

Vicky shuddered. "Don't talk like that."

Emily hugged her tightly. "It won't happen until we're married eighty years. We have it all planned."

Nettie shook a finger at Emily. "Don't make plans like that, or God will get out the monkey wrench."

"He already did. The birth control pills failed and I had to deal with Nicole—lordy, but I hate that name. In both instances it didn't pull us apart but made us closer," Emily said.

Nettie kicked off her shoes. "Like I said before, we got a smart kid."

The sun was setting behind the trees on the far side of the lake that evening when they arrived. Shane had a quilt draped over his arm as they made their way from Ryder's truck to the shoreline. He flipped it out under the drooping branches of a weeping willow tree. Emily and Ryder went on down the banks of the lake toward a swimming hole they'd all used since they were in high school.

"I love this place. W-we don't come out here often enough," Shane said.

"Never been here before right now," Jancy said.

"Ahhh, come on! Surely you w-went swimmin' wh-when you lived in Pick, didn't you?"

She shook her head. "Not one time, but I love it. It can be our special place from now on. I've always pictured a little white house with a weeping willow in the backyard. In my mind I can see the wind blowing the limbs and kids playing chase in and out around it."

"I'll plant one tomorrow," Shane said. "You said you had something to tell m-me and then the girls interrupted us."

"When my car first caught on fire, I thought I was the unluckiest person alive. Then I got to feelin' like maybe I was the luckiest, since I met you because of that fire and I've got these friends who are like family." She hesitated.

He moved over close enough to draw her to his side with an arm around her shoulders. "I like that you turned things around," he whispered next to her ear, his warm breath on her neck creating a quiver deep in her heart.

"Luck don't last." She sighed.

"We m-make our own luck, and love lasts when luck plays plumb out," he answered. "Look at all those beautiful colors reflected in the w-water. It's almost as gorgeous as you are."

"Okay." She inhaled deeply and told him everything about the probation, including why she'd been leaving Texas at the time she did.

"Is that all?" Shane asked when she'd finished.

"Every bit of it," she said.

"I have a confession to make," he said.

Her stomach tightened into a knot, and she held her hands so tightly in her lap that they began to tingle.

"I knew that three days after you got here and, Jancy, I don't care about any of it," he said.

Her eyes felt as if they might pop right out of her head and roll around on the grass until they reached the water. "How? What? How did you . . ."

"Now you are about to stutter." He planted a kiss on her cheek. "I had to get the papers in order to sell any usable parts of your car, and I'd let the rest go in the junk m-metal pile. Got a flag on your name and looked it up."

She pushed away from him and cocked her head to one side. "And you didn't mention it?"

He shrugged. "I told you. I don't care about the past. I just w-want a future with you, darlin'. I w-wish you could've stayed in Pick and w-we w-would have gotten together right out of high school. But that's not wh-what happened, so w-we'll have to m-make up for lost time."

"I love you, Shane Adams."

He grabbed her and rolled backward so that they were both lying down, facing each other. "Those are the sweetest words I've ever heard in my whole life. I'm the luckiest man in the state."

• • •

Vicky was sitting on her bed when Nettie knocked and pushed open the door. "Need some company?"

"In the worst kind of way." Vicky scooted to the middle to make room. "This is really happening, isn't it, Nettie? Next week there is going to be a wedding. And I think I'm going to be all right with it."

Nettie fluffed up two pillows against the headboard and propped her back against it. "Yes, and you can be thankful that she is coming home at night rather than moving in with him before the wedding."

"I am grateful for that, and Ryder has been so sweet that it'd be tough to stay mad at him. But what if he can't change? What if . . ."

Nettie laid a hand on her knee. "I heard Thelma say the same things about Creed, and you were seventeen and still in high school. Emily's twenty-two and has promised to finish her schoolin' with them online courses."

"And what did you tell Mama?" Vicky toyed with the tufts of chenille on her snowy-white bedspread.

"To be careful, because she didn't want to lose you. Hearts can be mended and problems fixed, but only if the lines of communication are open between the mother and daughter," Nettie answered.

"I'd rather it had been Shane."

"No, you wouldn't. Shane is a sweetheart, but he's not for Emily. She has to have someone who's on her mental level, who can talk her language. She and Ryder can do that. When the lust settles and the love is stretched, they'll still be able to talk. She and Shane would have grown apart fast."

Vicky sighed. "He was always such a bad boy."

"Like mama, like daughter." Nettie giggled. "And like grandma, too. And I thought you said you were okay with it. Where are these doubts coming from?"

Vicky jerked her head up so fast that it made her dizzy. "I don't know, but I need to get them out of my mind. What did you mean, like grandma?"

"Thelma Jane Green was the piano player at church from the time she was thirteen. Leonard's mama had been before that, but she died and Thelma had a right good ear for music, so she offered. Now put a girl like that with a boy that was twice as bad as Ryder."

"My daddy?" Vicky frowned.

"Was your dad and he could do no wrong. But before he got that title, he was the worst womanizer in Henderson and Anderson Counties. Your mama fell hard for him, and your grandma, God love her soul, couldn't do a dang thing to change her mind," Nettie said.

"Go on," Vicky said.

"That's all, but I wouldn't be a bit surprised to learn that your grandma was attracted to the same kind of man. You know"—Nettie lowered her voice—"that your great-grandma and grandpa made moonshine here in Pick during the Prohibition days."

"I heard that before. I hope that this baby is a boy."

"Will he be a bad boy?" Nettie giggled.

Emily knocked on the door. "Who's a bad boy? Can I join this party, or is it a private one?"

"Ryder is a bad boy, and you are welcome to come in. I hope your baby is a boy. Did y'all have a good swim?" Vicky patted the bed beside her.

Emily crawled up beside her mother and laid her head in her lap. "We sure did. The water was nice and cool. I hope this one is a boy, too, Mama. I want two boys and then a girl."

"Three is a big family in today's world." Vicky combed Emily's long blonde hair back away from her face with her fingers.

"Hey!" Jancy poked her head in the door. "All right if I have first turn in the bathtub tonight?"

"Come on in and join us first," Emily said. "There's room beside Nettie."

"You sure?" Jancy asked.

Nettie patted the pillows. "Saved this spot for

you. You are positively glowin', girl. What has happened?"

"I told Shane all of it and be hanged if he didn't already know about the probation thing. It was on my record when he applied for a car title for that burned-out wreck." She grinned. "And he's fine with it and I told him that I love him. Good grief, I'm rambling."

"Savor the moment," Emily said.

"I love this feeling, Nettie," Jancy said.

"Hey, this is Pick, Texas. It's a magical place where only good things happen," Emily said.

"That's just rainbows and unicorns talking," Vicky told her.

"But they're my pretty rainbows and my pink unicorns with glitter on their horns," Emily said.

Nettie chuckled. "For tonight y'all all can float around in the pretty fluffy clouds, but keep one foot on the ground and set firm in reality, because life is not all rainbows and unicorn farts. It's got pain as well as joy. Remember that."

"Will do," Vicky, Jancy, and Emily said in unison.

Chapter Twenty-Two

On Thursday night, their last night before the wedding preparations the next day, the four of them went to the mall in Tyler for some last-minute honeymoon items for Emily. Sarah had begged for a bridal shower and a bachelorette party, but Emily had promptly put an end to both ideas.

Music from a carousel greeted them when the two guys pushed open the doors into the mall. "Let's ride the horses," Emily yelled over the music.

"Are you serious? Aren't we too tall?" Jancy was doing all kinds of things for the first time and loving every minute of it.

"Never." Shane grabbed her hand and pulled her toward the carousel. He gave the man the money for four to ride. "Pick your pony, darlin'."

She chose one with gold reins and a sidesaddle. Shane put a hand on each side of her waist, picked her up, and set her on the horse. She loved that flash of heat when he touched her, even in the most innocent ways. He slung a leg over the black horse right beside her and reached for her hand.

When the ride ended and Shane had helped her off the horse, Jancy bumped her hip against Shane's. "Thank you. That was my first ever carousel ride."

"It wasn't m-my first, but it was the best one ever," he said.

Emily and Ryder joined them, and she pointed toward a cotton candy kiosk. "I've been craving that stuff. Let's share a big cone. After that I want to go to the food court and get a fat dill pickle, and then I'll be ready to go to Victoria's Secret."

"I'll buy two, because one won't go around among four of us," Ryder said. "Bag or cone for y'all, Shane?"

"Cone," he said without hesitation. "Them bags is pre-m-made, and they ain't as good as the warm stuff right out of the m-machine." He lowered his voice. "M-me and Ryder will go to another store wh-when y'all go to the panty place. He's got to pick up the rings and buy Emily a special w-weddin' present."

"What is it?" Jancy asked.

"Can't tell. It's a surprise," he answered. "But I think she's really goin' to love it."

"Are you for real or did you pop out of a romance book?" Jancy asked.

"Wh-what does that m-mean?" Shane grinned.

"You are so sweet and kind that I'm not sure you could possibly be real. I think maybe I'm dreamin' and you are a knight in shining armor."

One side of Shane's mouth turned up slightly. "Ahh, honey, not a one of them fancy knights ever stuttered. I'm m-more like Shrek."

"Maybe not, but you will always be my knight," Jancy said.

The lady handed Ryder two huge cones of pink cotton candy. He handed one to Jancy and the other to Emily. "Where to now?"

Shane grinned. "To the food court for this pregnant lady's pickles."

"Hey, at least I wore shoes, so I'm not barefoot and pregnant. And I don't crave pickles, just lots of sweet stuff." Emily picked a handful of cotton candy.

"And after that we need half an hour in Victoria's Secret," Jancy said.

"Why so long?" Emily asked. "I know exactly what I want and it won't take very long to get it all."

"Because it will take that long," Jancy said as they found seats in the food court and the guys went to buy bottles of water.

"Really, it won't," Emily argued.

"Did you get Ryder a wedding gift? Something that you give to him before the wedding? The bridesmaid is probably supposed to deliver it, since you can't see him that day, and believe me,

Nettie will stand guard outside the door with a shotgun to keep that rule in place."

"Oh, my gosh. I didn't even think of it," Emily said. "What am I going to get?"

"Does he wear a tie to work?"

"He will in the office." She nodded.

"Maybe a really nice tie tack with a personal note?"

"Jancy, you are a lifesaver."

Vicky set a bottle of cold water on the swing between her and Nettie. Andy sat down on the top porch step and braced his back against the post. Tomorrow it would all begin, and in forty-eight hours it would be over.

"So when do you start setting up?" Nettie asked.

"The bridal tent goes up first thing tomorrow morning so the girls can do all their primping and whatever it is that goes on inside those closed doors for two days. Tell Emily I'll get it ready and cooled down by ten o'clock. Then it's all theirs." He held up a six-pack of beer by the plastic ring. "Either of y'all want one? Things are about to get hectic around here. You might not have time for a beer and a relaxing hour until it's all said and done on Saturday night."

"I got water, but I might have one later," Nettie said.

Vicky hopped up from the swing and crossed

over to where he was sitting. "I'd love one."

He worked one out of the plastic ring and put it in her hands. "How did your day go? I bet you were so busy that your feet are killin' you. Will you be ready for a good foot massage after this wedding is over?"

"You have no idea, and yes." Rather than going back to the swing, she eased down beside him. Something about his presence brought calmness into her life.

"It's a date, then. Meet me on your front porch." He smiled. "Where are all the kids?"

"They've gone to Tyler for last-minute honeymoon things, plus Ryder needs to pick up the rings and Shane said something about a wedding gift for Emily. I hope she remembers to get him something. Hey"—she bumped a shoulder against his—"thanks again for making the cake on such short notice," she said.

"Hey!" Woody stepped up on the porch, grabbed a beer, and settled in beside Nettie on the swing. "I was out for a walk and decided to see if y'all might be on the porch. So what are they going to name the baby? Woodrow is a good boy's name."

"That's their job. Ours is to get them married and settled into the trailer," Nettie pointed out. "Y'all did a fine job of that porch."

"I just supervised. Them young'uns did the work. I still can't believe that Emily is going to marry Ryder. I love them both, but . . ." He hesitated.

"Everyone in Pick knows what he's been, and if I remember right, before you got married all them years ago, you might have given him a race for his money. You and Leonard both were pretty ornery in your day," Nettie reminded him.

Woody rubbed his chin with his hand. "But this is our sweet little Emily."

"I imagine Darlene's and Irma's folks felt the same way," Nettie told him.

Woody chuckled. "Probably so. I always felt like the luckiest man in the world just to get to spend my days with Irma. I imagine Ryder feels the same way. Hey, how much you bet me that Jancy and Shane are married by Christmas?"

"Christmas of which year?" Nettie teased. "It sure won't be this one. She's taking things too slow for that."

"Betcha a hundred dollars." Woody stuck out his hand.

Nettie shook it. "I'll take that in five twenties on the day after Christmas."

"I want mine in a hundred-dollar bill on the same day," Woody said, laughing.

"Have you met Andy Butler?" Vicky motioned to her right with a slight wave of the hand. "He's got the Southern Pastry Shop down in Palestine."

Woody stuck out a hand. "I know your dad.

Saw you at the picnic when Carlton was trying to hoodwink us into selling off our town. It's a pleasure to meet you."

Andy shook with him. "Glad to know you."

"My late wife loved them little macaron cookies that you make down there. I always got her a dozen for her birthday. We'd eat at the diner and share a tart. Then she'd eat one macaron a day for twelve days."

"Thanks for tellin' me that story." Andy grinned.

Nettie chuckled when Ryder's truck came to a stop in the front yard. "And here they are already back home. I figured they might be gone until midnight."

"Well, look here what the cats dug up," Woody called out as all four of them got out of the vehicle.

"Not cats, just part of a wedding party that's sugared up on cotton candy and who rode the carousel," Emily said as she crossed the last six feet toward them in long, easy strides.

It was near midnight when Vicky finally got to bed that night. Her feet ached so badly that she wished Andy had offered her a foot massage that night. She was already looking forward to the one after the wedding. Andy had better have been serious when he offered that.

For the first time ever, they'd decided to close the diner for two whole days. They'd need Friday for the wedding preparations, but Nettie insisted that they would be open on Sunday. Andy would take care of the cleanup, and if anyone needed them, they'd take turns helping him.

She wiggled her toes and shut her eyes, but her mind kept going in circles. Tomorrow morning by ten o'clock things would start popping. The dress had been bought, and it was exactly what Vicky had envisioned. Emily would look like a princess in all that fluff, and the train went on forever.

"Shoes!" She sat straight up in bed then fell back. "We decided she would wear the ballerina slippers that she used for her last sorority party. Lord, I'm losin' my mind." A gentle knock on her bedroom door brought her back up again. Nettie was sick again, she just knew it.

"Mama," Emily whispered.

Oh, no! Something was wrong with the baby. Cold chills covered Vicky's whole body as she threw back the sheet and hurried to the door.

"Are you okay?" Vicky voice quivered.

"I'm fine. It's just so late . . ."

"Are you sure?"

Tears flowed down Emily's face. "It just dawned on me that after I get married, you won't come into my room and kiss me on the forehead anymore. I'm going to miss that, Mama."

Vicky wiped away the tears with her hand. "You go on and get into bed. I'll come and kiss you on the forehead. I'll miss that, too, but now it's your turn to be a mother."

"I've had the best role model in the world. I only hope I can remember everything that you've taught me by example." Emily hugged Vicky and then went across the hall to her bedroom.

Vicky gave her five minutes and then slipped into her room and kissed her on the forehead. "Good night, my sweet little girl."

"Good night, Mama." Emily yawned.

That time when Vicky crawled into her bed, she went right to sleep and there were no dreams or worries.

Chapter Twenty-Three

Waynette had given Emily a mani-pedi right there in the tent, and now it was time to put the dress on. Jancy took it off the hanger and dropped it in a pile of fluff onto the carpeted floor.

"Just like the lady at the store said, you step into it and then be very still while we take care of all the rest," Jancy told Emily. "We need to avoid those pretty curls on top of your head."

"If you've got to go to the bathroom, go now, because it's an hour until the ceremony is over," Waynette said. "I had to cross my legs the last half of my wedding."

"I'm fine, but don't let me have another drop of water." Emily put one bare foot into the dress and then the other one. "I can't believe that I let Mama talk me into this thing. I wanted something simple."

"My granny told me that it wasn't my wedding"—Waynette helped Jancy pull the dress up—"it was my mama's affair, and when I had a daughter, I'd understand. We have this idea of what our wedding will be, but we have to remember that our mothers have been saving and thinking about it since the day we were born. My granny said that when she got married she and her mother had a big fight over how wide the ribbons were going to be in her bouquet. That's when she decided that all she wanted to be was married and she didn't really care about the wedding part."

"Yes!" Emily pumped her fist in the air. "Exactly."

That old familiar green monster hit Jancy right in the middle of her heart. Her mother would never get to argue with her about the width of the bouquet ribbons or whether to wear heels or flats, like Emily and Vicky had done in the bridal shop.

She and Waynette laced the dress up the back, making sure each ribbon was flat and the bow at the top was tied neatly. Then they carefully turned Emily around so that she could see herself in the mirror.

"Oh. My! Mama was right," Emily whispered. "I feel just like Cinderella, and it's a wonderful feeling."

"And she was right about our dresses, too. We talked about silver in the beginning, but this light-green floral is so much prettier for an outdoor wedding."

"Ryder's eyes are going to pop right out," Waynette said. "Now, I'm going to take my place at the guest table. I'll send Vicky in to put on your veil and put the penny in your shoe for good luck."

"Thanks for everything," Emily said. "Especially for my hair. I love it."

"And for mine," Jancy said. "I can't believe you got it to do this."

"I'm magic with a curlin' iron." Waynette waved to them with a smile as she left the tent.

"She's right about the expression on Ryder's face when you start up that strip of carpet," Jancy said.

She'd never wanted a wedding, especially since her mother couldn't be there, but she changed her mind that evening. To have Shane's eyes go all wide and to see his smile when she wore a dress like that, it would be well worth a big ceremony.

"Jancy, thank you for everything. For being our friend—not just mine, but Mama's and Nettie's. For being Shane's girlfriend. Ryder and I worried about him ever finding happiness. That's just the top of the list. I could go on for hours." Emily hugged her. "And darlin', Shane isn't going to be able to blink when he sees you in that gorgeous formal. You look amazing. Sure you don't want to just have a double wedding today?"

She'd love to, but she and Shane needed more time. She and Shane would have their day, maybe next summer when she'd saved up enough money to buy a beautiful dress and a wedding cake from Andy's shop.

"Thanks for the offer, but Shane hasn't even proposed. He'd run away so fast that his tux would catch on fire if we suggested such a thing now," Jancy answered.

Emily bent to hug the other girls, one at a time. "Y'all have been my friends since my earliest memories. I love you all, and thank you for helping make this day so special."

"And on such short notice," Sarah laughed. "Jancy, we will expect a little more time when it's your turn for this."

Jancy held up a palm. "I promise I will give everyone more than three weeks."

"Hey, I hear that it's time to put on the veil— oh, my goodness. You look like an angel." Vicky stopped right inside the door. "I knew that was the right dress the minute I saw it on the hanger."

"And you were so right," Emily told her. "The ballerina shoes were a great idea, too."

Vicky beamed. "I can't wait to see Ryder when he gets the first look at you. And Jancy, your hair is absolutely beautiful. We've got to get Waynette to fix it when you and Shane get married."

"One thing at a time, Miz Vicky. Today belongs to Emily. Besides, like I just told Emily, Shane hasn't even proposed. We need time. I'm never rushing into anything again."

Vicky had a million things to say to Emily, but suddenly Sarah's husband, Jimmy, poked his head into the tent and said it was time for them to go into the diner. It was only five minutes until the music would start for the ceremony.

Jimmy was in charge of the music, which he manned on the diner's small porch. The playlist for the thirty minutes before the wedding had included Shania Twain's "You're Still the One" and "Amazed" by Lonestar. When it came time for Jancy to walk down the aisle, Jimmy hit a button and "She's in Love with the Boy" started to play.

"You got everything but the music, Mama," Emily told Vicky as they waited inside the diner for Jimmy to give them their cue. "There won't be the traditional wedding music. When it's Jancy's turn, you can talk to her about that." Emily giggled nervously.

Vicky tucked her daughter's arm inside hers. "You know I don't like surprises and I've been good about this whole thing, so tell me, what are we going down the aisle to?"

"You'll recognize it." Emily slipped her hand into Vicky's. "And it's the truth."

"Mama, He's Crazy" by the Judds started playing, and Vicky bit back the tears.

"It's perfect," she said. "I couldn't have chosen better."

Emily took the first step on the way up the red carpet. When they reached the end, Vicky put her hand into Ryder's and sat down beside Nettie, who held a white handkerchief with lace around the edges in her hand.

"Loved the song. Fits perfectly. Look at that boy's face," Nettie said.

Jancy hadn't been designated as the maid of honor, but Emily handed her bouquet off to her and put both her hands in Ryder's. They faced each other with so much love written on their hearts that it put a lump the size of a grapefruit in Jancy's throat. Even that she was standing there in front of the whole town in her pretty satin dress was so much like a dream that she felt like she should pinch herself.

"Dearly beloved, we are gathered here on this beautiful night to join Ryder Jensen and Emily Rawlins together in holy matrimony," the preacher started.

Vicky sniffled into a hankie. Andy draped an arm around her shoulders. Something would come of that, maybe not for a couple of years, but it was pretty plain that they'd wind up together. Jancy would bet a week's worth of tips on it.

After the vows the preacher took a step back and said, "Emily and Ryder have decided to have their first dance right now. This song will be Ryder's vows to her."

"Love Can Build a Bridge" started to play, and Emily looped her arms around Ryder's neck. They danced together right there in front of everyone to the lyrics saying that love could build a bridge between their hearts, that when they stood together it was their finest hour and they could do anything.

When the song ended, more people than just Vicky were sniffling. The preacher stepped back up and went on with the ring ceremony, and then he said, "By the authority vested in me by God and the great state of Texas, I pronounce Emily and Ryder married. Ryder, you may kiss your bride."

He didn't rush the moment but held her cheeks with his big hands and brought her lips to his. In Jancy's eyes it was the perfect ending to the wedding. But then Ryder danced Emily down the aisle to "Amazed."

When they reached the end of the center aisle, Shane held out his hand to Jancy, who expected to loop her arm in his and walk toward the diner, but he pulled her to his chest and two-stepped with her all the way to the diner, where the bride and groom waited.

"It was perfect." Emily hugged both of them when they were alone for a few minutes.

Ryder touched her cheek. "You look like an angel. I can't believe that you are really married to me."

"You look pretty fine yourself." Emily pulled his face to hers for a long kiss. "I'm so happy that words can't describe the feeling in my heart."

"I want that," Shane said.

"So do I." Jancy nodded. "But we've got to give it time."

"You just tell m-me when there are no m-more *but*s and I'll be ready." He brought her hand to his lips and kissed the palm. "You are so beautiful that it takes m-my breath away. I can't believe that you are going to be m-mine someday."

In that moment, Jancy shed her wings.

She was home and ready to grow roots as deep and strong as an oak tree.

Epilogue

Six months later

After the wedding kiss, Shane scooped Jancy up into his arms like the new bride that she was and carried her down the aisle into the fellowship hall. Emily arrived right behind them, carrying new baby Victoria Rose in her arms. With her blonde hair and wearing a dark-green dress the same color as her mother's matron of honor outfit, the baby looked adorable. Ryder wasn't far behind with Henry Creed, Victoria Rose's twin brother, who had dark hair and big blue eyes.

Then the whole room exploded with people everywhere. Vicky and Andy quickly took charge of Rosie and Hank, which was what they'd nicknamed the babies who had arrived the week after Thanksgiving. Jancy and Shane posed for pictures behind the cake, feeding each other the first bite and toasting with glasses of lemonade. Then there was a picture taken of them holding hands and kissing over the punch bowl. Jancy loved every minute of the whole amazing wedding day—a dream that had come true.

Six months.

In one way, it seemed like she'd never left Pick, yet she was glad for those years, because if she hadn't had the bad times, then that day wouldn't be nearly as precious.

She'd opened the last letter her mother had left her that morning. On the outside it said it was to be read on her wedding day. Knowing her mother was there in spirit had brought tears to her eyes and joy to her heart. Then that evening in the dressing room, Vicky brought out the family pearls for her to wear, and she'd shed more tears. For the happiest day in her life, she'd sure had to use a lot of tissues.

"When are you going to give us some more of these wonderful presents, Jancy? You could follow in Emily's footsteps and start off with a set of twins. These kids are going to need cousins to play with." Vicky looked down at Hank. "I'd like a houseful of grandchildren by the time I'm fifty."

"Me, too." Andy winked. "I don't mind bypassing the father business and going straight to grandpa status."

"It fits both of you very well, but you'll have to wait at least nine months for cousins for Rosie and Hank." Jancy smiled. "When are you two going to make some kind of announcement about your wedding?"

"As soon as Vicky will let me, I'll get out the bullhorn and tell the whole world," Andy said. "But today is about you and Shane."

Shane tugged on her hand. "Everyone is waiting on the bride and groom to start the food line, darlin'. Are you hungry?"

"Starvin'," Jancy said.

Nettie looked up from behind the table. "There are two tarts on your table. One for each of you. Rules is rules."

"Thank you, Nettie." Shane grinned. "I been too nervous to eat today, but I'm about to m-make up for it now."

"We have a little midnight snack already made up for you to take with you. Don't leave without it." Nettie pointed toward a big basket with all kinds of food in it.

"Thank you. That is so sweet." Jancy leaned over the table and hugged Nettie.

"Don't get the sleeves of that gorgeous dress in the salsa. The red would never come out of velvet," Nettie scolded.

Oh, yes, Jancy was definitely part of the community and the family, and most importantly, she was Shane's wife, whether she was wearing white velvet and Chantilly lace or her jeans and T-shirts.

"You only have to stay an hour," Emily whispered when she took her place at the head table beside Jancy. "Ryder and I will take all the presents to your house and you can open them after the honeymoon."

"I don't want to miss one single minute of any of this," Jancy said. "And I'll let you in on a secret if you promise not to tell."

"You know I won't." Emily's eyes glittered.

"I didn't want a honeymoon. I just want to be married to Shane, so we're going to leave in that vintage car that he got all fixed up, drive out of town so everyone thinks we've gone to Galveston, and sneak right back to our house. We'll be opening presents in our home tomorrow, not next week."

"Smart woman," Emily said. "I loved the cruise, but I couldn't wait to get home to our trailer."

Ryder tapped his fork against a glass and held it up. "A toast. Shane has been like a brother to me since we were just kids. So I guess that makes Jancy my sister. Here's to family that isn't really blood kin but that are related by the heart."

"Hear, hear!" Shane touched his glass to Jancy's. "And here's to a lifetime of love and life together, M-Mrs. Adams."

Jancy leaned over and kissed him on the cheek. "I will never get tired of that title."

Author Note

Dear Reader,

I hope you enjoyed your visit to Pick, Texas. As I was writing, the whole cast became so real to me that I could taste the strawberry tarts and smell the aroma of Nettie's food coming from the kitchen at the diner. I'll miss the conversations with Woody, Nettie, Vicky, Jancy, and Emily, and even though I could have wrung his egotistical neck, even Carlton! I hope that you fall in love with Ryder, Shane, and Andy as much as I did—all three of them are really good men.

Folks say that it takes a village to raise a child—well, it takes a whole team to take a book from a simple dream to what you hold in your hands today. My Montlake team is totally amazing for all they do—from edits to covers—and each of them deserves more than a simple thank-you. But the appreciation comes from deep in my heart when I say thank you to Anh Schluep, my editor, who continues to believe in me; to my developmental editor, Krista Stroever, who always manages to help me take a chunk of coal and turn it into a diamond; to the whole team that has put together this amazing book; to my awesome agent, Erin Niumata, and to Folio Management; and once again, big hugs to my husband, Mr. B, who continues to support me even when he has to eat takeout five days in a row so I can write "just one more chapter."

And thank you to all my readers who buy my books, read them, talk about them, share them, write reviews, and send notes to me. I'm grateful for each and every one of you.

Until next time,
Carolyn Brown

About the Author

Carolyn Brown is a *New York Times*, *USA Today*, and *Wall Street Journal* bestselling author and a RITA finalist. *The Strawberry Hearts Diner* is her eighty-fifth published book. Her books include romantic women's fiction, historical romance, contemporary romance, cowboy romance, and country music mass-market paperbacks. She and her husband live in the small town of Davis, Oklahoma, where everyone knows what everyone else is doing—and reads the local newspaper on Wednesdays to see who got caught. They have three grown children and enough grandchildren to keep them young. When she's not writing, Carolyn likes to sit in her gorgeous backyard with her two cats, Chester Fat Boy and Boots Randolph Terminator Outlaw, and watch them protect their territory from all kinds of wicked varmints like crickets, locusts, and spiders. Visit her online at www.carolynbrownbooks.com.

| Books are produced in the United States using U.S.-based materials | Books are printed using a revolutionary new process called THINKtech™ that lowers energy usage by 70% and increases overall quality | Books are durable and flexible because of smythe-sewing | Paper is sourced using environmentally responsible foresting methods and the paper is acid-free |

Center Point Large Print
600 Brooks Road / PO Box 1
Thorndike, ME 04986-0001 USA

(207) 568-3717

US & Canada:
1 800 929-9108
www.centerpointlargeprint.com